Featuring the work of Gail Tucker, Agnes Hall, Sheila Skinner, Avner Kornblum, Vivien Johnson, Paul Shearer Walmsley, Jean M. Watson, Colin Hall and Deborah Grant.

All in

An eclectic collection of short stories from a mixture of nine authors with a passion for writing. From new authors to experienced and published raconteurs, all nine writers belong to The Jalon Valley Writing Group, a U3A Creative Writing Group in the Alicante Region of Spain.

From light tales to dark, from humour to pathos, from prose to poetry, this book has taken several years to evolve from a stray idea to fruition as a full and entertaining book.

It has been a pleasure to work on from start to finish. We hope that you enjoy reading it as much as we have collating it.

U P Publications

All Rights Reserved

No part of this publication may be reproduced or transmitted by any means, electronic, mechanical, photocopy or otherwise, without the prior permission of the publisher. This is a work of fiction. Names, characters, places and incidents are either the product of the authors' imagination, or are used fictitiously. Any resemblance to actual persons, living or dead, business establishments, events, or locales is entirely coincidental.

First published in Great Britain in 2016
by U P Publications Ltd, Eco Innovation Centre, PetersCourt,
City Rd Peterborough PE1 1SA, UK

Cover design copyright © G. M. Griffin Peers 2016

Copyrights © U P Publications 2016 (and Contributing Authors)

U P Publications Ltd and all the contributing authors assert their moral rights – Gail Tucker, Agnes Hall, Sheila Skinner, Avner Kornblum, Vivien Johnson, Paul Shearer Walmsley, Jean M. Watson, Colin Hall and Deborah Grant.

A CIP Catalogue record of this book is available from the British Library

Paperback Edition ISBN 978-1908135155

eBook Edition ISBN 978-1908135162

FIRST PAPERBACK EDITION

Published by U P Publications

Printed in England by The Lightning Source Group

www.uppbooks.com

All in the Mix

Short Stories

U P Publications
2016

Contents

INTRODUCTION 11
   Nine Authors 11
SHEILA SKINNER 13
   Taken For A Ride 13
VIVIEN JOHNSON 14
   Shooting Star 14
AVNER KORNBLUM................... 15
   Q is for Quagga....................... 15
GAIL TUCKER............................. 16
   Advice 16
AGNES HALL 17
   Another Life 17
GAIL TUCKER............................. 21
   Lost Sea 21
VIVIEN JOHNSON 22
   Newt 22
AVNER KORNBLUM................... 23
   The Glass and the Candle 23
VIVIEN JOHNSON 25
   Benissa Town 25
JEAN M. WATSON 26
   Going Away................................ 26
VIVIEN JOHNSON 29
   Police Box 30
VIVIEN JOHNSON 31
   Night Swimming......................... 31
GAIL TUCKER............................. 32
   Loss 32
SHEILA SKINNER 33
   Sacrifice...................................... 33

VIVIEN JOHNSON......................35
   5 Year's Old in Kathmandu........ 35
AVNER KORNBLUM 36
   A Table for Two 36
VIVIEN JOHNSON....................... 39
   Bygone Times 39
GAIL TUCKER 40
   Traceries...................................... 40
AGNES HALL............................... 41
   Every Cloud Has a Silver Lining 41
SHEILA SKINNER 45
   The Coin..................................... 45
VIVIEN JOHNSON....................... 51
   Vista Montgo............................... 51
GAIL TUCKER 52
   The Promised Land 52
AVNER KORNBLUM 55
   Lonely Hearts Letter 55
      To Her 55
      To Him 56
COLIN HALL................................ 57
   The Boss's Son........................... 57
VIVIEN JOHNSON....................... 59
   Your First Gift............................. 59
SHEILA SKINNER 60
   Missing.. 60
VIVIEN JOHNSON....................... 65
   Thoughts 65
JEAN M. WATSON 66
   Christmas Letters 66

AGNES HALL 68
  Just Rewards 68
VIVIEN JOHNSON 71
  Stallion 71
GAIL TUCKER 73
  Indoctrination 73
SHEILA SKINNER 74
  Message in a Bottle 74
COLIN HALL 80
  A Shirt Story 80
AVNER KORNBLUM 81
  Fire! 81
VIVIEN JOHNSON 83
  The Seascape 'Portichol' 83
GAIL TUCKER 84
  Villain 84
VIVIEN JOHNSON 87
  Second Post 87
AVNER KORNBLUM 90
  Neptune's Dilemma 90
AGNES HALL 98
  One Day Too Late 98
SHEILA SKINNER 99
  On Morning Air 99
VIVIEN JOHNSON 100
  Things Change 100
AVNER KORNBLUM 101
  Undiscovered Teruel 101
AGNES HALL 105
  Party Parrots 105
VIVIEN JOHNSON 108
  Investiture 108
AVNER KORNBLUM 111
  The Shoot-out 111
GAIL TUCKER 113
  Private Affair 113

PAUL SHEARER WALMSLEY 114
  Stormy Weather: Raining Cats and
  Dogs 114
AGNES HALL 115
  The Letter 115
GAIL TUCKER 117
  Passing Lives 117
COLIN HALL 122
  The Happy Couple 122
AVNER KORNBLUM 123
  A Chinese Dinner Stopped Me
  Smoking 123
VIVIEN JOHNSON 125
  The Chancer 125
GAIL TUCKER 131
  Inheritance 131
PAUL SHEARER WALMSLEY 135
  New Year's Eve 135
COLIN HALL 136
  Murder in the Showers of a
  Spanish Campsite 136
GAIL TUCKER 139
  Home and Away 139
JEAN M. WATSON 145
  As Green As Grass 145
COLIN HALL 148
  Winding Down 148
AVNER KORNBLUM 149
  Midnight Music 149
VIVIEN JOHNSON 152
  The Goatherd 152
  Violetta 153
GAIL TUCKER 158
  Good Neighbours 158
VIVIEN JOHNSON 162
  Pride 162

GAIL TUCKER 164	VIVIEN JOHNSON 211
Detachment 164	Inquisition 211
VIVIEN JOHNSON 167	JEAN M. WATSON 213
The Red, White and Blue 2005 167	Driving Home at Night 213
PAUL SHEARER WALMSLEY 168	VIVIEN JOHNSON 216
The Knee Job 168	An Encounter 216
GAIL TUCKER 170	VIVIEN JOHNSON 217
A Son 170	The Woman 217
VIVIEN JOHNSON 177	COLIN HALL 218
Europe's Idol 177	Boulevard Montmartre 218
GAIL TUCKER 179	COLIN HALL 219
A Fiction 179	Married Bliss 219
COLIN HALL 182	VIVIEN JOHNSON 220
The Last Supper 182	The Cooper's Art 220
VIVIEN JOHNSON 184	VIVIEN JOHNSON 223
Christmas 184	Autumn Tandem Ride 223
VIVIEN JOHNSON 185	JEAN M. WATSON 225
Gone 185	Obsessions 225
AVNER KORNBLUM 187	VIVIEN JOHNSON 232
A Novel Ending 187	Hamburg Christmas 232
JEAN M. WATSON 190	COLIN HALL 233
Crossing the bar 190	The Hot Dog Stand 233
AVNER KORNBLUM 194	COLIN HALL 234
Flowers in Barcelona 194	Snoring 234
GAIL TUCKER 196	VIVIEN JOHNSON 236
Graduation Day 196	A Surprise Trip 236
VIVIEN JOHNSON 199	JEAN M. WATSON 239
A Walk in the Past 199	The Photograph 239
JEAN M. WATSON 200	VIVIEN JOHNSON 241
The Ring 200	Comfort 241
AVNER KORNBLUM 203	COLIN HALL 242
Mr Grouchy's Holidays 203	Something Uninteresting 242
VIVIEN JOHNSON 205	VIVIEN JOHNSON 243
Faded Pictures 205	My Friend 243
COLIN HALL 209	VIVIEN JOHNSON 244
My Gloves 209	Opera and the Secret Service 244

GAIL TUCKER 245	GAIL TUCKER 273
Knowing 245	Setting Out 273
VIVIEN JOHNSON 246	VIVIEN JOHNSON 274
The Fall 246	Darkroom Senses 274
COLIN HALL 248	DEBORAH GRANT 277
Water Lilies 248	Purple Haze 277
COLIN HALL 249	GAIL TUCKER 278
The Zip 249	Spanish Spring Haiku 278
VIVIEN JOHNSON 250	One 278
An Act of Kindness 250	Three 278
VIVIEN JOHNSON 252	Two 278
Valentine's Day 252	Four 278
GAIL TUCKER 254	VIVIEN JOHNSON 279
Impatience 254	The First Day 279
VIVIEN JOHNSON 255	AGNES HALL 282
Old Faithfuls 255	A Table for Two 282
DEBORAH GRANT 257	GAIL TUCKER 286
Not Fade Away 257	Nets 286
COLIN HALL 260	VIVIEN JOHNSON 287
That Day Long Ago 260	A Short Break 287
VIVIEN JOHNSON 261	GAIL TUCKER 290
The Birthday Tea 261	Missing 290
GAIL TUCKER 263	VIVIEN JOHNSON 291
Parched Cures 263	Train to Work 291
AVNER KORNBLUM 264	GAIL TUCKER 292
When Budapest Became Istanbul 264	Sedge 292
	AVNER KORNBLUM 293
GAIL TUCKER 268	Pitchblack and the Giants of Dedlysinz 293
A Fib 268	
VIVIEN JOHNSON 269	AVNER KORNBLUM 296
A Painful Thumb 269	Lost Sons 296
GAIL TUCKER 271	VIVIEN JOHNSON 297
A Puzzle 271	The Scoop 297
VIVIEN JOHNSON 272	AVNER KORNBLUM 298
Grand Exit 272	Alcalali, 1990 298
	GAIL TUCKER 300
	Holiday Snapshot 300

AVNER KORNBLUM 301
   Do Fish Have Feelings? 301
SHEILA SKINNER 303
   What Will The Neighbours Think? 303
GAIL TUCKER 305
   Summer Storm 305
VIVIEN JOHNSON 306
   Big Mistake 306
GAIL TUCKER 308
   Transhumance 308

MEET THE AUTHORS 309
   Sheila Skinner 311
   Avner Kornblum 312
   Gail Tucker 313
   Vivien Johnson 314
   Paul Shearer Walmsley 315
   Jean M Watson 316
   Agnes Hall 317
   Colin Hall 318
   Deborah Grant 319
AUTHOR INDEX 321

Introduction

Nine Authors

Nine authors, nine very different styles and a myriad of subjects yet all these authors share a passion for writing – so much so that they are, or have been, members of the Jalon Valley Writing Group in the Valencia Region of Spain.

This bond has created a fascinating collection of stories and poems and it has been a privilege to work with them.

I hope that you enjoy the end result – after all…

…**It is All in the Mix!**

Gaile Griffin Peers
U P Publications
2016

Sheila Skinner

Taken For A Ride

Never a black cab around when it rains, so Kay waited outside, tense and shivering under the striped awnings. They'd assured her the Mini Cab was on its way. At least here she was dry, although already regretting her choice of linen swagger-jacket.

Kay decided against rummaging through her hastily packed case for something warmer. *I can't go back inside*, she thought to herself.

Kay knew that her earlier mobile phone conversation with Rod had been loud and bitter. She'd seen their faces inside the chic Wine Bar, they'd certainly seen hers, with the tears coursing down it after she hung up on him.

She'd had a second Sauvignon, not a good idea. The whole thing with Rod, she knew deep inside, hadn't been a good idea either. His call, although despicably last minute, wasn't really a surprise. She'd known all along that this was really her dream, not his ...but it didn't help much, standing here, alone, with her thoughts whirring.

Just then her mobile shrilled, her heart raced, Rod had changed his mind and was coming with her. No ...it was Star Cabs controller telling her that her mini cab was stuck on the other side of the road. It couldn't turn against the solid traffic that had backed up in the downpour of rain. She saw him then, flashers on, waving for her to come across to him. Kay struggled to the kerb with her suitcase.

Crossing nervously, picking her way between the lines of cars, she was soaked by the time she reached the old Rover saloon. The driver, cocooned, warm and dry, let her wrestle with the passenger door and she almost fell with her suitcase onto the back seat. *'P.O.B.'* he mumbled into his mike. Then, over his left shoulder, "Where to lady?" Pain suddenly searing her abdomen,

Kay gasped, "St. Bridget's Maternity Hospital and for Christ's sake hurry."

Vivien Johnson

Shooting Star

Did another person in some other pool see it?
A star losing identity eons away –
count them now see which one is missing –
a flare for astronomers to mull over.

Could it have been in my imagination?
Stronger than pool lights reflected in the trees.
A camera shutter's click; one naked breast-stroke
caught in a single ripple.

Astrologers look for hidden meanings;
Tuaregs huddle round night-time fires
my star unseen, extinguished, fallen –
hidden in Sahara sands.

Avner Kornblum

Q is for Quagga

The Q is for quagga, that beautiful beast –
He woke up one day, turned his eyes to the east
and spoke to the sun with a plea in his voice:
"I just cannot find a good mate of my choice.
In fact I can't find any friends, any herd,
my sisters, my brothers, they've all disappeared.
When two-legged creatures have tip-toed and stopped
there's been some loud thunder and neighbours have dropped.
The two-legged creatures then rush towards us
with sticks in the air and with shouts and a fuss.
I've followed my leader and galloped off fast
But what has become of my friends from the past?
My leader has fallen as well as my mates --
alone I survive, as the Sun-god dictates.
Yet here, in the dawn of a beautiful day,
I hope that a female will come my way,
then we can frolic and mate, and soon we'll have foals.
A new herd of quagga is the first of my goals."
But in the dawn of that day came a man with a gun
and shot the lone quagga, that very last one.
He returned to his base with a black-and-white hide.

"You won't see one like this!" he remarked with some pride.

Gail Tucker

Advice

*If I were you, I should give up
on the subjunctive – it's a lost cause.
Would that I could, that I were you.*

*I'm still one of the few, we are
becoming fewer, who stumble still
to find infinity split – rent in two.*

*It's not a given to be gifted, no longer
a gift to be born with just
something given, received, gifted.*

*Does this intermingling of cultures grow
more or less, with less not more
the final score? Whatever next
I give in, give up – not gifted.*

Agnes Hall

Another Life

The bedroom door is half-open from the night before when I had needed to get out of bed to go to the loo. It is early, still dark, as dad switches on the light at the top of the stairs. He appears in my bedroom doorway, already dressed. He is a big man, with grey trousers, the waistband falling below the round of his stomach, his belt fastened. As well as his belt he has braces, red and cream striped with gold coloured clasps that attach to his trousers. He already has his shirt on, the two top buttons undone. He has difficulty fastening these and I will do them up for him, when I am up and dressed. Despite everything, he tries to keep himself neat and tidy.

"It's time to get up," he says. He has followed this routine for the two months since my mother died, trying to take her place, doing the jobs that she used to do, but struggling. I roll over, rubbing my eyes.

"I'll have a shower and be down in a few minutes. You can leave the breakfast for me. I'll sort it out."

"It's already sorted, love," he says as he moves to the top of the stairs where he pauses, as he does every morning. I know that he will be looking towards the bedroom that they shared. He has slept in the spare room since her death, unable to sleep in the big, double bed without her. My heart aches for him. I know how much he misses her. I make myself get out of bed, and as he starts to descend the stairs, I cross the landing towards the bathroom.

When I arrive downstairs, he is standing at the cooker, stirring the porridge. The kettle boils and he warms the teapot before putting in a teabag and the hot water and then covers the teapot with the gaily-striped tea cosy. Was it only last Christmas that all the female members of the family received knitted tea cosies, the end products of my mother's latest hobby? Most of them were shaped like Christmas puddings with a sprig of holly on top. I find myself smiling as I remember the laughter as parcels were unwrapped and each of them was presented with a pudding tea-cosy.

My father spoons out the porridge. A slice of toast is all I need for breakfast, but I force the porridge down to please him. I notice the sandwiches, cheese and pickle, between thick doorsteps of white bread, which have been left ready for me to take to work. I don't tell him that I never eat them. I don't want to hurt his feelings. After I have eaten my porridge, I start to clear away the dishes.

He says, "I'll see to them. I've little else to do with my day."

As I sit on the bus on my way to work, I wonder again how my father does pass the time during the day. His life had revolved around mum and he is like a little, lost boy without her. He had retired early to spend more time with her, a plan thwarted by her illness and now he has so much time to fill that I am sure he would welcome the daily routine of going out to work again.

We are in the garden. It's Sunday, and I thought that my father had fallen asleep in the warm, September sunshine until I glance across at him.

"Your mother had neat ankles." He is staring at my feet, which are slotted into pink plastic flip-flops and I know that he would be comparing my ankles to those of my mother. I also know that my ankles bear no comparison to my mother's. She had been endowed with slender ankles in keeping with her willowy frame. Instead I have inherited my father's form, not fat, but tall and what could only be described as 'sturdy'. Nor do I have my mother's natural flair and style. She could have worn a sack and looked good in it. "Your mother's ankles were one of the first things that attracted me to her."

This is the first time that he has spoken of my mother since her death. Instead he has built a barrier with his grief, not sharing his pain with any of the family. It was my father who had found her when he arrived home from work. The usually immaculate kitchen still contained a draining-board full of dishes that, under normal circumstances, would already have been put away in the cupboard. A basket full of wet washing stood near the back door waiting to be taken out and pinned onto the washing line. My mother was nowhere to be seen and my father found her curled up in bed, white and in pain.

There had been no warning. She had always been healthy. The doctor was called and my mother admitted to hospital. After various tests and the usual cell-destroying treatment, she was allowed home to die. My father watched as her life ebbed away in front of him. Her death was a shock to us all. From being the focal point of the family, on whom we all depended, she ended up bed-ridden and dying. After her death, I often came across my father, sitting in front of a blank television screen, the tears streaming down his face.

He had always said that theirs was a special relationship, a true bonding of spirits. It had been 'love at first sight' and a relationship that lasted for almost fifty years and in all that time they had not spent a full day apart.

He begins to speak again.

"There was a group of us going to a dance in the church hall."

I know the story off by heart, but I want to hear it again. I want my father to speak about my mother. By doing so it might help to ease the grief he feels. There have been times over the last few weeks when I thought that he had no wish to remain alive without my mother and I even feared that he might take his own life.

"The dances were held once a month and most of the time it was the same crowd who went. There was a good turnout that night and there were a few new faces. Your mother was one. She had on a red and white polka-dot dress fitted at the waist with a wide, red belt and a big, full skirt." My father smiles for the first time in months. "Do you know what she used to do?" I do know because, of course, I have heard it so often before.

"She had, well, not only her, all the young girls had the same. They wore these petticoats under their dresses. Hers was made of stuff, sort of like net curtains and she used to wash it then soak it in a mixture of sugar and water and hang it up to dry. It used to dry stiff as a board. It used to make the skirt of her dress stand right out, like a bell, when she had it on. And when she danced, her skirt used to fly out around her, showing off her slim legs and her ankles. I spent ages watching her before I plucked up courage to ask her to dance. We were married within the year and neither of us ever regretted a moment of it." My father glances over at me to see if I am still listening. "And then when you came along, after two miscarriages, you were the icing on the cake. We decided not to try again. We had all that we needed and your mother had been heartbroken when the boys didn't survive."

We sit in silence for a while.

"She told me you know," he says, "just a few days before she died." I stare at him. I don't know what he's talking about. "She told me that you were pregnant."

"But I never…"

He interrupts me. "I know you didn't tell her but she knew. She'd guessed. She was so happy about it. Her only sadness was that she would never see her grandchild." He pauses. "She told me to look after you."

"Oh Dad! I'm so sorry. I didn't tell you yet because I thought you had enough on your plate."

He stands up and pulls his chair next to mine, sits and puts his arm around my shoulders. "I'm really looking forward to you having a baby you know. Having a little one about the house will be wonderful. Your mum said it would give me a purpose in life after she was gone."

There are no questions, no recriminations. No doubt the questions will come later. He smiles at me and strokes my hair as I lay my head on his shoulder.

"Your eyes are just like your mother's."

I feel the tears streaming down my face.

Gail Tucker

Lost Sea

Inside my childhood bed I hear below
The beating sea, while outside winds do rage
And storm's tempestuous moods disturb my rest.
In later years, across the world I'll roam
And wake to hear the absent rhythm roar.
What is it now keeps me awake at night?
Do you still call me from afar, across
The miles, and from the fathoms' deepest deep,
To leave the hills and head direct for home?
Or is the fancy folly merely mine;
Close companion time upon time.

Vivien Johnson

Newt

slips out of John's hand
toes spread wide, slithering
down the fire pond's bank

hides below the reeds, watches
nymphs rise to the shimmering surface.
Children's play slips quickly by.

The heron waits.

Avner Kornblum

The Glass and the Candle

The night the cockerel went missing was memorable. Frank said, "He is such a beauty and so unusual, Peggy and I were almost frantic at his disappearance."

Black and yellow is a strange combination, even for a sort-of bantam and, with his feathered feet and lack of a comb, one might have thought he was a bit odd, to say the least, but one look at him would convince even the most diehard chicken-eating cock-crow hater that this chap was spectacular.

Then came the night he went missing from the chicken-coop at Frank and Peggy's suburban home.

Frank and Peggy searched for him in the garden.

In trees, shrubs and bushes on a black, moonless night, it is very difficult to find a black cock – even one wearing plentiful splashes of yellow.

At Frank's suggestion, they went indoors and searched for a torch instead. They found three, none of which functioned, so Peggy suggested a magnifying glass and a candle, both of which were quickly located.

Frank held the candle aloft, below and in-between while Peggy peered through the undergrowth, her eye glued to the magnifying glass, to detect where Jasper might be hiding.

It all came to nought.

There was no sight of him, and unusually, no sound either. A fox must have taken him, as it took his father and several aunts a year earlier. Sadly, Frank and Peggy gave up the search and retired to bed.

Early next morning a neighbour rang the bell at their gate. "It's very strange," she said, "my friend up the road was awakened by a cock crowing in her garden at dawn. Could it be yours?"

She knew of no one else in Spain's seaside suburbia who kept hens and a cockerel and indeed it was, Mr Jasper Combless in person. Heaven knows who or what had frightened him out of his wits to such an extent that he flew or ran several hundred metres into someone else´s garden. Certainly, all his hens were safe.

So the glass and the candle were unnecessary. What Frank and Peggy needed instead were two more humans. The neighbour and her husband obliged, the errant cock was surrounded, captured and returned safely to his wives.

Vivien Johnson

Benissa Town

Pedro adjusts his Panama, gnarled knuckles clutch his stick;
eyes dulled by the sun – remembering thirty years ago.
Not just blocks of stone placed one upon another,
columns of basalt forced through the earth's crust.
Then his hands and cement-filled nails laid town bricks,
he shinned up scaffolding, ran along the boards,
ate bocadillos from a paper bag –
whistled at the girls below.

Houses huddled as the wind whistled round;
donkeys trampled the narrow streets,
laundry dangled from upstairs windows.
Housewives scrubbed pavements,
puppies tugging at their skirts.

But now it is the turn of others;
children sit on kerb-stones oblivious of passing cars –
soon it will be his son's turn to sit and watch the dancing girls.
Today Miguel plays the trumpet
between benign walls,
a Pied Piper visiting the Stations of the Cross.

Jean M. Watson

Going Away

My name is David now. I think it is a lovely name and the one that I chose for myself. David. Such a satisfying sound to it. David. I am glad that I chose it. It is so much nicer than Br... Hey, shush, don't even think it! Anyway, what my name used to be is not important. It belongs to that previous life, which I have abandoned along with my previous job and responsibilities. Today my plans for starting a new life are just an aeroplane flight away. Oh my goodness, just an aeroplane flight away. My heart is choking me with excitement. I checked in with my deliberately unremarkable luggage just a few minutes ago, trying not to draw unwanted attention to myself, trying to look absolutely ordinary. I find that quite difficult, but I must try. Time to be exotic and alluring when I get *there*. I daren't think the actual name of *there* even in the private parts of my own mind.

Now I must sit here in the airport café with this cup of tasteless liquid they call coffee on the silver, metal table in front of me. When I get *there,* the coffee will always taste perfect. My flight leaves in ninety-minutes. I am just ninety-minutes away from freedom and a new start. I imagine my luggage on a trolley, stacked high with an assortment of other people's luggage, labelled with addresses revealing destinations or houses possibly left empty, an incentive for criminal minds. How unwise. By contrast, I love the coloured straps distinguishing all those otherwise identical cases.

    Why does everyone have to go either to Marks and Spencer or to Argos for their luggage? Still, it suits me today that mine looks the same as theirs. Soon, so soon, that luggage will be loaded onto my flight and I will hear the call for boarding. I haven't missed it, have I? What's the time? Oh, that's OK. Only another eighty-five minutes to take-off.

    This coffee, in this ghastly polystyrene cup, has a skin on top. I bought it merely for something to do. Excitement makes it difficult to swallow. It would take something more tempting than airport coffee to make me want to eat or drink. I grip the polystyrene cup to disguise the shaking of my hands, and put the cup on the metal table in front of me. The cafeteria is noisy, crowded with people waiting for their time to board. All appear much more relaxed than I feel, unconcerned about anything more than their own flights. I press my knees together in my grey-suit trousers to try to control their shaking. If I could only look more relaxed, I would be more convincing in my role of businessman on my way to conclude a vital deal.

Well, that is exactly what I am, is it not? A man who works out a deal and steers it through all its tricky stages to that triumphant moment of completion. What admiration should come from one's colleagues, what envy should show in their eyes. However, that pleasure will be missing from this particular deal. This time the need for secrecy will have robbed me of my rightful accolade for my cleverness. This time it is very different. Oh, so very different. This time the deal has been concluded some time ago and the money is in the briefcase at my feet. Well, most of it. What would not go in my briefcase I have crammed into my hand-luggage.

Of course the other party, i.e. my former employer, is not yet aware of his part in the deal. If my luck continues to hold, he will not even become aware of his part in the deal until tomorrow. By then I will have flown away like a swallow to mingle with other swallows like me, becoming indistinguishable from the rest of the flock. There will be no looking back but, even so, it would have been very satisfying to see his face, probably very funny as well, after so many years of putting up with his pompousness and *'Nobody gets one over on me'*.

Of course not, sir. Until now, sir.

How long to go now? Just seventy-minutes to safety and freedom. They will be the longest seventy-minutes that I have ever lived through. What can I do for the next seventy minutes? Will the time never pass? Let me think for a minute. It might keep down these waves of panic that keep making me feel so sick …and they call this coffee? It has never seen a coffee bean in its life. How many coffee beans make a pound? How many pounds of beans in a sack? How many sacks…? Oh well, that passed a couple of minutes but it did not improve the coffee. Sixty-five minutes to go. Well, if the call to board comes twenty-minutes before take-off, it leaves only forty-five minutes to wait. I can loiter in the restroom for ten-minutes just before the boarding call, and take another five minutes to be at the boarding gate in good time.

Just another thirty-minutes to sit here with this cold coffee. I will just lean over and grab the newspaper that the chap on the next table has left behind. Lucky man, his flight has been called and he will soon be on his way. Hmm, not exactly 'The Times', but there is not much else around. Good Lord, what has that girl got on, or not got on? Ah well, just a little joke to myself. It does help lighten the tension. I hope it doesn't show. No, it probably doesn't. Nobody seems to be looking at me. If they were, they would have to admire the cut of my new suit. All they would see would be this prosperous businessman of some, shall we say forty-five years or possibly less. Or so I like to think of myself.

How is the time going? Just thirty-minutes of reading this newspaper and it will be time to move. I wonder what my wife is doing at this moment. It is a fine day so she is probably mowing the lawn. One day I will have to get in touch, through a solicitor I can trust not to reveal my whereabouts, to arrange the divorce. She can have the house. I won't need it anymore. I shall have a very impressive place of my own. Something white and colonnaded somewhere. Twenty-five minutes to waste. Time is passing at last. It is a shame she will not be there to see my new lifestyle, but it really is her own fault. She has been quite a good housekeeper all these years – I shall miss that – but she has got fat and talks only of her wretched garden and her stupid reading group. There will be no place for her in my new life. My new image calls for someone younger than me, who will look decorative by the swimming pool of my new place, and will be a good hostess at dinner parties. I need someone who can talk about more than pruning roses, thank you very much, but who knows how to shut up when I tell her, which is more than my silly wife did. Twenty more minutes to waste. I am glad I did not buy this newspaper. Nothing much in it to read: waste of money. I see somebody has won three-million on the lottery and, as usual, they don't think it will change their life. No point in winning if it does not change your life. How people delude themselves. At least I know how much this money is going to change my life. No doubt about that.

Still fifteen more minutes to waste? Has that clock stopped or something? No, the second-hand is still moving. What else is in this newspaper? Situations vacant: I wonder how they will describe my job when they advertise it – *Accountant with skill in side-lining money, Good prospects, Sunny future?* Now that would be a very proper description of the way I have fulfilled my duties over the last twenty-years. Twenty years of plotting and scheming are about to come to fruition. I can't believe that it is all about to happen. I am almost choking with excitement. Oh, please don't let it show. Look bored, Bri – no, no, David, I must think of myself as David. Ah well, it is almost time to move. Just ten more minutes before I go for a wash and a splash of cologne. I must look calm and groomed to keep the business man image intact. What is in the sports pages? Full of football as usual. You would not think anyone played any other game at all. Look at that team list there! They will not win, it is too weak in the defence, and even the goalkeeper is useless.

At last, only five minutes to waste. I think I will move now. If I go slowly I will get to the gate in perfect time. Oh lord, I am so stiff from sitting.

Pardon? What did you say?

You're not talking to me, are you? No, no, I am not Brian, I am David. Well, since this morning I am. Please take your hands off my new suit, whoever you are. From where? New Scotland Yard? No, Officer, you have got the wrong man. MY name is David. Well, yes, that is my coffee cup. Well, I suppose it will have my fingerprints on it. Why are you putting it in a plastic bag? Arresting me? For what? What do you mean embezzlement? No, I just did a deal with my employer. He knows all about it. What do you mean, he certainly does now? Who told him? My wife? How did she find out? She found the ticket? She can't have! How did my wife find the ticket? She is too stupid to look in my briefcase. Oh, when the new passport came in the post.

Look, I can't come with you now. I am booked on an aeroplane. Listen! My flight is just being called and my luggage is on board. I have been waiting here for ninety minutes, counting every one.

Oh, please, they are calling my name …it's David.

Vivien Johnson

Police Box

This Tadworth Tardis at the crossroads –
Blue paint, high square windows,
A crown of flashing blue light;
Telephone inside, 999 on the door.

1911 – he pedalled his bicycle,
Snakes of smoke coiled from under his helmet,
Cavernous cape around his shoulders –
To wallop apple-scrumping boys with.

I never did see inside the box
till I peeked at The Doctor from behind the sofa.
They pulled down his house and built posh flats;
He emigrated to another galaxy
to the sound of grinding metal.

Vivien Johnson

Night Swimming

He would watch her from the balcony,
entranced by her affinity with water,
her lithe body stroking the liquid
caressing it length by length.

Now with ripples wrapped
she glances up feeling him there –
his ghost risen from the ashes
scattered where he wanted to be.

Today she'd read their letters of fifty years ago,
She had forgotten how much he'd loved her.

Gail Tucker

Loss

These pre-dawn hours, I shall not hear
your foot-fall crush the stony path,
you'll not return to tap my door, to pat my head
or gently pinch my cheek.

Time was, I'd leap at door-key rasp,
heart catch click of latch. A blink before
you'd bow to plant your bags, I'd be there
at your feet, eager and meek.

Those signal sounds stay silent, there's no return
with tales to tell of that realm you now explore.
The daughter's world you left behind is
impoverished, raw and bleak.

It matters not the way news comes,
it could not matter more, or less, if brought
by gentle face or shrill insistent ringing – now!
I only have your tender smile, the crinkled eyes and
knowing grin safe to keep.

Though you were often absent then,
lodged in your child's heart – deep,
nourished by your stays at home
I never could a better father seek.

Sheila Skinner

Sacrifice

"Didn't have any of that stress what's-it in them days," says Dad, nodding in the direction of Gramps photo. The frail gnarled body I remember as my granddad, bore no resemblance to this straight-backed, proud young man in his 1915 khakis. The hand-tinted picture, familiar but fading, still shows those piercing, china-blue eyes. Bright and courageous, they dare you to question his commitment to *King and Country.*

A year later, those same eyes, seared by mustard gas, had already witnessed horrors that stayed locked in unseeing eyes, uncomprehending brain forever. Still he never questioned those who choreographed the chaos, the carnage.

"What is it?" Dad snapped testily, "that PT what's-it thing?"

"PTSD, Dad," I reply heavily. We've had this conversation before, I know what's coming and take a deep breath. "Post-Traumatic Stress Disorder, Dad." I speak the words calmly, but they still wind him up.

Lots of things do these days. November is always the worst. Poppy Sellers, Remembrance Sunday, people who ignore the two-minute silence, the lack of Union Jacks on public display. Any and all of it sets him off but now, with the centenary of the outbreak of WW1, he is even touchier.

"Load of bloody nonsense if you ask me" he snarls.

Not that I blame him, of course. He has his convictions, still – believes it was all a glorious victory, even Dunkirk. It got him through North Africa and home safe, that belief.

Gramps and all those brave, young men must have believed too, but at least you could argue that they couldn't see the bigger picture a hundred years ago …just their own patch of mud and misery: just the camaraderie and courage and faith that they were fighting on the side of good against evil. They *had* to believe, to keep going forward against all the odds.

There's my Dad too, in his 1941 full-length army picture, next to Gramps. Dad, too young at eighteen to ask the wreck of a man who had come back, if it had all been worth it. It wasn't the kind of conversation you had with your Dad in those days.

My Dad's here now, over ninety-years-old. I still haven't had that conversation with him either: never had that kind of courage.

He and his generation knew about the millions who perished in the *War to end all Wars.* They knew about the criminal waste of life and limb, the annihilation of the youth of Europe, let alone Britain. How *could* they have fallen for that *King and Country* crap all over again, just twenty years later?

We've all made the supreme sacrifice these last one-hundred years: truth.

Vivien Johnson

5 Year's Old in Kathmandu

*Gilded temples all around
she sits among the holy cow-pats
filthy fabric shrouds her bones,
stumps where arms should be.
Legs?   No legs.*

*In Durbar Square shutters click –
all caught on film
to be shown in cosy drawing rooms.*

*The hippies are long gone –
but a girl like her will always be there.
The child with the dark brown eyes.*

Avner Kornblum

A Table for Two

In a dark and miserable year we experienced a moment of light. It occurred when Pru and I saw a lovely dining table in a second-hand shop. The frame and legs were of a bright and cheerful wood and the table-top was an even brighter and more cheerful marble. Better still, the table and its six chairs were a perfect match for the existing furniture. Best of all, the price was downright reasonable.

We bought the seven-item set and arranged for them to be delivered, but neither Pru nor I know how the table and chairs got into the villa. We came home from an outing and there they were, stacked up in the lounge. It did not require much effort to push – no, to slide – the table a metre or so across the glossy, tiled Spanish floor into the right position, yet that was enough to tell me the table was heavy …very heavy.

Some months later my wife exercised her divine right as a woman to move, change and re-organise the complete components and contents, furniture and furnishings of the villa´s lounge, dining room and kitchen. Of course, I am not only her husband, I am also her general factotum. Thus it was her idea that caused us to drive 300 kilometres to our Teruel watermill then 300 kilometres back the same day in snow, rain and frost, to fetch the large, wooden, expanding table, so beautiful and so solid, at which twelve people can sit in comfort.

Fortunately for the factotum, this wonderfully-designed table divided into five parts, only two of which were almost hernia-inducing when carried to the car.

Back home, slightly warmer, slightly drier, I carried the five-part table into the villa, still resisting the hernia threatened by two of the parts. Having brought them in, I re-assembled them. Now we had three very attractive tables in the lounge-dining room: the modern marble-top wooden table, the older expanding table from the mill, and the antique round table (painted cracklewood, no less) with its glass top. Seating accommodation for everybody we were expecting, and more.

Pru commented. "This place looks just like a car-boot sale. Why don't you take the marble-top table and its chairs out onto the *naya*? Guests enjoy eating outside in sunny weather. Then we could close the expanding table into a six-seater, and the round table could have four chairs instead of six. That would make this place far more friendly, don't you think?"

To tell the truth, I don't think – not when Pru speaks. I obey. So I proceeded to move the marble-top table. No problem to slide it to the glass door that opened onto the *naya,* but it was four inches (sorry, ten centimetres) too wide! After I had tried angling it and wangling it, all fruitlessly, I was forced to admit there was no other solution than to place it on its side, and get it out two legs at a time.

Suddenly it seemed considerably heavier than before. I needed to exercise the greatest care in turning it on its side, so that I did not break the legs nor scratch the sides. I placed a mat where its edge would come to rest, then groped around the joints where its legs and sides met until I found reinforced sections at each end. Clinging firmly to these, I succeeded in turning the table sideways with its heavy top resting on the mat and slid it halfway through the door. Here I faced three more obstacles.

The step down from the lounge to the *naya* was hazardous; the position Pru had chosen for the table was a good ten feet (oops, three metres) from the doorway where it now lay, which meant a great deal more effort on my part; and the paving stones were rough, so they would scuff the edge if I dragged it there on its side, or would hinder its progress if I stood the table upright.

Discovering a hitherto-hidden inventiveness, I placed two runners and a small mat in a line to the exact destination of the table. Then, employing physical flexibility and strength I thought had long deserted me, I lowered the table down the step and along the runners to its final position astride the mat. The task would now be completed, except that the table was still on its side.

After this long story I won't bore you by reciting the efforts I made over an extended period to stand the table up. Every attempt failed. My new-found inventiveness deserted me as suddenly as it had arrived. When I was completely spent, physically and ideas-wise, Pru appeared. She admired what I had achieved, bless her. "Wait for Sam," was her profound contribution, and when our son, Sam, arrived, it was astonishing. I swear it took no more than ten seconds for him and me to right the table, and to place it correctly.

The exercise taught me something about such a table. One person can lay it, one person can lay it on its side …but when it's on its side and has to be lifted onto its legs, it is definitely a table for two.

Vivien Johnson

Bygone Times

Blue sky, dotted clouds, a storm on the way.
Serfs bend over the small plot
scraping the earth with rough-forged trowels.
Seeds dropped into dibbed holes in reddish earth.

The master gallops through the land;
like undertow peasants draw back,
genuflect as their crops are trampled
by the charger's hoofs.

The man, a god, his golden embellishments
glitter in sunlight's shafts.
He extracts his dues.
When he is gone, they start all over.

Gail Tucker

Traceries

Cake is displayed on a pedestalled stand,
white doily visible below the missing slice.
Delicious criss-cross of fine white sugar masks
vanilla rich custard, airy sponge rosewater fragrant.

The customer reads the name, Alcazar,
Indian ink on crisp white, sharp edged card;
in a Bath teashop called The Canary
a name adds to exoticism of cake.

A decade later in another city, another country,
an Englishwoman looks up from cool flagstones
to delicate tracery of exquisitely fashioned ceilings –
Real Alcázar, Moorish Seville.

'Good enough to eat,' says her greedy companion,
'How delicious!'

Agnes Hall

Every Cloud Has a Silver Lining

Jane hated the very thought of holidays. The extra washing and ironing, the packing, the cleaning out the fridge, arranging for the dogs to go into kennels. It all simply added to an already stressful life. This particular holiday was going to be even worse than usual because they were going camping ...in Ireland. It always rained in Ireland. Wasn't that why it was called 'The Emerald Isle', because of the lush greenness, a result of the constant rain? That was not all. They were not going alone.

The idea of a camping holiday had originated with Megan, the wife of one of Jane's husband's workmates, Kevin. Jane tolerated Kevin but secretly thought of Megan as 'The Welsh Witch' and not only because of her large hooked nose. Despite Jane's protestations that a camping holiday in Ireland was not a good idea (in fact as far as Jane was concerned, a camping holiday anywhere was not a good idea), Graham had managed to muster the troops in his favour, by persuading their two children, Helen and Mark, that camping could be a great adventure. It had not taken much to persuade them, particularly when Graham had promised them that they could have a small tent of their own and would not have to share with their parents. Jane, despite her misgivings, capitulated under the pressure.

On Jane's insistence, one of the tents they hired was a large frame tent so that she could stand up whilst she cooked but, as Graham had promised, they also hired a small, separate ridge-tent for the children. The tents, along with all the other paraphernalia that a camping holiday demands, were packed into every available orifice inside the car and what would not fit inside was balanced precariously on the roof rack secured by multi-coloured bungies.

Graham's secretary had been asked to book the ferry tickets from

Liverpool to Dublin and, remembering as they approached Liverpool that she had seen directions to the port on the back of the ticket folder, Jane took the tickets from her handbag. Her eyes scanned the folder and then the tickets. "I think you'd better pull over. We have a problem." Graham glanced sideways at her but did as requested when he saw the expression on her face. "We're not going to Dublin," she said, "we're going to Belfast."

She passed the tickets to him. "Don't even think about it." She snapped, not giving Graham the opportunity to open the expected tirade against her for not having previously checked the tickets. "We need to get a message to Kevin and let him know what's happened." They both groaned when they remembered that Graham had left his mobile phone, which was normally an extension of his right arm, on the kitchen table. It was something that they had only realised when they were halfway across the M62 and it was too late to turn back. They also realised that the only source of Kevin's mobile number was the address book in Graham's mobile phone, so it was not even possible to contact him easily from a public phone.

The plans for the holiday itself had been rather vague, to be discussed in greater detail on board the Dublin ferry, where they were supposed to meet up. There had however, been mention of the Dingle Peninsula on the west coast of Ireland and a place called Castle Gregory and they decided that the best thing that they could do was to take the Belfast ferry and head in the direction of the Dingle Peninsula the following morning.

The crossing was rough and Jane was not a good sailor. Coupled with that, the fact that their destination was a much farther drive from Belfast than from Dublin reinforced Jane's dread that the holiday was doomed to be a disaster. The only bonus point Jane could see was that there would be one day less to spend with 'The Welsh Witch'.

They were all tired by the time they reached the Dingle Peninsula and eventually Castle Gregory and on edge knowing that their tour of local campsites, in the search of Kevin and Megan, was still to begin.

"I think that we should stop and have a drink before we start searching. The kids are tired and I'm thirsty." Jane said, secretly hoping that Kevin and Megan would have forgotten the vague mention of Castle Gregory. Her hopes were dashed when the first bar they came across was Fitzgerald's Bar and sitting outside were Kevin, the Welsh

Witch and their two sons.

The rain started, confirming Jane's fears, as she and Graham followed Kevin and Megan to the campsite where, aided by Helen and Mark, they began to unload the car and erect their tents. Jane carefully noted that Kevin, Megan and the boys crawled into their two small ridge tents, to shelter from the rain, not offering any assistance.

When the tents were finally erected and the airbeds, sleeping bags, table and chairs were all in place, Jane breathed a sigh of relief. She began rummaging about in the cardboard boxes full of food that littered the tent, looking for something that she could cook quickly for supper.

"Coo-eee!" Megan appeared at the entrance to the tent. "Mind if we join you. It's a bit cramped in there," she said, nodding in the direction of their own tents, from which Kevin and the boys were emerging. "We haven't eaten yet, so we may as well join forces." Jane soon found herself being jostled for position at the camping stove as she attempted to cook their evening meal and, as the evening wore on with no sign of Megan and family moving back to their own tents, she became more and more angry.

As soon as the uninvited guests had gone and the dishes washed, scarcely able to bring herself to speak to Graham, Jane settled down to sleep. She awoke some hours later, feeling cold and realised that she was not just cold. She was wet. The rain had persisted all night and seeped up through the ground sheet and their two tents were flooded. They hadn't realised that the area selected by Kevin and Megan as their camping plot was situated at the bottom of a shallow slope, where rain collected.

The morning was spent in silence as both families packed their sodden belongings back into the cars and moved farther along the coast to a campsite on higher ground. The rain continued, each night a repeat of the first, with both families sharing the living accommodation that the larger frame tent provided.

"I've had enough," Jane said, after a few days, when Kevin, Megan and family once again appeared at the entrance to the tent. "I'm going to book a room at Fitzgerald's Bar. You lot can do what the hell you like." She grabbed a bag, stuffed a few items of clothing in it and drove off into the night leaving everyone else with their mouths hanging open. Mark and Helen had also had enough. Sitting around a campfire, singing songs, had not materialised. They were permanently wet and uncomfortable, there was nothing to do and only the tent to escape from the rain. The following morning, when Jane returned with the car after a cosy and comfortable night at Fitzgerald's Bar, her family had dismantled their two tents and all the provisions and equipment were packed up. "Good," she said, "I've booked us into Fitzgerald's Bar."

Kevin and Megan appeared from their tents as they loaded up the car.

"Sorry folks," Jane told them, "I've booked the last two rooms at Fitzgerald's. The rain is forecast to stop, or so I've been told, but as far as I'm concerned you can sod camping for a lark, I'm all for a comfy bed and a warm fire. See you around."

She knew it was unlikely that she would be seeing much of the Welsh Witch in future. Something that she was very happy about.

Sheila Skinner

The Coin

Just a couple of statements in my mail box, so I'm surprised to see a squashed Jiffy Bag laying on the hall mat. I close the front door behind me and slide the bolts across, a good habit for a young woman living alone. I bend and pick up the package.

A4, obviously too large for the box outside and unceremoniously stuffed through the letter box, it looks a bit worse for wear. It has also, judging by the claw marks and loose bits of stuffing, already been investigated by Bella, my Siamese.

She's scampering down the stairs to greet me, vocalizing as always: that mix of 'welcome home' and 'you'll never guess what kind of a day *I've* had', that always makes me smile. I scoop her up for a cuddle, she nuzzles and murmurs but denies all knowledge of the packet when waved at her. Jumping down she heads for the kitchen and her food bowl.

The same routine every evening for the last four years ...I walk home from the Vet's Practice on the Promenade, where I work with Rodney Willis, my partner: strictly work partner, a nice man but twenty-years my senior and happily married, thank goodness. I've shared this two-up two-down terraced cottage, with Bella, since she was brought in as an abandoned kitten. I've tried sharing with one special man, but that didn't work out, so it's pretty much the same this evening as always. Shoes off, kettle on and supper. Tea and biscuits for me – tuna, Bella's favourite, for her and the TV news that we watch together.

Settling down I read the neat sender's label on the reverse. *'Creighton & Warren Solicitors, The Shambles, Canterbury.'* Mm-mm ...I'm impressed by the posh address but still wondering what on earth a Solicitor, who I'd never contacted, wants with me?

It's addressed to me under my full name, Donna Helen Moss, that's curious too, I never use Helen. Putting my cup safely on the side-table and the biscuits out of Bella's reach, I peel open the package.

As soon as I do Bella's back on my lap, curiosity turning her pretty head from side to side, like a ventriloquist's dummy as I slide various items out onto the coffee table: a single typed sheet, obviously from the Solicitors, a small plastic wallet, which seems to contain a few handwritten pages together with an even smaller, lumpy package, tissue-wrapped and sealed with tape.

My tea cool enough to sip now, I start to read…

Dear Ms. Moss,

We are writing to you as instructed in the last Will and Testament of Helen Bernadette O'Farrell, late of Flat 7b, Chestnut Court, Ashford.

That's not that far from here I'm thinking, but the name and address mean nothing to me.
 As my curiosity increases, so does a slight feeling of unease.
 Someone has died, someone I don't know, so what can this possibly have to do with me?
 The dry official language continues.
 I sip my tea and share a ginger snap with Bella…
We are requested to forward the enclosed private letter addressed to you, together with the wallet and contents, neither of which, under instruction from the deceased, have been seen nor read by any other person.
 Should you feel it necessary to contact us further in this matter, we are obliged to advise you that we have no further knowledge of the deceased or her affairs. There is, to our knowledge, no question of inheritance.

The word inheritance adds to my feeling of unease.
 This is worrying me now.

Ms. O'Farrell's last Will and Testament was signed here in November 2014 and remains the only contact made with us. This matter has recently come to light with her demise, her death certified on 8th April 2015. The delay is due to the extensive enquiries we have had to undertake in order to trace your current whereabouts. We would be *most obliged for written confirmation of receipt of these items. There are no charges levied for this service and this, we trust, brings this matter to a satisfactory conclusion.*

'We remain' etc. etc., the usual jargon, obedient servants and all that rubbish.

A package, a few paragraphs of a letter and my mind is in turmoil, my heart racing. Ring Colin, that's my first reaction always, if I'm not sure what to do …but no, I try to calm myself. My tea was cold by the time I read the letter through again and again. This woman died in April, that's months ago now, but that doesn't help. I still don't know who she is or what she has to do with me and my quiet, ordered life.

I need something stronger I decide, so jump up, still cuddling Bella. Stroking her always calms me and I pour myself an Amaretto, she sniffs it, wrinkles her nose in disgust and jumps down. As contrary as ever, as soon as I sit down again down she rejoins me on the sofa. She's looking for attention but I'm too caught up in the thoughts that are racing around my head.

The only link seems to be Helen, my second name, the Bernadette O'Farrell sounds really Irish. No connections there either, or none that Doreen and Bob my loving parents had ever spoken about. Officially my adoptive parents, they had been totally honest about that in my teens and, on my 18th birthday, I was handed a file of papers and the choice, whether or not to find out about my birthmother.

Colin, my brother, 6 years my senior and always my protector assured me that none of them would mind if I wanted to know. I never did. Nothing in my childhood or upbringing had ever given me reason to doubt that they chose me, they had wanted me and had loved me.

Whoever had given me away obviously had not and I never felt the need to find out who they were or why. Never.

When Doreen and Bob perished in that awful ferry disaster I made Colin promise to burn that file. It seemed even more of an insult to them after their death.

We never mentioned it again.

We were both reeling in those awful weeks and months after the accident. Newspapers were full of stories and pictures of the victims and their bereaved families: reporters and local radio interviewers at doors, and even at funeral services.

Our local papers fed off it for weeks covering the inquest and coroner's reports. All that pain and grieving makes great copy, of course. Colin, with his medal-winning service record in Iraq, had already been a local celebrity. He'd featured a lot.

Bob who had also been a RAF man, was so proud of him, he had cut out all the Press articles and photos and kept them in an album, together with my graduation from Vet College and my first day when I went to work for Mr. Willis as a young, nervous assistant.

Later, with the money that they'd left us, I was able to buy a partnership in this same practice and Colin bought a couple of properties. This one I rent from him and the other he lets out to students at the nearby Language Academy. He's due for retirement in eight years and then figures to move in there himself. He's still my big brother and I will always be happy to have him nearby. I know that I'll need to talk to him about this, but first, I tell myself, I have to find out what's in these packages.

Another slug of almond liqueur and the folded, hand-written pages are on my lap. Bella has decided there's nothing interesting in the small package that she has batted around the coffee table a few times.

I rescue it and she goes back to preening herself.

With slightly shaking hands I smooth out the small, blue-lined writing paper, four pages in all.

"Here goes," I say out loud and start to read.

No address I notice, just the date:

October 22, 2014

Dear Donna,
I was so happy to learn that they had kept your name, that was all I had to give you and it was when I read about the ferry tragedy and you and your brother losing your parents, that I realised who you were.

'Realised who you were' …I repeat this out loud.

It doesn't make sense – then I make the connection – the accident, early December 1983. Mum and Dad were coming back from their pre-Xmas caravan trip to Tuscany, they loved autumn there, went every year, but always came back for a family Xmas.

This lady had obviously read about it, seen the pictures of Colin and me, but so had everyone.

What did she have to do with my name?

What could she want to give me if I never knew her? My brain is scrambling now, I take a deep breath and read on:

How sorry I was and what a lovely service, you and Colin even look a bit alike. I never knew your Mum and Dad, of course and it took me years to find out that they had taken you for their daughter.

I hope you don't blame me for coming to the Church anyway. I know they loved you and cared for you as I never could, but I couldn't thank them whilst they were alive, could I? Not without barging into your lives and upsetting everything. When your 18th birthday came, and went, I realised that you had chosen not to find me. I can't blame you Donna, I just wanted to tell you, before it's too late, that after you were born and until the day I die, you and Don, your father, were my first thoughts every morning and my last every night, you are still.

Donald, Don, was your Dad, he was a serving US pilot, based at Cranton USAF Air Base.

Our story sounds cheap now, but I need you to know that it wasn't like that at all. We loved each other and, after a year, we were planning to get married when he came back from Vietnam, only he never did.

Officials at the Base were very sympathetic. He'd only been over there two months and their priority, of course, was his family and shipping his remains back to Oregon.

He'd mentioned me to his family, even sent a couple of photos, but they were wrapped up in their grief, not mine. I got a letter from his Mum saying that they were sure that Don would have wished me to find someone else and be happy. It sounded as if they really hadn't taken us seriously.

Don was a lonely young man, miles from home, who had met a nice local girl, why not? So neither Don, nor his family, ever knew about you, our darling baby girl.

I was 19, of a strict Catholic family back in Cavan. As a trainee nurse I could have found a way out, but I loved Don and I loved you from the moment I held you. I loved you when I signed the papers to give you up so that you would have a chance of a decent, respectable and loving upbringing. I know that's what your Mum and Dad gave you and I was always so grateful to them. I wanted so much to comfort you at their funeral, but knew that would be so selfish of me, I just lit candles for them instead.

This will be a shock to you and maybe a terrible disappointment, but now that we are never going to talk or meet, I feel it safe to let you know that I still love you Donna and never wanted to do anything to upset you or the life you have made for yourself. I needed to tell you and you need to know that you were born of a loving relationship.

Don would have made a great Dad. He had our two initials and his service number engraved on this silver dollar. It was to be our lovetoken to keep him safe 'til he got back. I've worn it every day.

It's yours now Donna and I am so sorry that this is all I have to give you, apart from my everlasting love. I never married so for the record, your natural parents were Helen Bernadette O' Farrell, Cavan, Co. Cavan, EIRE and Donald Festor Brightman, Eugene OREGON USA: If you believe in God and I hope you do, we are together now looking over you.

Yours in truth and love,
Helen.

There wasn't any more; just as well, as the tears welling up in my eyes were making it hard to read further. Running down my cheeks they were wetting Bella's head too. Bless her, she was nudging and rubbing against my cheek, picking up on my distress as animals do and trying to comfort me.

I grabbed some tissues, drained the last of the Amoretto and unwrapped the small package.

Inside lay the silver dollar on a thick Belcher silver chain. There were the initials, linked with a cupid's arrow on the front and a serial number on the back. Gingerly I trace the H & D. How could a few grams of silver be such a weight in my heart?

The linked, silver chain slips easily over my head and I'm sitting here, rocking Bella gently on my lap.

The letter and the story I'm going to read again, tears or no tears.

Then I'll phone Colin.

Vivien Johnson

Vista Montgo

The elephant mountain watches the river's mouth,
trunk trailing in Mediterranean water.
He kneels in fields of vines and orange groves.
Pine trees bowing to the wind cling to scarce soil,
cushions of needles settle on rock;
the sun's evening rays rage on the slopes –
new life will blossom there tomorrow.

A patchwork quilt on a mother's birthing bed
a squawking infant and
morning blood with stains of pain,
a child of Aries launched into the world.
Ruled by Mars in anything she'll do,
a firework that flares –
mother will not forsake this cherished child.

As years wheel by
Montgo still kneels
trailing his trunk in the water,
watching for every new birth.

Gail Tucker

The Promised Land

"B'Jesus Colm, will you stop squirming!" Mammie reached out a hand across my shoulder to still my brother. "If your daddy wakes again, you'll catch it." I could hear the fear in her voice, tired though she was. I shifted my back to another spot on the wall of crates that blocked our view of the city. Ahead was only the cold grey water lapping the jetty. "Here, Rita, take the babe a while, there's a good girl," Mammie eased the bundle from her breast and into my lap.

Trapped as I was behind Colm and The Daddy, I could barely reach a hand to catch at the shawl. My legs were numb with cold, I'd have given anything to stand up and stamp about a bit. We'd done nothing but sit or tramp about for days now. First had come the tramping – well, I was not too sad about that, it took us steadily away from the mud patch and streaming-wet walls of the place we called home. With no work, The Daddy made life a misery and with nothing coming up in the patch, Mammie had less and less to put in the pot to feed us.

It was Uncle Rory that went first. He told the old ones he'd be back within a twelve-month if it didn't work out. He did not come back. He did not send word.

Granddaddy went up to the top of the rise every day for a month after that Christmas but was back with a shake of his old head every evening when the light failed. He just sat on his old chair by the hearth and chewed his pipe with a dreamy look in his eyes.

Every day at noon, The Granny would comb her wisps of hair. One day I said, "What are you doing that for?"

She looked at me and smiled such a sad smile, sort of empty and full of hope at the same time, "Today our Rory might be back."

The Daddy went off one day soon after she died. The place was all sixes and sevens, even Mammie seemed distracted and I'd never seen that before. She didn't even clip Colm when he took a fist of porridge from the cooking-pot on the side.

We heard them coming home together, Granddaddy had his arm thrown round The Daddy's shoulder – they were arguing like the blazes.

"Well you'll go without me," said the old one. "I'll not stand the voyage but take the rest. Start a new life. There's nothing for you here," he drew away with a punch on the arm.

"I'll not leave you, so I'll not …" The Daddy swore a word I'd not use but I could tell he meant it kindly. He pulled at the old one's sleeve but it was no use, he was only pulling the stitches; it was Granddaddy that held firm in his resolve.

"Would you tear the sleeve of the only rag he's got now?" cautioned Mammie.

"It's not the sleeve to be tearing," declared the old man, wagging his big, bent finger in the air at her, "remember the lining – even the pocket!"

The way he said it, it sounded biblical, like something about The Day of Redemption from the pulpit.

It was his last word anyway. He went to bed there and then: just lay down and slept.

The next morning, he was gone.

When The Daddy came back to say that the priest would be along later, he had important business up at The Big House before he could come, Mammie was busy with the kitchen knife.

"What in God's name are you doing now?" he whispered, angry at her but mindful of her dead father lying with his eyes open, staring into the room.

"I'm doing his bidding," she said as she slit the lining to part it from the jacket.

She had not even asked me to help as she'd rolled Granddaddy and tugged off the old tweed he wore day and night. All she'd said was, *'Watch the babby'* and once, *'Stop snivelling, Colm',* and there it was, suddenly, a bright gleam that flashed three times as the lining pulled free of the coat. "Take them," she said to me now, "into the babe's crib. Quick sharp!" While The Daddy still stood gaping, Mammie pushed the knife away and gathered up the lining.

When the shadow of the priest, always scenting the whiff of money, fell much sooner than expected across the threshold, the old man was already shrouded in his best for burial.

I expect he was used to the scene, the priest, and he'd have doubted there'd be money for Divine Rites anyway. He hesitated a bit I noticed, as if something puzzled him. Perhaps he'd come sooner than later because he had smelled money and now saw it could not have been here at all, that his instinct must have been confused with the thought of luncheon at The Big House. I caught his eye as he stood looking at me, once he got used to the gloom. It was creepy, he should have been looking at Granddaddy. I never liked him, the priest. Mammie didn't either, I could tell.

Anyway, it was all quick after that. The quick and the dead, you might say. We left without a backward glance. No time for questions about what we all quietly referred to as *the wherewithal*, and forever grateful to the dead Granddaddy.

They say New York is paved with gold; our wherewithal is only three coins; America will be our heaven on earth, The Daddy says.

Avner Kornblum

Lonely Hearts Letter

To Her

I was just about to give up the ghost
when I saw your advert in Today's Post,
so I'll put pen to paper once again
in the hope my letter won't be in vain.

You asked for a man who's honest, mature,
well-bred and well-heeled. I am that, for sure.
To prove that I'm honest I'll tell you strictly the truth:
I'm more than mature, I am pretty long in the tooth.
I'm well-bred for certain, from a long line of cads –
my mother conceived me through a pal of my Dad's.
I am very well-heeled, I have money to burn –
did a night-job on Barclays. (Will banks never learn?)
You said you want a handsome man, fairly slim and tall:
on those three points I fear I don't measure up at all.
Your ad requests a single man who has no family ties:
now this request I can oblige without my telling you lies.
My wife left me a year ago for a glib insurance man
'Twas shortly after he sold me an expensive five-year plan.
My children are grown, I'm completely alone.
I want a companion of under nine stone,
a good-humoured good cook who's preferably pretty,
unencumbered and sexy and just about thirty.

To Him

I thank you for your letter and for telling me the truth.
I'm glad you have admitted that you're past the peak of youth.
As a bank-robbing husband with a wife on the run
you are not very safe, but then you're bound to be fun.

You want a little lady whose weight is just nine stone:
I'm thirteen kilos over that, with superb muscle tone.
I am excellent at cooking, thanks to instant frozen food
and I fry up eggs and chips at times –that's if I'm in the mood.
My friends say I am pretty yet I know they're being kind
I'm not exactly wrinkled but my face is fairly lined.
I'm completely unencumbered as my husband died at sea;
Since my kids learned that I pushed him in they never speak to me.
At your age you want me sexy? I can do a thing or two
but don't think you can just lie there with no work for you to do.
I long ago passed thirty; you can be kind and say I'm mellow
but who the hell of thirty would want a short, fat ugly fellow?
I don't meet the needs you stated and you do not meet mine.
We are such a perfect mis-match it has to work out fine.

Colin Hall

The Boss's Son

The suggestion that had just been made caused his spirit to rise. It made him feel better inside, about life in general and what the future might have in the offing. The last 16 years had not been entirely happy. There had been the highs of football and cricket and riding his bike. Those times had been spoilt by the hours sitting in classrooms learning boring dates in history and chemical symbols, all delivered by disinterested teachers. If they weren't interested in what they were saying, then why should he be?

At a previous meal-time, he had said that he fancied becoming a missionary. Going off into Africa to spread the Good News and improve their living standards. His dad had said it was a stupid idea and to forget it.

Now came the offer he just couldn't refuse. The promise of his own car and independence excited him. The thought of real money in his pocket and the chance to get out and about and see more than just the immediate locality enthused him. The prospect of never having to go to school again energised him. The thought of meeting grown-ups and being able to talk with them about important matters motivated him. The prospect of making new friends and joining in their interests awakened him. All in all, he was charged with a freshness at the prospect of replacing the sterility of the institutional surroundings of his Grammar School with release into the outside world.

The offer came at the dinner table. "Why don't you leave school and come and work for me?"

It didn't take forever for him to make up his mind and so, within the month, he was to be found on the shop-floor of a joinery shop in Manchester, albeit sweeping up and fetching nails and glue from the storeroom. Every morning at 11.30 he went round all the joiners with his paper and pencil, collected their money and walked up the road to the local baker's. It was more fun sitting with the lads around the open wood-stove in the middle of the shop and listening to their tales of what they got up to outside work hours, than being stuck in the school canteen. At school, nobody dared to swear or spit on the floor. Here it was obligatory.

Gradually, over the course of the following months, he was encouraged to use some of the men's tools. He was helping to construct all sorts of things out of timber. He had done woodwork at school, but this was different. There were shortcuts to be followed if the job were to be completed on time. Whereas, it used to take hours to make a mortise and tenon joint, now it was a matter of minutes. One year it had taken a whole term to construct a bird-stand for the garden. He was eager to please his new colleagues and, in turn, to impress his father. Sometimes he wondered if it would be all his one day. That was something to aim for.

To this end he went beyond the call of duty. There was one machine, which instilled fear in most men. It was called a spindle moulder. The machinist who normally operated it had three fingers missing from one hand and a thumb from the other. The central blade spun at the speed of light and gouged out anything in its way. Many had witnessed its devastating effects. Not a few had driven an operator of this malicious machine to the Accident and Emergency department at Ancoats Hospital. He had to show he was not afraid and machined many a dovetail joint on it.

Flushed with his safety record on the spindle moulder, he next volunteered to do something else that many shied away from. The material very much in vogue at the time because of recent fire regulations, in construction, was an asbestos insulating board, which went by the trade name of 'Asbestolux'. He would stay behind after the rest of the men had gone home, tie a handkerchief over his nose and mouth and, working from a cutting list, cut up sheet after sheet of the stuff. When he had finished, he was covered in the white dust. It was in his hair and all over his clothes. The joinery shop looked as though a snow storm had blown through it. After sweeping up he went home.

Now, fifty years later, he lay in his bed remembering those happy times of leaving school and proving himself to the boss, and his coughing grew worse.

Vivien Johnson

Your First Gift

*Was it my innocence, your good looks or
getting wet in the bishop's garden?
Perhaps it was the horse fly and the cream cheese;
you lent me your sock for my swollen foot.
The cheese remedy didn't smell;
you carried my Rollieflex up the Salsgammergutt.*

*I wrote to my parents,
I have met this boy – they worried –
no one had ever touched my camera!
On the coach back seat we held hands, later
sat by the lake watching the reflection of stars
on noiseless ripples – it rained at eleven.*

*In St. Wolfgang you bought me an edelweiss pendant –
black velvet around my neck and silver mount;
it has lain in my jewel box all these years.*

*Travelling home
you ran down the Tyrolean track spilling the collected water –
I worried we would abandon you there;
the train gathered speed – eager hands dragged you aboard.
Only a tiny drop left.*

*My father met us at London's Victoria
we caught the last train out – stopping.
We kissed at your station
Daddy's jaw dropped.
We changed at East Croydon
I glowed all the way home.*

Sheila Skinner

Missing

A bit tearful, now that they've gone, Raymond gives me a squeeze to let me know he understands, then goes back to his book. Sitting together on the sofa I'm thinking back over these last two weeks, how quickly that precious time went by. I'm only half watching the afternoon news.

Robert and Marina kept to Jo-Jo's routine for meals and bedtime, but gave us lots of time with him. Marina, bless her, knows how much we need to hold and spoil him. "But not too much Betty." I hear charming accented English; Jo-Jo will probably have that too, I muse. A week from his third birthday and he already has a smattering of English among his Italian vocabulary. Sensibly they are bringing him up bilingually in faraway Sicily.

Raymond's bypass operation went well but meant we couldn't fly out there as planned so Robert, our only son, brought them over to our new retirement home, here in Spain. It's their first visit here and these two weeks have formed a wonderful bond between all of us. Robert, a husband and father himself now, seems to have grown more comfortable with his Dad. Rob and I were always close and when we've seen them, Marina, cleverly, has always given us time together.

We'd agreed that Granddad and Grandma sounded far too formal, apart from making us feel ancient, so we happily settled for Nono and Nona: easier for Jo-Jo and us.

His early shyness melted that first afternoon, when Raymond took him down the garden to feed the rabbits. That was their daily routine then, that and helping Nono to water the allotment. Raymond is so proud of that, it's almost as good as the one in Bournemouth.

Marina was really impressed with his Mediterranean vegetables and cooked us a lovely pasta dish with our own peppers and aubergines, even praising the local olive oil. She's a joy as a daughter-in-law. She and Rob, so suited and still in love, make great parents, and they do appreciate that we are missing out, as grandparents.

Phone calls and photos don't fill the gap, especially in these early years. They rent a delightful apartment, one wing of a huge old house just outside Palermo where Robert works setting up bilingual IT systems. Now that Jo-Jo goes to a morning nursery Marina has gone back to teaching English part-time. They live just over an hour away, on the islands twisty roads from her parents.

Like Robert she's an only child and Rosina and Stefano are lovely people and doting grandparents. No-one knows how much I envy them their time with our first grandchild. Marina's blossomed, still very pretty but more womanly now. A great Mum and a good wife, but not the old fashioned type like Rosina. Rob admits to sharing the chores too and it was a joy seeing him so patiently showing Jo-Jo, over and over, how to match his tiny feet to those beautifully made little leather Italian sandals. I didn't dare ask the price!

On their last full day, yesterday, Raymond took his parents down to our local Bank, where we opened a Savings Account for Jo-Jo's third Birthday, they had to sign too. That was a sensible present we all agreed, but not much fun for Jo-Jo. Weeks before, thinking just that, I hadn't been able to resist the huge Victorian rocking horse, a rare find in our local Spanish Rastro: not at all sensible – neither was the price.

When Rob and Marina protested that it was too expensive a present for a three-year-old, I countered that Jo-Jo, as our first grandchild, was bound to be an exception and he would grow into it on future visits. I added, teasingly, that of course it would do for future grandkids too. They grinned sheepishly and I won that argument hands down.

Jo-Jo just stood and gaped when we took him into the spare room. His eyes lit up and he gasped with delight when his Dad swept him up into the saddle. His little feet didn't reach anywhere near the stirrups, but he soon had the hang of the reins and the movement. He sat gazing around at us all with a smile that would have lit up Oxford Street. I took loads of photos, not only for us but to share that moment with Rosina and Stefano by email. I plan to send them this weekend and get a couple printed off and framed to add to the collection scattered around our living room.

Yesterday was a special gift for me too …a couple of hours, just the two of us …Jo-Jo sitting next to me on this same sofa, watching cartoons, pointing and chattering away in mixed up Italian and English.

I almost hurt with happiness and tried not to think of them leaving so early this morning. We went for a last ride on his rocking horse, he was already loving it, I could tell. Catching sight of himself in the long wall-mounted dressing mirror he was even more excited. We waved to each other in the mirror and when it was time to lift him down, we patted GiGi and made our goodbyes. Then with the innocence of a child that warms your heart he went over to the long mirror and patted the reflection of the horse there too. "Ciao, ciao GiGi."

The perfect tiny palm print looked even tinier when I patted my own palm next to his. "Bye- bye GiGi." I took a super photo of the two palm prints touching each other on the mirror's surface. Somehow in my heart I decided not to polish those prints off. Sounds daft now, doesn't it? I didn't mention them to the others.

This morning was tough on Raymond too, I know. Smiles and tearful farewells at the door, luckily Jo-Jo still too drowsy at that early hour to get upset. We waved them off in their hire car, promising us an early evening call on their return home. I check the clock, again. It won't be for a few hours yet and little Jo-Jo will be tucked up early in bed this evening, it will have been a long day for our little man.

Raymond murmurs something about a cup of tea, bringing me back to the present. I'm looking again at all the lovely digital photos we've taken only half-listening to the early evening news reader. Raymond is getting to his feet to put the kettle on and then, one of those awful grave-faced interruptions, the newscasters face warning that bad news has happened, somewhere, to someone.

There was only one flight from Alicante to Palermo today, we don't need to check the flight number. I stand up, Raymond's arm goes around my shoulder, tight. We stand there numbly staring at the screen, listening in horror. Their flight is missing and overdue into Palermo. My knees buckle, I slump down onto the sofa. Raymond goes quickly through to the hall phone, I'm repeating the emergency contact number he is already dialling, like some kind of mantra, over and over.

He comes back, ashen-faced, bends over me, taking both my hands. "They say there was a Mayday call about twenty minutes out of Palermo, Bet. They don't know any more yet, it could just be a technical problem, but they can't say anything till they know." I hear the words, but it can't be happening.

"But they were here just this morning, they're flying back, they'll be home soon and they're going to ring us," I tell him, stupidly, as if any of that will change anything.

He's still holding my hands but won't look at me.

Palermo, I'm even trying to picture the airport, willing them to land there safely as we did, nearly four years ago. Raymond and I flew in for our first visit to Robert's new home and new life. He'd met Marina in London, where they'd got together as language students and we were there, meeting her parents and family and all their welcoming friends to celebrate their Sicilian wedding.

Look, here they are on the mantelpiece – lovely wedding photos. Robert and his beautiful young bride, radiant, full of life and over there on the sideboard – all of us at Jo-Jo's christening, just sixteen months later... Loving parents with Stefano and Raymond, proud godfathers and Rosina and myself, beaming grandmothers ...all so happy, all caught up in the miracle of this tiny child ...and there he is on his first birthday: Guiseppe, Joseph ...Jo-Jo as we called him, only this morning.

I hold the framed photos, clutching them to my heart. Praying. "Please God, let them be safe." Raymond is speaking to me, or someone. "I won't go the Airport, no point," he says. Janet agrees. Janet, our next door neighbour has suddenly appeared. She's trying to make me drink some tea but I can't hold it, can't stop shaking.

The phone rings, Raymond jumps up. It's Sicily: Leno, Stefano's young nephew: tortured questions in tortured English, relayed from the frantic parents and Raymond, desperately trying to believe his words of comfort to them. "No, we have no more news. Yes, yes, we are praying too, we know they're going to be alright. Yes, we will ring if we hear anything. Yes, goodbye, ciao, ciao."

I grab the digital camera again, look, look, here they are all safe inside.

Nothing can have happened to them. "Look Raymond, here's Jo-Jo on Gi-Gi yesterday."

Raymond just sits; shaking his head he turns away. I'm looking for the one with the palm prints on the mirror ...little Jo-Jo's next to mine – next to his Nona who won't let go of his hand. I kept it, kept him, next to me, safe, safe – but something's wrong – I can't find the photo.

I jump up, teacup crashing to the floor and run crazily to the spare room.

To the mirror, but it's clean, no palm prints, no Jo-Jo next to his Nona.

Then I know I've lost him, lost all of them.

I sink down on my knees. Someone is screaming, Raymond hears them too because he comes running in and is on his knees next to me.

Here we are, both on the floor next to GiGi.

Holding each other and rocking backward and forwards, backward and forwards and crying.

Vivien Johnson

Thoughts

*Thoughts like ghosts come and go
only to return in the middle of the night
or on a bus,
they grow like nurtured plants.
If only I had pen and paper –
it's cold out of bed.*

*I don't want to wake him –
the torch won't work.
I feel my way around walls
stub my toe on the door post,
feet freezing on stone –
wish we had put down carpets.*

*Boot up the computer –
Please wait –
find the poetry folder, click
on a blank page, type the title.
Power cut – thoughts forgotten!
Narrowed eyes peer at a blank screen.
I sit and shiver,
wish I had donned my dressing gown –
sexy nightie inappropriate now.*

*I peer out of the window at the moon –
does the man have thoughts?
Or is he just moon-shine reflected in frozen earth?*

Jean M. Watson

Christmas Letters

26th. December

Dear Mother,

I am so very, very sorry that I, Lucy, your beloved only daughter, should have sent you such a dreadful Christmas present. How could I have done anything so silly?

It was all the dog's fault. When I was wrapping up the Christmas presents for the family he came bounding in through the door and threw it wide open. Well, it was such a windy day and a whole storm of leaves blew in with him. It was like a brown snow storm. All my labels and cards scattered over the carpet and the sofa mixing themselves with the leaves and dust. I absolutely flew over to close the door.

What a mess it all was.

By the time I had cleared up the mess and found all the labels I was not sure which parcel was yours and which was for my super-sexy friend, Gemma. The parcels looked so much alike in their red and gold paper.

I know now that I got things muddled up because Gemma phoned and thanked me for the fleecy dressing-gown and matching slippers, which were meant for you. She said that it was the nicest present I had ever sent her. She really sounded as if she meant it, but I expect she was only being polite. So Mother, if you would return the lacy bra and thong to me, I will go to the shop and exchange them for something more suitable for your age.

Once again, Mother, I am so sorry for the mix-up.

Love from Lucy.

26th. December

Dear Lucy,
Thank you, thank you a thousand times for the gorgeous underwear you sent me for Christmas. It has certainly woken your father up.

Sorry, I haven't got time to write more just now – life has taken a most interesting turn.

Love Mother

Agnes Hall

Just Rewards

The villagers called it the 'Chicken Shack' because of its resemblance to the units, long since gone, that used to be used for the commercial rearing of chickens. The building was single storey, long and low and constructed of concrete, set back a long distance from the road. The presence of windows was not obvious to anyone who managed to get close enough to examine it.

High electric fencing surrounded the building, with a secondary row of electric fencing approximately fifteen metres within the first. Both sets of fencing had large electronically controlled gates so that any vehicle, either entering or exiting had to stop for security checks overseen by the armed men in black who manned each set of gates.

At each corner of the compound and sandwiched between the two layers of fencing were observation towers manned by more armed security personnel. Lights at the top of each tower were automatically controlled by a photo-electric cell, which activated the lights as soon as it was dusk. The lights scanned an area of a 360-degree circumference at controlled intervals.

The villagers knew that the 'chicken shack' was a secure unit, owned and controlled by the state, a fact made patently obvious by the many official signs around the perimeter, warning of the penalties for trespassing, but they knew better than to ask questions. Those who appeared to be expressing too much interest in the building were known to disappear, never to be seen again.

The ground inside the compound was uncultivated.

The grass was dried to all one drab colour by the harsh winds, but this was of no interest to the occupants of the building nor to the staff who were permanently resident there and never used the outside space, for their outlook was a contrived one. Inside the building there were what appeared to be windows, with white painted frames but the view from these windows never changed. They did not show the scrubby grassland of the compound, nor did they show the changing seasons;

no russet leaves falling from the trees in autumn: no snow, frost or rain in winter: no buds slowly unfurling in spring. All the windows displayed were bright blue skies, trees in full leaf, and verdant green grass with meadows always in flower. This synthetic state of weather had been proven to be useful in maintaining a permanent state of happiness and contentment within the building for most of its occupants.

Silver vans with blackened windows made regular trips to and from the site, but nobody outside the site knew from where they came, nor where they went.

The vans secret cargo was that of vagrants gathered from the streets. In the new book of rules known only to those in power, it was stated that anyone who was slothful and did not contribute to the community in terms of their work ethic, had to pay a price. The price was to have their freedom removed and to be 'processed' by the state.

On arrival, each new group of arrivals at the compound was kept apart from the existing inhabitants. When they first arrived they were in a dazed state as a result of the drugs that had been administered to them and had to be transported from the silver vans on stretchers. Once inside the building they were washed and shaved of all bodily hair, dressed in clean garments and placed in rooms where they were seduced by soft music until they had recovered from the sedation.

It was necessary for careful supervision at this time because some became violent as they realised that their freedom had been taken away.

After a few days, if their behaviour was approved, they were moved to stage two of the process.

During the second stage, they were able to relax in comfortable surroundings, on sofas with thick, feather cushions. They were given food and drink, which best nourished their bodies. Their every need was catered for, but often, as the days passed, one or two would kick at the process and begin to feel uneasy. It all seemed to be too good to be true. Who had brought them here and why? The few who persisted with the dissatisfaction were gradually removed from the group and transported elsewhere, to where they could do no harm. The officials were well-versed in handling these situations.

After a few more weeks, those who remained were processed to the next stage, pampered and allowed to grow bigger and fatter, unknowingly making way for the next intake.

The rumours about the 'chicken shack' were held in check; the vagrant-free streets an encouragement not to ask too many questions. The plentiful supply of food that was transported to stores throughout the country in silver refrigerated vans, kept silent a previously starving community.

The 'chicken shack' served a valuable purpose and the community had never had it so good.

Vivien Johnson

Stallion

He moves
   as the wind
      as the sunlight
         as a storm driven wave.

He comes
   as siloed grain
      as a field of wheat –
         as a mountain stream.

He goes
   as the rolling clouds
      as well filled sails
         as a rainy squall.

He's wild
   as a fire on the heath –
      as a swaying tree
         as swirling leaves.

He thrills
   as regimental colours
      as a warrior's charge
         as the glint of steel.

He is
   as the hunting horn
      to a hunted hind –
         as a rhythmic dance.

Muscles strain,
*   hooves beat*
*   tail flies*
*   mane flows*

Ears prick,
*   lips quiver*
*   teeth gnash*
*   eyes blaze.*

He rears
*   as powerful as Victoria Falls*
*   to cover his mares*
*   his sons will carry his genes.*

Gail Tucker

Indoctrination

Husband your resources, the nun instructed;
serried ranks of easels shook with stifled
laughter. In 1962, convent girls were not
quite innocent, though silly enough.

Buttons as large as five shilling pieces!
outraged Reverend Mother. Sixth formers
smirked – bursting their blouses, clutching
those buttons, feeling foolish.

To be well dressed is to be suitably dressed.
How many convent old girls look aghast
at twenty-first century grunge and secretly
admire its flagrant unsuitability?

Sheila Skinner

Message in a Bottle

"*How* many billions?" Even Ralph's ample intellect did a mental double-take.

Diane's voice came round the edge of the weighty Sunday paper. "Four-hundred and fifty-billion, every year," adding, "that's countries where they can get statistics, of course, they reckon it could double in fifty years."

"It's got to stop, the world's gone mad." Ralph shouted, as vehement and as passionate at fifty-eight as the eighteen-year-old she'd met at college. Diane had joined all his causes, marched all his marches, echoed all his rhetoric and spent 40 years alongside him, fighting the good fight. Against nuclear armament, de-forestation, toxic dumping, carbon emissions – and now this – the latest pollution threat to mankind – packaging.

He'd brought their breakfasts through on a tray, together with the broadsheets, this was their usual Sunday morning ritual. Some slow but determined muscle-wasting disease had put paid to Diane's pharmacist work. That was over two years ago now. During the week the nursing team saw to most of her needs, allowing Ralph to continue his campaigning work. He'd taken early retirement from teaching last year, when her condition worsened suddenly.

Sunday morning, late breakfast in bed with the papers was their *normal* time. Normal that was until Diane slowly, but doggedly, got herself out of the drop-sided bed and into her wheelchair. The specially adapted bedroom and bathroom allowed her the independence she fought hard to retain. She insisted on managing whilst she could.

Ralph didn't argue, he couldn't.

Their years together had been full of arguments, but she'd stuck by him, backed him in all his social and political protests.

He knew, as she did, that without Diane he wouldn't have made the mark he had. The French Green Party had honoured him, calling him an 'ecological warrior'.

Diane had been his strength, now he had to be hers and with her prognosis they both knew they were running out of time to make a difference

They were still determined to make one last stand together. A dramatic protest at this growing mountain of non-degradable packaging that was slowly choking the planet.

Not so slowly chemicals seeped from the very packaging itself, leached into the product it contained and eventually, in the case of consumables, into the very people that bought and ingested it.

They'd chosen their last target carefully.

One of the worse culprits, they knew, were children's fruit drinks.

They'd identified a nearby distributor's warehouse that supplied hundreds of thousands of plastic bottles, each week, to supermarkets up and down the country. Ideal for their purpose.

To this end Ralph had been working a couple of nightshifts a week there for the last few months.

They'd been delighted for an all-rounder who could handle the forklift, sort out the computer printouts and, for a couple of quid on the side, would clock you out in the morning, so that you could slip away the night before and still get double bubble for night work.

He had little in common with his workmates there, he kept his head down, got on with his own tasks and they left him to it. He had become invisible, background to their little clique and all their dodges.

No threat, nothing to draw attention to himself; half of them didn't even know his name.

Ralph worked carefully, no damage to the shrink-wrapping on the pallets. Randomly choosing bottles from six-packs of June consignments, not due for delivery for some time. As planned with Diane, six with the poison and six with the benign mix. They'd identify and lead them to a couple of each, to authenticate their seriousness. That in itself would mean the whole delivery would need to be ditched.

They'd already bought a dozen selected brands from a handful of major supermarkets; they'd shopped some distance away for safety, making sure that the sell-by dates and barcodes were noted exactly, as Ralph had done at the warehouse. They'd already doctored them. A long fine syringe had introduced a benign solution. These were in the garage, scheduled for their visits to far-flung supermarkets over the next few days.

These harmless ones would be the first line of attack, locations identified to the supermarkets and the media in good time, just to get things stirred up, the rumours circulating.

Then they would target with the real thing, no danger of course, as he would be able to identify where and when they had been delivered in good time to have them pulled out of the receiving warehouses long before they hit the shelves.

That would be enough. The panic would set in. Ralph knew that he couldn't risk tampering with anything else at the warehouse after that.

The bottles at home would be in reserve, dropped off here and there, just to extend the impact, really get the message home.

The public would demand something safer.

The media would trumpet the danger of plastic bottles that could so easily be targeted and contaminated.

The sales would drop through the floor, the whole design of their packaging would be questioned, be rethought.

It would take time for any major change, they both knew, but this could not be ignored. The media and the public wouldn't stand for it.

What could be more dramatic and effective? They'd thought of everything. They were ready to go. Tampering with the bottles, inserting the chemical compound that Diane had formulated, had been relatively easy. Odourless and colourless these chemicals were harmless actually, but the supermarkets couldn't take any chances they *could* be some of the potentially lethal ones that they warned would be out there too.

Anonymous letters had been posted over these past weeks from various places, some on a day-trip to France. Major supermarkets, TV and Press had all received the warnings.

They'd also driven to three distant major supermarkets.

Diane's blanketed legs in her wheelchair only drew sympathetic looks.

It was easy to slide two tampered bottles at the back amongst their brand names at each store.

Two each should do it.

They'd experimented at home. The chemicals hadn't affected the colour of the juices; there was nothing to distinguish them.

The syringe introduced expertly just under the sealed cap hadn't caused any bubbles or leaks. Ralph and Diane considered this some of their best work and agreed this was going to be a fitting last stand for the two of them.

Billions of non-degradable plastic bottles were causing toxic and chemical pollution around the world, even in the oceans themselves.

Their effect was a slow time bomb, all that they were doing was highlighting the dangers, accelerating the process to educate and save the world.

That was all they had ever tried to do, this time the world would listen to their message in a bottle.

On Wednesday morning, TV news had the first hint. The top supermarket announced that they were pulling their own brand juices, *'As a precautionary measure'*.

By Friday, TV Radio and Press were full of the threats received by the retailers and the discovery of suspect tampering with popular kids' drinks.

The media slant was of course that this was an attempt at consumer terrorism – Ralph and Diane smiled at the new hook – or just plain extortion. Either way they were ecstatic. All that weekend TV news featured the threats that had been received, even BBC World News too. They were able to follow the follow the story online as it bounced around the IT world.

Ralph and Diane of course, still had the winning cards up their sleeves.

Plenty of time.

They'd already alerted the supermarkets, warning of the actual poisoned consignments that Ralph would release tomorrow, the Fifth of June. Coded pallets would arrive the following day.

Ironically they called it D for delivery Day.

The sixth of June anniversary somehow seemed apt.

Ralph knew that the new stock was then called off within the retailers' own warehouse, it would be days before it was destined for the shelves.

They would find the bottles amongst the incoming pallets, they would test positive for poisoning this time. The coup de grace of course, they wouldn't know how many of them there were.

It had been a hectic few days and Diane was feeling the pace, he knew. He left her reading in bed as he went off for his usual Thursday night shift.

He wasn't surprised to find that Geoff the foreman actually stayed on all night.

He usually crept off as soon as Ralph clocked in.

Their usual deal was for Ralph to clock Geoff out with his own card on the Friday morning.

Geoff and the other lads were slagging off the nutters who had messed with the kids drinks. "No one was really sure what had been found in those bottles were they?"

"What kind of sick bastards would poison a kid's drink?" They were all incensed. Ralph bit his lip hard, so as not to remind them that no kid had been poisoned, it was all just warnings at present, wasn't it?

He kept his mouth shut and went off to move those pallets.

Far away from everyone, he gunned the forklift up and down the rows looking for the barcodes that he had to pick out and move to the loading bay.

Here we were into the second week in May, so what bright spark had moved the June consignments and where to?

He raced up and down. He had to find them, had to make sure that nothing could go wrong. There was nobody that he could question without implicating himself, of course.

Getting a bit panicky now, he doubled back, up and down the pallet stacks but no, there was no sign of the Fifth of June stack he'd barcoded himself.

Suddenly, as he tried to make sense of it, a sick, cold feeling crept over him. That cocky young Romanian who worked on Fridays had already cocked-up a couple of times. Where could he find out, discreetly?

Heart thumping and his armpits damp with nervous sweat he jumped off the forklift. Ralph knocked on Geoff's cubicle, squeezed past him muttering something about fucked-up call-offs and tapped in the barcodes that he had carefully isolated.

The computer figures were there all-right.

They stopped his breath and he could swear his heart too. Instead of keeping them with the Fifth of June consignments, Drago the Romanian had mistaken the fifth of the sixth month for the sixth of the fifth month. He'd sent the poisoned June ones out in May.

They were out there already and, God help him, Ralph didn't know where.

He knew he mustn't panic, he carefully deleted all the references to barcodes for May and June, Geoff had little knowledge of the workings of the computer and was only too happy to have Ralph tapping away, assuring him that, after all, everything was OK: no worries.

He went into the poky Gents toilet, his mouth dry and his hands shaking.

He tried ringing Diane but her mobile was off. Ralph stayed there a few minutes, splashing his face trying to compose himself.

Struggling to think of his next step, his mind had blanked. He pressed redial, but no luck. Diane hadn't watched TV in bed, she'd finished her book just as the sleeping tablet kicked in, so she missed the late-news flash.

Walking slowly back towards the cubicle offices, his mind in turmoil, needing so badly to talk to her, it was then he heard the shouting. A few of the men were suddenly racing towards a white-faced Geoff, who had come running out of their restroom. Most of the lads seemed to spend their shift in there, the TV was always on, usually on the adult channels but, tonight, it was the TV news that was stirring them up.

It had just flashed across the screen, Geoff told the stunned group. Sitting at the back of a school coach, returning from an inter-school tennis tournament, two lads had been sharing a fruit drink. Owing to the usual teenage noise level, and messing around, it was minutes before their mates realised that something was wrong.

With the driver desperately trying to get off the motorway to reach the nearest hospital and the games master uselessly trying basic first aid the two youngsters had died, painfully and horribly, in front of their weeping, screaming school-friends.

"God help us." said Ralph aloud.

"Yeah mate," said Geoff, "and God help those two poor kids too." The others nodded silently, huddled in a group, united in their disbelief and shock, for once they'd included Ralph in with them.

Only he knew they weren't talking about the same thing at all.

Colin Hall

A Shirt Story

During a visit to London, I remembered that Charles Tyrwhitt had a shop on Jermyn Street, close to Piccadilly Circus.

From Euston station I travelled as far as Oxford Circus on the Victoria Line. There I changed to the Bakerloo Line, which dropped me at my destination.

Only a ten-minute walk and I was outside the shop.

I nipped in and selected a bright yellow shirt with a red collar.

It was ghastly, but well made.

I write this in the hope that it makes the small book of <u>shirt</u> stories.

Avner Kornblum

Fire!

"Fire!" she shouted.

Her agonised shriek resounded around the concrete square.

On command, the firing squad raised their rifles, took aim and fired.

She sank limply to the ground, sobbing, "Why am I alive? Why didn't you kill me?"

Lieutenant Schroder lowered his rifle and knelt down to untie the knotted rope around her arms and legs. He spoke gently. "General Martin, our boss, your husband, gave the orders, ma'am. And you should know, you're married to him, he prefers to inflict torture rather than death."

She remained huddled up and wailed, "But why me? I've done him no harm! I've done nothing wrong!"

"For General Martin, ma'am, you don't need do anything wrong. He enjoys murder and torture as others enjoy a game of football. We acted on his orders, practically frightening you to death instead of shooting you dead, while he watched the performance. He has now gone off, bored stiff with your recovery and my attempt to help you. Get up, straighten out your clothes and hair and decide on your future. I will return in a few minutes to ask if there's any way I can help."

With that, Lieutenant Schroder rose and led his silently 'at-ease' squad from the enclosure.

Angeline Martin remained hunched and desolate for several minutes.

When she stood, the expression on her face had changed from anguish to steely determination, her form from round-shouldered resignation to a cold, erect bearing.

The brigadier's daughter had returned from the slough of despond.

Later that night General Martin awoke with a start.

Smoke filled the bedroom, huge flames encircled the door and windows.

For him there was no escape.

Angeline Martin emerged from the bushes opposite, her clothes and hair carefully disarrayed.

"Fire!" She shouted.

Vivien Johnson

The Seascape 'Portichol'

Let's pass through this picture's portal
to the stairs with banister for sliding down,
to the creaky boards on the landing
popping and cracking at night
and the daemon hanging on the bedroom door.

That winter room as cold as frozen steel:
see the ragged join in the green linoleum,
the deer rug by the bed,
the nightlight spluttering on the mantelpiece.
The North Wind scraped through
the window that would never shut.

In summer I listened to them in the garden,
watched as they mowed the lawn below.
Happy, Grumpy and Dozy twitching
on my Snow White curtains.
I wished I was a grown up,
and
didn't have to go to bed.

Dreamt I was on a sailing ship.
Wind blowing sweet scent of tamarisk trees,
filling the sails into my seascape
to the other side of the island;
seagulls screaming overhead.

Gail Tucker

Villain

Maisy moved the photo of the boy with the hare-lip to the back of the group; he'd had pride of place yesterday, Monday, district nurse day. Tuesday's child was the girl in her bridal frock: Maisy, before all those children had torn and swollen her body. Gimlet-eye met gimlet-eye as the gnarled hand shifted the frame into pole position. Pursed lips involuntarily mimicked the self-satisfied smile of the sitter, before Maisy was forced to acknowledge the figure that shared the space with her younger self. The stocky man was dressed in the uncomfortable, stiff collar of an alien culture, a culture that would cause his family to leave home and cross to the cold, unfriendly land they now were pleased to call home. Maisy tossed her head in derision. Her misguided children had thought they could sever links, start afresh – clean white sheet. Maisy knew better.

There had been a time when she'd been minded to crop the photograph as she had cropped her life; she had gone so far as to remove it from the frame and was offering it up to a sharp pair of scissors when a trick of the light had brought her up short. As the reflected beam from the blades had crossed the man's face, she realised that she did not care anymore. One way or the other. She had disposed of the living reality – why ruin the myth she had created, or waste a good frame. Mistress of Destiny, she had not regretted the decision to put everything back together exactly as it had been: the glass, posed portrait of a happy couple, sugar-bag-blue back-board – all held tight against the ebony frame by the four flat, metal fingernail, clips.

Today the home-help would say, on cue, as she lifted the picture to dust, "Such a lovely couple, Mrs M."

What a fool.

Maisy turned on the radio. Rabbi Lionel Blue was in the middle of his *Thought for The Day*. Not yet eight o'clock. There was plenty of time to enjoy her breakfast and think of that little extra for Joan who had, some weeks ago, left the laundry on the line where it had got wet again and hung dripping for two drizzly days. An embarrassment of drooped knickers for everyone to mock.

Octogenarian Maisy prided herself on her memory and seldom let an error pass unpunished. Nowadays she had to be careful, she couldn't exact retribution too soon after the offence or the trick might be rumbled; Joan might be a fool but she was not stupid. In most respects she was excellent, Maisy regularly got her to do things outside the remit of a home-help. Maisy could not risk a face-off with that man from social services who read her the riot act the last time she drove one of his team to resign. He'd made it quite clear that Joan was Maisy's last chance. She did not doubt he meant it. Life in *a home* was not how Maisy planned to end her days. Nevertheless, having spent a lifetime helping others to correct their mistakes, it was a matter of honour to see to Joan.

She went through to the tiny kitchen and put on the kettle. Last week's envelopes lay piled beside the caddy on the adjacent shelf. Empty now of course, the envelopes were her Sunday evening ritual. She had always been fair about that, always given everyone maximum time to meet the weekly deadline. Her move to London had been to help her off-spring, it had been hard for them while she remained in Barbados. Now she was a widow in a strange land. What sacrifices a mother had to make. It never stopped.

Tomorrow, she would have to take a taxi to Fulham to find out why Earle's envelope was missing. Eight years ago she'd have hopped on the tube, these days if she wanted to go anywhere she had to take a taxi.

In fact, she had a more or less regular booking for Wednesday afternoons; if she did not need to visit one of the children, she took a nice trip to Guildford and treated herself to afternoon tea.

Tomorrow, however, would be reserved for Earle or rather Earle's wife who was probably the cause of his error. Maternal instinct told her that it was invariably the daughters and sons-in-law who failed in their obligations to their mother-in-law. Maisy never failed to put them right and they were usually acquiescent for a long time afterwards.

She felt the teapot, too cold for a third cup; she'd get Joan to make her a nice mug of coffee when she'd done the bathroom. Maisy heard the gate click. How time had flown! She nipped into the living room and slumped into her leather armchair. Joan's footsteps halted at the back door.

"Damn!" Maisy realised she had forgotten Joan's surprise but the rasp of the key unlocked an idea.

The contents of Maisy's bladder flooded the rug; her look of triumph altered to one of contrition, "Oh Joan, I'm afraid I've had a little accident."

Easy!

Vivien Johnson

Second Post

I had been tucked in a drawer with my relations, gradually getting nearer to the top of the pile. Whichever way I looked at it I would always be at the bottom, the last sheet to go; hoping to be first one day and be the most important sheet of a letter. My brothers and sisters had gone to all Corners of the Earth and I wondered where I might go. Hopefully not in a waste paper basket! However, it was unlikely that I would be written on for the next fortnight; Harry was getting married and, straight after the wedding, would be away on his honeymoon in Arundel. I knew all this of course, because my older brother had taken a message to an hotel there, requesting a double room.

It was seven a.m. on July 5th 1930 when Harry woke up and drew back the curtains. He'd had a restless night, worrying about the arrangements for the next day and been in a state at the wedding rehearsal on the previous day. His younger sister, Jane, who was Mary's bridesmaid, had tripped on a tombstone as she approached the main aisle of the church and Mary had burst into tears, the best man had been late and the vicar had to go to a meeting of the Mothers Union and now, because of the kafuffle, he would be late.

Harry wanted to talk to Mary on the phone but her parents were not connected.

He had to reassure her that everything would be all right, to tell her that he loved her and could hardly wait 'til half-past three to see her.

The early morning sun streamed into the small masculine room, it needed a woman's touch, he was so lucky to have found the love of his life. He so wanted to go round to Selton Street and see her. No, he mustn't, it was supposed to be unlucky to see your bride on the day of the ceremony. He looked at his new suit, bought especially for the wedding, hanging on the end of his wardrobe. His white shirt and dark tie would look impressive and give the feeling of his dependability, to reassure Mary's parents.

He mused that you could always tell the newly married staff at the bank where he worked, because of their extra-smart new suits. His black shoes stood neatly together on the brown linoleum; they were as highly polished as though just placed there by a valet who'd recently buffed them up. He gazed at a pair of black socks folded together on top of the chest of drawers. He wondered if Mary was awake yet. Was she thinking of him?

A shaft of light fell on the socks and shone on the handle of the top drawer. Harry remembered the letter pad. In one bound he crossed the room. If he were quick enough, he could catch the half-past-eight collection from the post-box on the corner. With luck, the letter would reach Mary by the second delivery, at one o'clock. Excitedly he fumbled with the drawer handle... He must calm down!

Opening the drawer, a little wider, his fingers touched the pad. To his dismay it felt empty, then, he remembered, he had meant to replace it two days earlier. As he pulled it out, he hardly dared look at it but, to his relief, there was one pale, crème page left. He sat on a plain, wooden chair in his pyjamas, unscrewed his fountain pen and started to write.

Dearest Darling Mary

Our wonderful day has come at last; I could hardly sleep all night for thinking about you and our new life together. Thank you so much for agreeing to marry me. I am truly the happiest man in the world today. I so much want to come and see you this morning, to take you in my arms, hold you and kiss you but I know I must not. My heart is full. I am so looking forward to having you by my side for ever, you are my sweetest flower. I know that you will look like an angel in your wedding dress but for me there is no need for you to dress up, you'll always be my angel and I am so proud and lucky to become your husband.

I want to go on telling you these things but I must catch the post, so that you have read this before we see each other at half past three.

I love you with all my heart and kisses, My Darling Flower,

Harry

Harry said that he was proud and happy but you can just imagine how I felt. This must be the most important letter he had ever written and he was using me to convey his true feelings to his future wife. His fingers trembled as he put me in the matching crème envelope. To my absolute horror he put me down on the dressing table. Had he decided not to send me after all? Was I going to be torn up and thrown into the waste paper basket? Had he changed his mind about the wedding? I could hear him moving about, the wardrobe door opened and closed, the chest of drawers roughly opened and shut with a slam. Harry must be dressing. At last I heard the clump of his brogues on the linoleum as he walked across the room once more, picked me up and placed me lovingly in his tweed jacket pocket.

Harry hurried down the stairs, out into Warwick Street and leaped the few yards to the post-box. Then he kissed me tenderly saying,

"Don't be late!" as he dropped me through the slit into the dark. I floated gently down to the bottom of the box and rested like a butterfly on top of the other letters. How could I be late? I was on the most important mission of my life.

Avner Kornblum

Neptune's Dilemma

There was an ear-bashing din in the reception area of Neptune´s palace. From the largest creatures of the sea, the great blue whales, to armour-plated sturgeon, boneless jellyfish and shell-encased lobsters, right down to tiny sea-horses, the huge hall was filled with marine creatures large and small: broad and thin, spiky, spindly, toothy, eight-legged and legless. Albatrosses, cormorants and gulls dived in, every now and then, adding their screeches and hoots to the puffing, blowing and ear-splitting sirens of whales and whistles of dolphins.

This was, of course, only a fraction of the enormous marine population, and consisted of the bravest or the most outraged of the oceans´ inhabitants. The sardines and pilchards, scared of the huge appetites of the whales and sharks, had chosen not to attend, and nominated the sea-horses to represent them. The swordfish community had been kindly requested to stay away in case their terrifying spears damaged some innocent delegates. The sharks had been asked – ever so gently – to keep their mouths shut during the meeting. All had agreed that this event was too important to spoil with age-old tiffs or insatiable appetites.

The one unifying factor was that all these creatures, large and small, had one common enemy: human beings.

Humans were tiny compared with whales, they had neither teeth nor stings and were not protected by shells. Yet they had weapons deadlier than anything available to those who dwelt within the waters of the world. From fishing-rods to vast nets, from spears to harpoons they were equipped to help themselves to any waterborne creatures they fancied. However gross, barbaric and indiscriminate this may have been, if the purpose had been for feeding their ravenous and growing populations, the marine creatures would have found it forgivable. Every one of them recognised the need to eat. Because of the vast numbers of fish in the sea, they had tolerated the human game of fishing for fun; they had even put up with whaling for the manufacture of stupid little things like buttons and figurines and corkscrew tops.

Humans had been polluting the seas for many centuries, starting off with wooden boats, gold coins, glazed crockery, metal urns, graduating to metal hulls, airplane wrecks and human bodies in all types of clothing. Then came mines and torpedoes, their explosions taking much marine life as well as men, women and children. The indignation of the marine creatures had just about reached boiling point when the oil-spills started. That was the final straw. "Pouring oil on troubled waters" did not have the same meaning for them as it did for English-speaking humans. Just the opposite, in fact.

Two penguins suddenly appeared at the far end of the lobby, at the entrance to the Great Court, where Neptune entertained his guests or listened to his messengers' reports. "Silence, silence!" they called. The hubbub subsided, but not enough for them. "Silence, silence!" they called again. This time, the reception hall became totally still. One could hear a pin drop.

"Enter in Noah-fashion, two by two," ordered one penguin.

"Whales, sharks and other large creatures on the right, medium-sized creatures in the centre, and everyone from soles and salmon to sea-horses on the left," ordered his companion.

The mammals were quick to follow the instructions, a la sheep, humans and other land-creatures. The fish and shell-fish behaved exactly as normal. Pretending to be deaf (in fact, some of them were!) they swam in shoals, in schools or singly, depending not on what the penguins had said but on how many of each kind there were. Nevertheless, it took less than three hours to arrange themselves with the help of the penguins into the places that had been allotted them.

Then the Grand Vizier of the Whales raised himself up onto his tail, with his snout on high and blasted a single trumpet call that echoed through the palace, out into the ocean and travelled far and wide, even being heard in some seaside towns on faraway continents.

Neptune, King of the Deep, surrounded by a squad of penguins, swept into the court as the sound died away. He mounted his throne placing his wand at his side, signalled the penguins to retreat, arranged his robes, stroked his beard into tidiness and, finally, spoke.

"Greetings to you all. Before we start the business of the day, I ask all here to convey my greetings and very best wishes for a peaceful life to your families, your species and the species you represent.

"Today we will attempt to solve the problems that everyone has. We regret you will not all be allowed to speak, for there are so many here that the seas may be destroyed while we talk. Suffice it to say that my messengers have travelled throughout the oceans and seas, and have even visited lakes and rivers. We have studied the enormous number of complaints they received, so now we will hear only a few examples. Each section must choose one case to report."

A huge babble of noise erupted, as the groups swam and crawled and flapped around their sections, until each had chosen their speaker. An hour later all three groups had decided. Neptune returned to his throne, adjusted his robes and waited for the rowdy gathering to settle.

"The smallest are not the least important," he boomed, "although their voices are rarely heard. Let us start with them."

He turned to his right – the left-hand side for the creatures that had entered – and called out, "Who is to address us?"

Cornelius the Cod, leader of his school, swam to the front, flapped his tail and waved his fins in deference to the King of the Deep, introduced himself in the usual formal manner, and then told his sad tale.

"I, Cornelius, declare, sire, that the Portuguese, the Spanish and the British are the main offenders against us. Humans have apparently made rules somewhere on land, far away from us, that they may only take a certain number of us so as not to destroy our population but the Portuguese play tricks, pretending they are catching other species while their nets sneakily haul shoals of us in. The Spanish are quite unconcerned and go freely into banned areas and British waters, while the British ..."

At this point, the big, strong Cornelius broke down and cried, his tears making little difference to the already salty sea, but seriously affecting his audience. "The British," he sobbed, "we thought they were friendly..." He could not say more without choking, so he resumed his place.

Neptune shook his head sadly, and waited for a while so that the audience could regain its composure. Then he spoke.

"At this stage we do not wish to declare what action we can take, but rest assured, Cornelius, we will do whatever is in our power to do. Let us remind all of you that we do have power against land-dwelling invaders, for we control four-fifths of the planet. We will tell you more later. Meanwhile, let us hear from the next section."

Salome the Seal skidded to the base of Neptune's throne, stood up on her tail and performed a backwards leap, turning a complete circle and landing again in an upright position, standing on her tail.

"Why did she do that?" exclaimed Louis, a surprised lobster.

"Because she has the wrong shape for a bow or a curtsy," whispered his mate. "Now shush, this is important!"

Salome had difficulty expressing herself through her grief and anguish. A glib TV commentator, unmoved by the dreadful facts that Salome revealed, later said, "She blubbed through her blubber." In fact, what Salome told Neptune and the vast audience was horrifying.

Speaking delicately about their habits, she reminded Neptune of how seals had functioned for centuries before the Europeans arrived in Canada. They spent most of their lives on land and, in the appropriate season, thousands gathered in one area and enjoyed a huge festival. Unarmed and unaggressive, they were no match for the brutal Canadians who rushed in with clubs, guns and any weapons they could lay hands on. The Canadian humans mercilessly killed thousands, turning the ice red and utterly regardless of leaving orphaned youngsters to cope without their parents, or grieving parents who lost their offspring. She tried to describe the awful bloodbath, but, like Cornelius, she broke down and sobbed uncontrollably.

"Oh, Salome, I am glad your tears spared us a recital of the scene created by these human trespassers and murderers," said Neptune. "Every fish in the sea has experienced their brutality, either personally or by losing some family member. Your story will add to our determination today to teach humans how to behave. If they do not respond positively, we will teach them a different lesson, one they will not forget. Now we call on the representative of the mammals."

Walter the Whale, who had kept his eyes fixed on Salome from the time she rose up, now followed her example precisely. Instead of bowing to the King of the Deep, he rose up onto his ponderous tail, and performed a backward somersault.

Louis, the lobster who had gasped at Salome's performance, seemed bemused. Olive, an octopus alongside, leaned across and whispered, "That's nothing. Whales do really amazing things . . ."

"Hush!!" exclaimed Louis' companion. "This is too important for chit-chat!"

King Neptune was a large being by human standards, yet Walter, at 60,000 kilograms (or 30 tons), towered over him. For all his size, though, Walter was so gentle and quiet that several times creatures in the audience asked him to speak up. In his soft voice he told a tale at least as savage and cruel as Salome's.

"Good sire, I, Walter the whale, assure you that we have been remarkably decent to humans right down the ages, ever since Jonah's day. We have helped them when they have fallen into the sea and when they've been lost. We and dolphins and porpoises have also helped their ships overcome many problems. Yet throughout this planet, humans are guilty of abusing our gentleness and friendliness towards them. They have been merciless in their pursuit of us, using our fat, flesh and bones for a host of purposes, some of them utterly inane and pointless.

"Recently, under a great deal of pressure from the more noble-minded of their species, a host of nations agreed to control their acts of decimation of the whales. Not all countries agreed, and some of those who did still secretly enjoyed hunting us. For today's meeting I particularly wish to complain about the Japanese and Norwegians."

Walter then recited the unrelenting pursuit of whales by the Norwegians and the blood-curdling horrors committed by the Japanese. He spoke of the attempts by the tiny Greenpeace vessel, Rainbow Warrior, to halt the mass–murder of the whales, and the efforts of their sailors, at the risk of their own lives, to interrupt the Japanese desecration. Painfully and sadly he described the entire slaughter procedure, and said he knew of some photographers who had been captured by the whalers and had their cameras thrown into the sea. His address lasted nearly an hour, by which time virtually every member of the audience was in tears and Neptune's face was sombre indeed.

Ending his long-drawn out tale of human savagery, Walter looked the King of the Deep straight in the eye.

"Sire, something must be done! You have to help us and the seals and the cod to overcome this barbarism. Even so, our three species are not the only sufferers. I am sure that every member of the ocean population has suffered either directly or indirectly through humans."

Neptune stroked his beard again, and again he was silent for a long while. The audience was under the impression that he was thinking out some dastardly strategy. Only those closest to him could see that he was so moved he did not trust himself to speak right away. Eventually, though, he did speak.

"We will not thank you for so devastating a picture as you have painted, Walter. Know that we and all this audience appreciate what you and the seals and other tribes – in fact, the whole of ocean life has suffered. We have already undertaken to do whatever is possible to remedy the situation, so now we will take the first step of our plan."

"No, sire, please hear me first!" cried a cormorant that had dropped down from the sky. "I can only stay under water for a minute or two, so let me speak quickly."

"Quickly, then!" Neptune commanded her. "Tell us!"

Coleen the cormorant blurted out, "It's the oil-spills and oil-slicks I wish to complain about. Thousands upon thousands of birds, from seagulls to pelicans and storks, plus untold numbers of fish, penguins and other marine mammals have suffocated to death from the oil that humans have drilled from the sea or spilled into it. It affects every ocean, every sea and every coastline of this planet. Sorry, sire, I must leave."

In a flash, Coleen disappeared upwards, leaving the great mixed throng to mull over the four dreadful tales they had heard.

The King of the Deep stretched to his full height and spoke in his most regal manner. "We have decided that there are two approaches to adopt. One is soft and gentle, the other is hard and relentless. We have decided that we will use both if necessary. First, we will approach the humans peacefully, telling them that we have no objection to fair fishing practices, for they must eat to live, just as all of you have to. Some of you, like the whales and sharks, prey on thousands of smaller fish at a time. But those very same fish prey on others. So you should cool your anger to some extent, remembering that everything – yes, everything, including coral and plankton and sea-anemones – lives by consuming something else.

"We will object to their maiming and killing fish as pastimes or for profit-making baubles. We will tell them that their hauls of lobsters, oysters, whelks, prawns, cockles and crabs as well as sardines, cod, hake, herrings, swordfish and others is excessive. We will complain in the strongest terms to their use of huge nets that capture vast quantities of fish and kill dolphins in the process. We will point out that the Norwegians and Japanese are in defiance of their human rules that were intended to protect whales from extinction. We will make it clear that their barbarism and that of the Canadians will not be tolerated and must cease immediately.

"We know that sharks, sting-rays and jellyfish have accounted for a number of human beings. Here we must sternly rebuke the sting-ray who killed our great friend Steve Irwin." Neptune interrupted himself to address the sting-rays, all of whom squirmed uncomfortably under his malevolent glare. Then he continued. "Be warned, however. If they do not obey, there is nothing you as sea-creatures can do, regardless of size. All your efforts will be insignificant in the light of there being billions of humans on this planet, many of whom eat fish constantly, using the disrespectful term 'sea-food' for all marine life.

"If they do not comply with our reasonable approach, there is a different, more devious yet extremely effective remedy. We will teach them a very severe lesson, and we have the means to do so. We do not wish to disturb our marine populations or the non-human land-creatures but if we are severely enough hampered in our desire for fairness, then we will adopt that method."

The monarch ceased speaking and relaxed. Instantly a babble ensued as the rival merits of his alternatives were discussed, weighed up and chewed over including considerable speculation as to what his second remedy involved. The reactions ranged from blind, enthusiastic support for anything Neptune proposed to a more cautious, doubtful attitude, depending on which family one belonged to and what their experience of humans had been.

Olive the octopus waved a floppy arm (though she was not at all as lazy as her languid arm implied). King Neptune nodded for her to speak.

"Is there nothing that can be done to the humans who live inland, sire?" she asked. "Many of them have never seen the ocean but are dreadful offenders, too."

"There is nothing we can do. We are confined to the sea. However, the damage that we have outlined will affect every human being throughout the planet, the land-locked as well as the seashore-dwellers, the innocent as well as the guilty."

Neptune, King of the Deep, looked around his vast court full of creatures of all sizes and shapes and checked the tears that were welling up inside him.

"I will consider what to do, and meanwhile bid you now farewell," he said gruffly as he stood up and gathered his robes and his wand. His penguin bodyguards formed a circle around him to escort him to the Inner Court of his palace.

All the creatures of the seas and oceans fell silent and slowly disbanded to go their separate ways.

In the minds of most of them were questions. "Would there ever be a limit to human rapacity?"

"Can Neptune halt their ravages of the oceans?"

"Will our planet, which has survived so many changes through the ages, survive the damage that humans are doing?"

Back in his palace, Neptune was asking himself the same questions, and facing the dreadful dilemma: Should he leave it to the humans to continue destroying the waters of the planet and all the creatures that dwell in them, his creatures, or should he, in order to punish humans, become a partner in the destruction of all sea-creatures?

Agnes Hall

One Day Too Late

He was due to meet the man again on the first Wednesday of the month.

He had already paid him a percentage of the money, the remainder to be paid when the job was completed.

His wife had a regular hair-dressing appointment, late in the day, on the first Tuesday of every month and always parked her car in the multi-storey car park, where the deed was to be done.

On the first Monday of the month his wife visited her solicitor and changed her will, leaving everything to her neice in Australia.

He was one day too late.

Sheila Skinner

On Morning Air

Fooled by leaden skies and the tossing branches of olive and pine, used to welcoming the early morning sun through the bedroom window, I judged the day harshly.

Surprised then by the treacly warm swirl that greeted me outside, carrying with it waves of orange-blossom perfume.

Fists of showy, creamy-white flowers poised, impatient with the old fruit clinging on stubbornly.

Wrinkled bruised skin, decayed, shriven flesh leaking foul fluids, fading oh so slowly. The earth and worms await. They will not be denied for long.

On the same tropical, buffeting breeze, came the ebb and flow of Church bells, tolling first the hour and then, that unmistakable discordant dirge: a death in the village.

With wrinkled bruised skin, they'd clung on stubbornly, decayed shriven flesh leaked foul fluids, faded oh so slowly. The earth and worms await.

Vivien Johnson

Things Change

Edward hadn't thought of Sara for fifty-years, until he drove through the village of his birth. Then he saw the house with the turret, where they used to play trains together.

The Southern Railway line and station looked the same; just the same as he remembered them, except for the new logo.

He stopped the car and entered the ticket office.

He'd been half-expecting to see his old friend Jim at the counter, behind the glass screen with an oval hole to speak through and, at the bottom, a hole shaped like a tunnel entrance, where money and tickets were passed between traveller and railway clerk.

Edward felt a pang of deep disappointment. He shuddered remembering the passage of time.

Now, all he saw was an empty space where the counter had been and, standing by the platform entrance, a ticket machine …like a policeman on duty.

Avner Kornblum

Undiscovered Teruel

Teruel is more-or-less equidistant from Madrid, Barcelona, Valencia and Zaragoza, whence come most of its visitors.

'Teruel Capital' is the capital of the province that bears the same name.

The city is also known as 'Teruel Mudejar', relating to the era when Moors, Christians and Jews lived and thrived together, still reflected spectacularly in the city's architecture.

Here, better than anywhere else, can be seen the gracious and unusual blending of Romanesque, Moorish and Gothic architecture in individual buildings, surmounted by beautiful – specifically Teruel – tiles.

Tourism has had its impact. Signposts, which used to indicate 'Teruel' now point to 'Teruel Mudejar'. The new, four-lane highway from Valencia to Zaragoza via Teruel has been officially named the Autovia Mudejar.

Teruel is also known as the city of the lovers (Ciudad de los Amantes). This medieval tale, with its romanticism and sad ending, has been adapted to operas, musicals and literature. The mausoleum wherein the blighted lovers lie has attracted thousands of visitors.

The city is small, quaint, and fascinating in its juxtaposition of old and new. Narrow, winding streets lead onto large, open plazas; dark, lugubrious bars yield delicious food at low prices; uninteresting, jaded shop-fronts conceal bright lights and brighter fashions; rows of old, shoulder-to-shoulder buildings suddenly give way to gracious public-gardens and an astonishing variety of trees.

Its inhabitants are warm and generous. The local bank, the city and the province, jointly, host a biennial International Folklore Festival, which attracts troupes of 60 or more performers each, from countries as far afield as Mongolia, Ukraine, Ireland, Mexico and Colombia – as well as the provinces of Spain. The festival, in an open plaza from 8pm to 3am on an August night, is free. One may come or go at any time during the show, armed, if one wishes, with food and drink.

At the heart of the city is the Plaza Torico (Little Bull Square). The huge, wide and tall pillar in the centre of the plaza is unmistakeable. If you crane your neck as high as you can, you will see, atop the pillar, a very little bull. Why is it there? And why so small? Like so many other questions, the Spanish don't have the answers. In fact, they don't care.

For example, the third and fourth largest towns in the province, Mora de Rubielos and Rubielos de Mora, are only ten kilometres apart yet as different as night and day. Nobody knows or cares why they are called what they are, why the names are inverted, nor even what the names mean. Rubielos de Mora was Franco's northern headquarters, and – much earlier – a centre of great wealth and grand homes. Mora de Rubielos was famous for its 20-hour-a-day five-week-long summer fiesta in its restored castle until a few years ago when it was obliged to share the festival with its neighbour.

Fourteen kilometres from Mora de Rubielos is Alcala de la Selva, another old town with a great, forbidding castle protecting it. Under its wing is the quaint village of Virgen de la Vega. This has developed apace in recent years, because of its closeness to the Valdelinares ski-slopes and its accessibility to the main road.

Valdelinares, an out-of-the way mountain village, had no claim to fame until someone bright developed, there, the only ski-slopes in the 900 kilometres between the Pyrenees and the Sierra Nevada. Since then, another ski-slope has been opened at Javalambre, fifty kilometres away. One would not expect six slopes, plus a snow-making machine when Nature lets us down, in this dry, dusty region. But that's not the only contradiction. Valdelinares is officially listed as being the highest village in all of Spain – yet its name means *Valley of Linares*! In summer the huge ski-slope area is devoted to entertainment, even offering rock-wall climbing and horse-riding.

Many villages prosper through the snows of Valdelinares, boasting houses, hotels and bars that didn't exist five years ago. A lucky young Englishman converted the last run-down mill in Alcala de la Selva into a hostel and restaurant. A few months later, the vacant plot adjacent was turned into the town's coach cum car-park, bringing hordes of visitors into the restaurant!

From Valdelinares (altitude 1860m / 6045ft) the twenty kilometres to Allepuz is worthwhile travelling. The magnificent heights, unexpectedly grassy in summer, the breathtakingly beautiful spring flowers and the nightmarishly pot-holed road, which one should not attempt in winter, are all so out-of-character with the surrounding area as to seem placed there by a playful deity. Three kilometres before Allepuz, a large, off-centre, virtually purposeless, roundabout was recently sited at what had been, and continues to be, an adequate T-junction; no playful deity here, just clerical error. Here we will veer to the left. Before we do, though, look down! There, 150 metres below, on a bank of the Rio Sollavientos, surrounded by chopos (poplar trees) stands Molino Tormagal.

The immediate surroundings of this isolated mill currently house seventy different species of butterfly.

Outside these two hectares of uncultivated wilderness one is hard put to find other butterflies, yet each year new species arrive. The mill is being declared a butterfly sanctuary because elsewhere so many species are becoming extinct as human needs expand.

High above the mill lives a family of ravens. Vultures scavenge the area in the warmer months. Eagles, too, are no strangers here. Apparently, all are descended from the dinosaurs who once roamed this area in huge numbers and in a variety of shapes and sizes. *Teruel Capital* hosts *Dinopolis* – a modern re-creation of the dinosaur experience, particularly enjoyed by children – but the tiny dead-end village of Galve, some 40 kilometres away, boasts the greatest number and variety of dinosaur remains in Europe.

Three kilometres beyond Moñino Tormagal is the village of Allepuz. It has only one shop, a bakery converted into a general dealer´s store ...so high up the mountainside a visitor cannot see it. Close by and equally high up, was a five-star hotel built where the village's great mansion once stood: a five-star hotel where the village school has only two pupils and where the population (900 a century ago) is only 90. Amazing! Especially as the two newly-renovated bars have eleven guest-rooms, and there are other upmarket places in the area.

Fascinating, too, are the names of several inhabitants. Amongst the Juans and Marias and the twenty-two shepherds are Melchior, Serafin, Agustin, Eleuterio, Hilario, Angel, Aurora, while Ascension is a four-foot-ten young woman married to one of the two Ezekiels.

On the way to Teruel city via Jorcas, you will once more be confounded by the rapid changes of scenery. Outside Aliaga, there is an astonishing fossil concentration in the rock-face on a short stretch of road. From Aliaga we pass through delightful grassy and forested areas – interrupted by some pretty (and some pretty-awful) villages.

It is worth deviating to Escorihuela to see and smell vast banks of lavender growing wild along the road. The old, tumble-down village itself has been modernised to an extent; some houses have been painted green from top to bottom, others black or red. A few villagers have confined their painting to the fences or garage doors.

West of Teruel is the magical town of Albarracin. Built high up in the huge rocks by a Moorish prince some 700 years ago, Albarracin has recently been declared a World Heritage Site. It is usually full of visitors, mainly Spanish.

Our journey through a small part of the province has been punctuated by many changes of scene. Yet the most dramatic change of all takes place five kilometres beyond Albarracin. Rounding a bend in the road, the green-brown shrubland has gone! In its place are gigantic blood-red rocks. These provided shelter for the earliest humans in Spain, as proven by 10,000-year-old rock and cave-paintings. The public, free to go from cave to cave without interference, do exercise great respect. While the towns and villages are full of graffiti, there is none here newer than eight-thousand years.

Now we can return to *Teruel Capital,* thence north to Zaragoza and France, south-east to Valencia, or north-east to Barcelona.

Albarracin, though, is itself another gateway out of Teruel province, via the mystical Montes Universales in the west.

Whichever way you choose – buen viaje!

Agnes Hall

Party Parrots

I started working for Mrs. Watkins when I left school six months ago. I help George look after her garden. George is 'getting on a bit' and he was finding Mrs Watkins' garden a bit too much for him so I was employed to help with the heavy work, the digging and that sort of stuff. My dad said that was all I was good for …digging, that is! He said I was a big lump and as thick as two short planks and I was lucky that anyone wanted to employ me. I don't think my dad likes me very much.

Mrs Watkins' garden is big. It's far bigger than you'd think when you stand outside the tall, wooden gates and there's plenty of work for both of us, to keep it looking good. George lives in a flat above Mrs Watkins' garage and works full-time for her, partly gardening and partly driving her about. I only work there three mornings a week. George usually opens the gates at eight o'clock sharp and if I arrive early and he hasn't unlocked the gates, I have to stand outside waiting for him.

One day when I arrived, there was no sign of George and it got to a quarter-past-eight and then it was Mrs. Watkins who opened the gate. "George isn't well. He was supposed to be taking me shopping today but he isn't well enough, so I'd like you to come shopping with me, instead of doing the garden."

"But I can't drive." I told her. She looked at me as though I was an idiot.

"I know you can't drive. I only need your help to carry the shopping to the car. I'll be doing the driving."

I wondered why, if she could drive, it was always George who did the driving, until I remembered my dad saying that Mrs Watkins was a jumped-up nobody with ideas above her station and that the only reason that George drove her was that she liked people to think that she had her own chauffer, which I suppose in a way, she did. I don't think my dad likes Mrs. Watkins either.

I waited around while Mrs. Watkins got herself organised, fetching her bag and keys and backing the car out of the garage and out onto the road.

"We're going to Leeds," she said and handed me the keys to lock the gates after us. We set off to Leeds where she parked the car in a multi-storey car park near one of the big department stores. In the store we went up in the lift to the third floor and Mrs. Watkins told me to wait for her by the lift doors while she had a 'browse-around'. When she came back, she handed me her scruffy shopping bag and told me to carry it carefully.

When we arrived back at the house she asked me to put the kettle on for a cup of tea and while I was doing that she opened the shopping bag and took out a piece of pottery. It wasn't wrapped up or in a plastic bag or anything. It was a bird, a budgie or something. She asked me if I would like to see her collection. I just wanted to go home but she took me by the arm and led me into a small room at the back of the house.

"They come from all over the world." she told me. I gasped as I looked into the room, which had lots of shelves, stacked with piece after piece of pottery, all birds. When I saw so many together, I thought that they could have been parrots but I still wasn't sure. Many of them looked the same as the one she had just brought home.

"Some of them are worth hundreds of pounds," she said proudly.

I was never very good at maths at school but I knew all of those birds must have been worth an awful lot of money. She told me that it was our secret and I wasn't to tell anyone about her collection.

A few days later, when I was working at Mrs. Watkins, again, George was back at work. "Did you have a good shopping trip?" He asked me, grinning.

I remembered Mrs Watkins orders not to mention her collection to anyone so just said, "She didn't buy anything."

George laughed. "Well she wouldn't have, would she? Not if she could nick it."

"You know what she does, then?" I asked, surprised.

"Of course I know. She's been doing it for years. She's got away with it so far but one day she'll be found out. Mind, she's got her head screwed on. She never shops on her own. She always insists on having someone with her."

I shrugged. I didn't know what he was getting at.

I only worked for Mrs. Watkins a few months longer. I was always nervous and ready with an excuse in case she asked me to go shopping with her again. I was relieved to be able to leave when I managed to get a full-time gardening job with the council.

One evening a few weeks after I had left Mrs Watkins, my dad and I were sitting in the sitting-room after our tea. He was reading the local paper and I was watching TV.

"Hey just listen to this," he said and began to read:

'Richard Evans, aged 18 years, of 3 Cardigan Way, was today convicted, in Leeds, of shoplifting. He protested his innocence, when a piece of Lladro porcelain from the Parrot-Party Collection, worth approximately £900, was found in the bag he was carrying, when he was stopped by security personnel, as he left a department store in Leeds. He was accompanying his employer, Hilda Watkins, aged 75 years, to assist her with her shopping. Mrs. Watkins was extremely tearful and expressed horror at what had happened. She said that Richard had only been working for her for a short time and his references had been very good.'

I know now, what George had meant when he said that Mrs Watkins always took someone shopping with her and was glad that I had escaped the same fate as Richard Evans. For once, I also agreed with my dad and could have added a few more choice words to his description of Mrs Watkins as a 'jumped up nobody'.

Vivien Johnson

Investiture

"The trouble is," Samantha George confided to her friend and colleague, Jade, one morning after a busy night in town, "work in Soho has changed. Men used to be after a quickie, never mind if the girl looked like the back of a bus, but now all they want is long legs that can perform all sorts of unimaginable tricks. Know what I mean?"

"Oh yes I do," Jade replied, "only the other day I had this client who wanted me to hang upside down from the ceiling. Well at my age I ask you! Anyway I told him that the best I could do was a handstand. Of course I didn't say anything about age, you have to keep up the illusion don't you?"

"Well," continued Samantha, "my body has had so many nips and tucks that it doesn't recognise itself in the mirror any more. Unfortunately, I know that I'm fifty-four-years-old and I need a change. I'm going to try a new beat. I fancy settling down, with someone sensible and wealthy. I thought outside Buckingham Palace might be a good pitch. The pigs around there won't know me… Just think of the rich, lonely Americans needing entertainment at night. Perhaps I'd get a good meal or two, as well. Imagine all those dollars!"

Later that day Samantha wondered what to wear. Mini skirt up to her buttocks and fishnet stockings didn't seem quite appropriate for the Queen's front garden. If the royal personage should happen to look out of her window, wave the royal wave and spy Samantha in her normal working clothes, she might be offended and then what? The tower for sure! No, black trousers, red jacket, medium heels and a black ribbon to tie back her normally-unruly, bleached, blonde curls.

It was investiture day. Samantha stood a little apart from the crowd, watching intently as people and limousines entered the palace forecourt. Suddenly she was aware of a man standing beside her; he was obviously hesitant about going inside. She smiled, in return a glimmer of a smile played on his lips.

"You look worried, can I help?" she asked, thinking she might get lucky and it wasn't even lunchtime yet! The tall, slim-built man should have looked extremely elegant in morning dress but his bulging pockets completely spoiled the sartorial effect.

"Perhaps you can," he replied as he moved closer. "I'm Jacob Peterson, by the way." Samantha reeled away from his breath. The eligible man had the most dreadful halitosis she had ever come across. Normally all she had to do, while at work with men with this condition, was turn her head away, but this man was different!

"You see," he continued, "all my life I have eaten garlic. My mother insisted it was good for me so I'm afraid I am addicted; every day I chew on a few cloves. In the past, I always wondered why I'd never been able to make friends; of course, now she's gone, I realise why."

"So how can I help today?" She enquired turning away, taking a deep breath and trying not to inhale while she spoke.

"Well, now I have been summoned to the palace to receive an award from Her Majesty." He practised a little bow. "The gong is for starting a charity to assist multi-millionaires who are down to their last ten million. I've stuffed my pockets with mouth fresheners but I don't think they'll let me in through the gates, they are all aerosols, you see …"

"Would you like me to keep them for you until you come out?" Samantha seized the opportunity; at her age two wealthy men were not likely to pop up in one day. She fished in the bottom of her bag. "Here take this, it might help, security can't object to a packet of Polo's." Like a couple of drug-dealers they palmed the items across.

"Thank you so much, I can't tell you how relieved I am and of course you needn't wait." He waved his admittance card to the sentry and disappeared through the gate.

"See you later." Samantha said under her breath, knowing she was onto a winner.

Over dinner, back at Jacob's house in Birdcage Walk, Samantha sat and listened patiently as the whole story tumbled out.

"Samantha, I have never told anyone this," Jacob began. "Mother always sheltered me from the world and the evils of women. From the time I was five-years-old she gave me raw garlic to eat. I was too young to realise that it could become an addiction and the shield of garlic breath forced other people away ...but now I'm forty-six and I'm lonely." He blew his nose hard into a silk handkerchief.

"How could a mother do that to her child?" Samantha crooned. She placed scarlet eagle-talons soothingly on his arm. This quarry would be as easy as grabbing fish out of a river.

"Well, when she died I inherited the family fortunes and Petersons Multinational Enterprises, which I run via computer. I sit inside a sealed glass office; she had it built especially for me. You've probably heard of the company. Mother arranged my marriage, for respectabilities sake, she'd said. Because of my problems the marriage has never been consummated. My wife enjoys all the luxury I can provide, she lives in a large, country house with servants etc. and I think of her as a leach. The marriage has never been annulled – I have felt too embarrassed."

Here at last was Samantha's naïve, lonely man, just the man she'd been looking for. A comfortable meal ticket and absolute luxury for the rest of her life. She'd never need to work again. Taking his mother's place would be easy. Persuading him to get rid of his wife through the courts, if necessary, would be a doddle. She could wean him from his addiction even though, for a while, she might have to join him in a daily garlic clove. Later she'd gradually wean him onto full-power tablets, then after a while, odourless tablets.

Her name wasn't Samantha George, 'wizard of Soho', if she couldn't find plenty of ideas to occupy Jacob Peterson's time. She had discovered that he was a virgin and she could definitely teach him a few tricks!

Avner Kornblum

The Shoot-out

They shot the white woman first. Then it was the turn of the black lad, barely fifteen, yet he had a protruding belly and several gaps in his mouth where once there were teeth.

"Get rid of him next!" barked Fred, 'The Boss' as he was known to his gang.

"He has his hands up. Shall I shoot him like that?" asked Mick.

"No, tie them behind his back, so they make his belly stick out more. Aim at his belly …that will justify his suffering."

The Boss was terse and unmoved by the lad's confusion and woe.

After all, it was not Fred's fault if foreigners of all colours came to settle in Britain without being able to speak English.

After he'd shot the gap-toothed youngster it was the turn of the crazy Italian. Mick wondered if he were really crazy, or was his peculiar behaviour something he had learned so as to get out of doing things he didn't enjoy and to be accepted wherever the crowd was strange enough.

Mick was jerked out of his reverie by The Boss shouting at him. "C'mon, Mick, shoot the bugger! It's hot out here, and in any case we don't have all day!"

That's true, thought Mick, looking at the gathering rain-clouds. "Say, boss, shall I just shoot him and leave the rest for later, or tomorrow?"

"Yeah, shoot him quickly then let's grab a bite of lunch."

The Italian had a doleful expression on his face. "You want shoot me before lunch? Bang, bang, and I finished. You not want me have lunch also?"

"I'm sure you can join us if you're up to it after I've shot you!" replied Mick, with a fiendish grin on his face. "Now put on the stupidest expression you can manage, because that's how you'll be best remembered."

The Italian grimaced then adopted a ludicrous pose. Mick took careful aim and shot him twice as he stood, once as he went down and again as he lay on the ground. "Okay, that's him done," growled Fred. "Let's go have some lunch."

With that, he and Mick strode off to the canteen, leaving the Italian to pick himself up and the gaffer to collect all the equipment before they too joined the white woman and the gap-toothed youngster for lunch.

Gail Tucker

Private Affair

With a sigh, Mavis settled back to enjoy the prawn.

She could not remember when or how she had first lit upon a prawn but it had served her well: you could always eat a prawn, afterwards.

You couldn't really buy just one prawn so she had taken to buying a baby Hovis too, having it handy with some nicely salted butter and a little white pepper.

She had always had a good appetite and it was not diminished now.

All in all, jolly nice …and quite harmless – in private, of course

Paul Shearer Walmsley

Stormy Weather: Raining Cats and Dogs

It had been raining non-stop for two days and two nights. Janet stood at the front door of her semi-detached house and sighed, will it ever stop she heard herself say out loud.

Just at that moment a large van stopped in front of the house. On the side of the van, painted in big, red letters, were the words, 'We collect stray dogs and cats'.

Well that takes the biscuit, thought Janet, I can't get out because of the rain, and animals are collected and taken to a dry place. So who is the animal? I wonder; they will have overnight hotels next, where they can stay until a good home can be found for them.

I give up. There is no justice for we poor humans

Agnes Hall

The Letter

The Cells
No 4 Parkhurst Camp
Salisbury Plain.

31st May 1917.

My Dear Anne,

Today I have been paraded once again before the troops and subjected to abuse and ridicule. As you know, since I have been here, I have not co-operated with orders to do work that would help the war effort and, as the result of my latest refusal, I have now been sentenced to my third term of 'hard labour', which has forced me to make another decision. Today I have decided to refuse all orders given to me, whether associated with the war or not. I have not made this decision lightly nor yet made this decision known to the authorities. Once they know of it, all basic 'rights' will be taken away from me. That will include the 'right' to send and receive letters, so this may well be the last letter that you receive from me.

I know that you have always withheld your approval of my decision not to fight in this accursed war and I also know that you, personally, have suffered as a result of a brother who is a 'Conchie'. At least you know that my decision not to fight was not out of cowardice but out of the belief that we should not harm our fellow man. I am not a coward and nor are many others who are imprisoned in this place for standing firm in their belief. If we were cowards we wouldn't have placed ourselves in a position where constant humiliations are heaped upon us, and as we have recently heard, there is an opinion voiced that those who refuse to fight should be shot.

The first thing that will happen after I have disclosed my intentions to the authorities is that I will be placed in solitary confinement. I have been told that the cells are bare, without any item of furniture, not even a bed and without any windows. As I have said I will not be allowed to write or receive letters nor be allowed reading material of any kind. Nor will I be allowed any visitors. My diet for most of the time will consist of bread and water and there will be little or no exercise allowed. I am not telling you this so that you will feel sorry for me but to make you understand how serious my intentions are.

I have tried bringing the conditions under which we are imprisoned to the attention of various outside authorities but, so far, with little response, so this letter is also an appeal to you, to try and make people aware that we are not cowards and do not deserve the punishment that is meted out to us. Please pray for me.

Your ever-loving brother
John. [1]

---

[1] This is not an actual letter but based on research about the conditions that some Conscientious Objectors suffered in WW1 All mail was censored and the letter would not have been sent.

Gail Tucker

Passing Lives

The patrolling security man watched the smartly dressed young woman open small sheets of paper and smooth them onto her lap with practised care. An envelope slid off the charcoal-grey skirt to lie for a moment against a gold-heeled, red shoe. An immaculately manicured finger and thumb quickly pinched the escapee under control and tucked it into a flat document wallet which hung from a gold chain across the woman's chest. The man observed all this as he observed other subjects of scrutiny during his nine-hour shift in the airport departure lounge.

He could not read what held her attention, that was for his companion – way up in the cctv control room – if he could. There had been a lot of ruined film of late. Security shrugged, not its concern, it turned its eye to the young man with a beard and a rucksack who browsed the book-stand.

Ignorant of all around her, the confident woman traveller, immersed herself in the document on her lap:

My Dearest Tanya,

A fortunate child is one raised by loving parents: two people who enfold the helpless infant in their love and care for its daily needs. Today, on this your 16th Birthday, I am certain that you know you have enjoyed such love.

I only met your mama once, but we women of a certain nature do not need time to recognise one another; in my world, friendship and love can be both instant and eternal, even when circumstances force a separation.

Who do you resemble, Tanya? I know you will have your father's bluest of blue eyes, and I expect you are tall too like each of your parents, but sometimes when I look in the mirror I wonder if you have a freckle on your cheek now or whether it faded as your baby-self grew.

You see, Tanya, I am trying to do the impossible here – I am trying to tell you gently that you are my Tanya too: that I am your mother: that you have not only the love of two but the love of three parents to keep you safe, cherished in all of their hearts. You are indeed a love child, a child of love.

Before I met your mama, Valerie, that one time, I had 'un di felice, eterea' with Gregor. I first saw him on the stage of the opera house at Covent Garden. Yes, your London stage of such renown. I was enduring, as I remember, the rehearsal most tedious for performers, the technical one where we must stand and move into places around the stage to find the lights – or be found. Our voices are at rest while our bodies must stand still, at times till our feet go numb while a lamp is tilted or a gel-tone changed.

At such moments these days my mind wanders, sometimes exploring the libretto but, more often than not since that fateful day, I have wandered the world of my imagination with you. Your first steps, your nursery rhymes – do you have a voice, Tanya? Do you like to sing? You will have music in your soul, you were on stage many times before you were born. But I digress – how not! Sixteen years is a lifetime – your lifetime after all.

Well, to the day I first saw your father. Dazzled by a spotlight, I could see nothing but an intense whiteness, black, pulsing waves. Unsteady, I stumbled and was caught in the bearlike hold of a stagehand who turned out to be Gregory Mason, scenery painter. Mi Gregor.

From that moment 'Di quell amor ch' è palpi to' – do you know it, Tanya? 'All that has life has its breath from you'.

The Company was in London for more than a month and by the time we took the boat train for Paris, you were with me. I carried my secret across Europe to Vienna and Milan – the farthest point of our tour in The West before we must return to Mother Russia – to Moscow, that had so proudly displayed our talents to glorify the Soviet State. Politics has no place here in this letter but I realise it cannot be discounted from our decisions, the passionate actions of we three. The Company was scheduled to return for a final week in London where we were to give two concert performances at The Royal Albert Hall.

Thanks to good health & good luck your presence was not betrayed. The big, fur coats we had been given to wear by Moscow, helped to disguise you when I was not on stage. My dresser is a very old friend whose family belonged on the estate of our ancestors since the days of Great Catherine. Rita does all and says nothing.

The day of your arrival, in the sleeping-car between Marseilles and Lyon, Rita barred the door and declared that Diva Tatiana needed complete rest. She carried you swaddled, in a basket with other luggage, and we prayed that you would not sing too soon. You did not, my darling Tanya.
You lay and smiled and screwed up your eyes as though from a great light; you sighed and fell asleep.

In the waiting room on Waterloo Station, you and I met Valerie. "Darling!" – does she still do that? Come into a room already speaking to those inside so that she is with them before she is there? A wonderful trick! Well, I think it so. "Darling!" she said and crossed the cold space and gripped my shoulders, turning me so that we looked together at you in your basket on the waiting room bench.

I think she said 'Darling' once more but whispered it.

Beyond that, I can remember nothing. The mind finds ways to mend even the deepest sorrow.

Your father held his three girls together in his enormous embrace before I slipped under his arm and left you with your mama.

I doubt this letter's arrival will be a surprise to Valerie and I hope Gregor will recognise the paper I use to write, its colour has faded but he will know it I'm sure, we bought it together in London. I shall send the package via a London law firm as an insurance against State interference here; after Rudi leapt the barrier, we artists have been carefully monitored. We had hopes of a softening once or twice but we are still walled by what I think you know as The Iron Curtain. Perhaps that curtain will rise one day in my lifetime – who can tell.

You are old enough now to learn of my love for you, Tanya. You are my only child and I hold you, with Valerie and mi Gregor, for ever in my heart,

Tatiana K.

Tan Mason almost knew the words by heart, she had carried them with her for nearly two decades. She folded the sheets carefully and tucked them into the worn envelope that bore her baptismal name.

She looked up to see her return flight to Heathrow flash, *Now Boarding*. It was time to close the door on a past that had never seemed part of her life, no matter how hard she tried.

Carefully, she folded the envelope in two.

The scarlet nails creased the fold. With her left hand she held the wad tightly and with the thumbnail of her right hand picked a tiny split in the fold she had just created.

With a deliberate, swift movement she tore the wad in half. Repeating the tear several times, she reduced the single rectangle to tiny fragments.

A lad in a grubby bomber jacket collided with her, as she reached their targeted bin she did not miss a step. She pressed forward and cast the fistful of paper into the trash-can to free herself from her history.

The paper fragments fluttered to the dark base before a larger packet thudded softly to lie among them.

None of it would be there long.

Tan joined the queue at the boarding gate and reflected that nothing could have prepared her for this trip. She ought never to have come. Fate had dealt her a strange hand but she was done with it all now.

When she went to work on Monday, she could put all her mind to the task in hand.

There would be nothing to distract her from the role she played in her country's national security: no glimmer of conflicting personal loyalty.

Her colleagues would continue to rely on her dedication to the hunt for terrorists, a beautiful woman with an iron will.

Behind her in the queue, the young man checked his watch against the clock on the wall and hoped the flight would take off on time.

So far so good. The margin for error was always very small, a delay could cost him his life and he had more work to do, if God would allow.

He concentrated his gaze on the gold heels of the red shoes that moved swiftly through the entrance to the gantry.

Keep your eyes down and distant, had been part of the drill. He flashed his boarding card across the desk.

The female flight attendant slotted the long narrow slip into the machine.

Silently, he began to pray.

Colin Hall

The Happy Couple

Inspired by the painting 'American Gothic' by Grant Wood

Never had two people been so happy.

Inside, they were full of spiritual peace and evangelical zeal and fervour. Somehow these feelings didn't quite make it to the outside world. They lay hidden behind the stern facade of their glum faces and the austere cut of their clothes. In some way, the colours just served to dampen any celebratory feelings. They had dressed up for the big day.

The new toaster, on order from the on-line catalogue store, had failed to arrive in time for his birthday bash, so it was back to the old, reliable toasting-fork once again. He probably preferred the tried and tested method with the fork, as he was sure it gave a better and more even shade of brown to the individual slices. He also had more control over the process, being able to 'do' one side more than the other.

Having signed the pledge all those years ago, the tipple of the day was to be a lethal mixture of sarsaparilla and dandelion-and-burdock. He, being in charge of the catering, thought this would complement the egg-on-toast being served to the privileged guests.

He could not help wondering what presents to expect this year. He had read and reread the books from last year. "The Power of Positive Thinking", "Laugh and the World Laughs with You" and "Fanny Craddock's Guide to the Perfect Egg-On-Toast". He was hoping for something a little less positive and more downbeat for this year. He wondered if his friends were trying to tell him something, but he had built up an immunity to the threats of indoctrination, by the optimistic forces, which threatened his relationship with his wife.

They were happy as they were.

Avner Kornblum

A Chinese Dinner Stopped Me Smoking

It was December 30th, 1978, a balmy summer's night in South Africa. A glass of wine was on the table in front of me, a cigarette glowed in my left hand and the young woman I had married a week earlier sat beside me, holding my right hand. All was right with my world.

"Have you decided on your New Year's wish?" she asked.

"I'm not making a New Year's wish," I replied. "I made five at the beginning of this year and they have all manifested. There's nothing more I want."

"How about giving up smoking?" she asked innocently.

"That's a good idea. I'll make that my New Year wish."

"That's too vague," she said. "You have to state a date or circumstance."

I reflected on all the times I had given up smoking in the twenty-eight year since I'd started. At 16 I had been elected President of the Papyros Club (our school's illicit smoker's group) by its ten members because I was the only one who did not smoke. I had tentatively tried one cigarette at University two years later. Next day I accepted two from friends, and within a month I was an addict, smoking forty to fifty cigarettes a day.

Like most smokers, I had tried to kick the habit at times, once for three months and once for six months, convincing myself I was finally free. Then I attended a serious 6-hour business meeting with 17 men and 2 women, all heavy smokers. In that time I, quite unthinkingly and unhesitatingly, accepted ten proffered cigarettes. Next day I was back on forty.

"Tell you what," I said, "I'll make a New Year's wish to give up the first time smoking a cigarette makes me feel ill."

December 31st was a hectic day. We were hosting 100 carefully-selected high-profile members of my Professionals Club to a New

Year's Eve dinner at the `Club House´ in my garden.

In my perceived wisdom I had arranged for a top-class Chinese restaurant to deliver 100 four-course meals while I went to a huge liquor superstore and loaded my car to the hilt with beer, wine, soft drinks, liqueurs and twenty bottles of champagne.

It was a wonderful evening, a memorable event for all of us.

At 8 o´clock a hundred people descended on my garden, in which chairs, light-weight couches and long benches had been strategically placed.

In the centre we had arranged long tables, laden with plates, glasses, cutlery, ashtrays and the variety of beverages I had brought. My wife and I and my two sons added the Chinese dinners and the guests – all strangers to each other – ate, drank and chattered away long after the midnight-bell tolled, stopping only to sing `Auld Lang Syne´, as though they were Scots and to toast the New Year in swigging champagne, as though they were thirsty.

By four-o`clock on New Year`s morning the last guest had finally left and I realised that I had been so busy introducing guests to each other and chatting and serving that I had not eaten at all. As we tidied and cleared away the spoils and leftovers, I nibbled on various items that had been left untouched. By this time, they were all cold and to some extent congealed.

From five-o`clock on I was in agony. My stomach was heaving but it refused to discharge anything I had consumed. Not from the top nor from the bottom. All stayed within me and I became more and more nauseous. I drank soda-water. It did not help. I took every remedy available though in my disturbed state I neither noticed nor cared what they were. Finally, I did something I had been too ill to think about during the preceding two hours. I lit a cigarette, certain it would help me settle the upset caused by the glutinous conglomeration deep within me.

It did not help at all. It made me feel worse. Much worse. I stubbed it out. I have never smoked since. Never wanted to. Never missed it. I recommend cold Chinese dinners to all intending abstainers. It`s better than cold turkey.

Vivien Johnson

The Chancer

"Sold for 2,000 guineas." The horse was mine.

Going to the Ascot Sales is a monthly occurrence for me. Buying quality ex-race horses and turning them into eventers or show-jumpers is the way I make my living. I enjoy the work, in the fresh air in all weathers but now that my daughter Susie has joined me in the business, doing the day to day management, it is easier for me to get away to sales. I usually have about a dozen horses in at a time, for schooling, so as well as my two hardworking grooms I needed more knowledgeable help.

I am fortunate to have Susie working beside me; she'd been a travelling groom with international show-horses and had recently decided to put down roots in the spare cottage beside my yard, so we aren't under each other's feet all the time. She has her privacy, even though we have always got on. I'd bought her first pony, Nutmeg, when she was only three-years-old. We're lucky to agree on most horsey aspects of training and stable management.

My heart pounded as the auctioneer brought down his hammer. The groom looked relieved, the Gelding shook his head and snorted down his nostrils. The man led him away to the stables.

I didn't usually buy horses on a whim. My hand shook, half with anxiety and half with excitement, as I raised my bidding number for the auctioneer to see. Unsuccessfully trying not to worry, I hurried after my fast-disappearing horse …*what had I bought*? I always had doubts after my bid had been accepted. I had, of course given the horse a good once-over before the sale started and had decided that he didn't fit what I had imagined him to be. I'd seen his details, but no picture, on the internet catalogue a few days before: *16.2hh Chestnut gelding, eight years old, T.B.*

This part of the description was true enough but he was also said to be of good temperament with no vices. For 2,000 guineas I had been willing to take a chance but now warning bells sounded in my brain. A basically good stamp of a horse like this, sold without warranty? There must be something wrong with him. I reached the stables just in time to see the groom scuttle away.

"Wait a minute! I've some questions to ask you."

He turned and looked uncomfortable. "Me, Sir?"

"Yes you, Sir. Can you tell me anything about the horse? He looks a bit poor."

The man gave a wry smile. "He's a difficult ride. He was too much for his previous owner, so he let him down in condition and turned him away. His passport says he's by Extra Snake. That's all I can tell you."

Unmanageable was a word that lodged in my mind. Never-the-less, I paid my 2,000 guineas plus commission to the auctioneer and prepared to take the horse home.

The horse had travelled well, showed no signs of sweat, even though it was a warm day. I led him down the ramp into the sunlight. Susie stood in the yard, barrow-in-hand, on her way to the muck heap. She dropped the handles and the barrow clattered onto the concrete, spilling its contents everywhere. The horse reared, shied and turned tail. I just managed to control him before he galloped off down the drive. Susie's voice rang clear above the commotion.

"Dad why on earth did you buy that rat-bag?" She yelled after me. "I thought you went for a show-jumper and, in any case, it would have been a better plan to spend the money on a new car!"

Susie, always spoke her mind, which is why we get on so well.

I had to admit she was right about the car. Our old Ford Focus had spent more time in the garage lately, than it had on the road. However, horses were my passion and livelihood, a car wouldn't earn me money if I sold it!

"Well dear, I felt sorry for him and he was cheap enough."

"You felt sorry for him! Are you going soft Dad? You are supposed to be a professional, not a namby-pamby do-gooding amateur!" She'd gone red in the face.

"I'm sure I can make something of him. I promise you he'll be worth the effort..."

She stomped off down the yard whistling loudly. She always did that when she was in a strop. She turned and said, as more of an accusation than a question,

"I don't suppose he has any papers or anything? We need to turn him round quickly, sell if he hasn't. He might make a good hunter if we're lucky."

Fortunately, she didn't wait for my answer. I didn't want to admit that I wasn't sure, I only had his passport. If not registered with the British Show Jumping Association, we would have to work up through the grades. If registered, I needed to know which classes he was eligible for.

In the meantime, I was dying to try him out; building up his fitness would take several months. I didn't even know if Susie, or I, could manage him under saddle.

During the next few weeks, the horse began to put on condition. He wasn't an easy ride but he seemed to have jumping ability. The BSJA had been a bit slow with his registration. I was on tenterhooks, had to stop myself phoning up every day. I pounced on the long-awaited envelope, knowing what it was the moment it dropped through the letterbox. I skimmed over the details.

Master Serpent, 16.2hh, T.B. Chestnut gelding, etc., Grade A. I didn't read any further. For the second time my heart was thumping with excitement over this animal.

"Susie, Susie, he's Grade A!" I couldn't believe my luck and sploshed down the rain-sodden yard in my slippers. "I can enter him in the county show in two months. The series' first prize, you know, is a car. As you never stop reminding me we desperately need that new car." All our money is invested in the horses – winning the car would solve a lot of our problems.

I spent even more time with Serpent, I had to get between his ears, as an old Irish horse dealer had once said to me, find out what makes him tick. More grooming, special feed supplements and exercise. He seemed to enjoy the extra attention and a bond was forged between us. Susie couldn't ride him; every time she tried he bucked her off, he didn't even like her going into his stable. To show his displeasure he'd put his ears flat back on his neck and curl his lip, showing two rows of large, white teeth.

"Don't you have a go at me you chestnut object; you are not going to intimidate me in any way. I told Dad that you would have been more value to us as a car." Bustling into his stable, laden with hay nets or dung forks, she'd busy herself with mucking out, tidying his bed. She'd talk to him all the time. "Now Serpent, you be a good boy and we'll get along fine. You try any of your tricks and you'll soon find yourself in a dog-meat can." So eventually, over the weeks, they reached an uneasy truce.

The day came for our first major show together. We had to qualify four times to enter the class with the car, wins, or being placed second. I loaded the lorry the night before with a picnic and food and water for the horse. I packed the tack, my best leather boots and everything else I could possibly think of; I am a belt and braces person.

I drove out of the yard at six a.m.

It would take us three hours to get to the show; we'd have a rest, then I'd tack up.

Serpent had travelled well and everything had gone according to plan. I put his saddle and bridle on and warmed him up over a few jumps before going into the ring. Of course, I had jumped him in affiliated shows before but never in a class of this calibre. We would have to jump against some well-known people with good horses. I hoped he would settle to the job.

He went clear in the first round, even jumped the huge water with ease, I was delighted. In the second round Serpent got a bit hyper and hit a couple of poles quite hard but to my relief and amazement they stayed in place. There were four horses in the jump-off, Serpent was second to go. The first horse went clear. I decided to try to go fast, he felt ready. All went well until he hit a brick out of the wall, four faults. However, we finished in a very fast time. This horse was proving to be a real star. The last two horses both had four faults but slower times, so we finished second. Our first qualifier for the car.

The horse heard his name over the loudspeaker system and I swear he grew another two inches. We pranced off to the ring to collect our rosettes, one for coming second and one for qualifying. As the sponsor of the class reached up to hand me our prize, Serpent reared up, spun round and bucking violently, galloped off across the ring, scattering people and horses in all directions. I finished up hanging around his neck and only just managed to get myself back into the saddle. I really thought I was going to end up on the ground. Eventually, order was restored. I collected my rosettes from the show office later.

Susie saw the rosettes hanging on the cab windscreen as I drove down the drive. Leaving her hay bales and trolley in the middle of the yard she ran to meet us, waving her arms above her head. She opened the yard gate to let us in and jumped into the cab almost before we'd stopped.

"Dad you did it! Tell me all about it."

"I'll tell you later, first let's get him unboxed."

This was only the beginning of course; we had three more qualifiers to go. The next one was nearer home, only an hour away. Except for a heart-stopping moment when he stumbled after a big, wide parallel, he easily won the competition with three clear rounds and the fastest time.

The next two outings were pretty uneventful. Serpent came second in each, being beaten by one-tenth of a second and half-a-second respectively. So now we had our four qualifiers and the county show was the next week.

An overcast sky greeted the dawn, a nice temperature for jumping. I hoped it wouldn't rain. Serpent hated the rain and always danced around in a crabwise-fashion trying to keep the water out of his ears.

I gave him ten-minutes lunging before we left home to loosen up his muscles and had plenty of time to get to the show ground, which was nearby, and to find a parking-place in the shade. I'd taken horses to minor classes there, many times before, and had been very successful. That day I felt lucky. Serpent had given me wonderful qualifying rides; he'd proved that despite my original doubts, water held no fears for him. Although there would be some tough opposition, international riders with really experienced horses, I felt confident. I always enjoyed these occasions; I chatted to old friends and caught up on horsey-news and, better still, horsey-gossip. It was also an opportunity to buy and sell a horse or two. Susie always came with me to the county show; for her too, it was a social occasion, as well as an opportunity to ride in the minor classes. That year, however, she came to watch …to watch me win the car!

We were last to go. The first round went without a hitch. Serpent sailed over the fences as if he were an international horse. In the second round the jumps were raised and he had to make a bit more effort. He was on top form. Susie stood by the ring, her fists clenched around the perimeter fence, her knuckles white. I passed her as I positioned myself for the start of the jump-off. The bell went, we cantered off.

The first fence, an inviting rustic, presented no trouble at all but we were now jumping against the clock: a sharp right-hand turn to an upright of planks: eight strides to an enormous parallel: left turn, a big, red wall. I felt the big horse give me everything, every ounce of his energy and his ability.

Two more jumps, then the stile followed by a big oxer and we were through the finish at breakneck speed. I knew we were clear and we were fast.

The only other horse in the jump-off had gone clear too.

I felt sure we had been faster than he was and I knew that the car was ours!

We left the ring amidst tumultuous applause and then, through the noise, I heard the tail-end of the loudspeaker announcement… *'Tangmed wins by one-tenth of a second. Master Serpent takes second place'*.

Gail Tucker

Inheritance

"Strange," thought Louisa inclined over the canvas, alternately spitting and rolling, deftly controlling the fat cotton bud across the dark folds of the skirt. Each time the fibres made contact with the crackled surface, the skirt fabric seemed to move aside to show a glimpse of something Louisa felt certain was there. Something hidden.

People were often amazed at how simply a painting could be raised from the dead in the hands of an expert restorer. She never used saliva when a client was present but Louisa liked the fact that her own juices could contribute to a work of art. For an initial assessment there was nothing quicker or safer than what she was now doing.

Usually the rhythm of the initial delicate exploration, moving in time to her own heartbeat, was a steady revelation. Cleaning away the layer of dirt built up over years of domestic life: the soot of open fires, the tar of cigar smoke, the grit of dust all became a new landscape to be explored by the restorer.

Once in a while, Louisa had felt the thrill of the unexpected. Those were the times she was drawn to a section of canvas, impelled to work with tireless delicacy to find an unexpected pet dog in the lap of an austere bishop or a sheet of paper clasped in the elegant fingers of a courtly lady. On such days Louisa's fingertips tingled with excitement although any casual visitor to the workshop would see only a serenely absorbed woman working deftly among the assorted paraphernalia of her trade. Today, however, was different.

For three months the Willoughby canvas had been stacked against the wall, put to one side; the owners were away until July so there had been no urgency. The delayed start was due to more than that. When she had first taken the work out of the frame to assess the extent of the damage and give them an estimate of costs to expect, Louisa had felt unaccountably apprehensive. This was, on the face of it, a routine cleaning job. The present owner had recently inherited the painting and his wife saw it as a potential trophy, a signal of background and breeding, to flaunt.

Mrs Willoughby had hoped Louisa would find brighter colours beneath the grime as she clearly knew that her husband would not want to hide their heirloom on the landing. He was always keen to please his second wife and allowed her much more license than he had his first, who had been a mere child when they had married. The present Mrs Willoughby was an altogether different animal and that's exactly what he loved her for: the animal. So long as she pleased him, he pleased her and she could do as she pleased when he was busy elsewhere.

Professionally, Louisa generally reserved her opinions for the art works themselves, having little interest in the owners so long as they paid their bills. Privately, the restorer labelled her clients worthy or unworthy, depending upon how much they truly cared about the objects in their care. Louisa believed that art belonged to no one, no matter what sums were paid at celebrated auctions, the buyer could only ever be a custodian. She had thought Mrs Willoughby exceedingly unworthy. The woman had swept into the old stables one September morning.

"Get your man to fetch the picture from my car, dear," opened the encounter.

"Good Morning!"

Mrs Willoughby looked at the slender form in the loose overalls.

She waved the car keys in the air, presuming instant attention from a minion.

Louisa advanced, outstretched hand ready to shake in greeting, not to take car keys, "I'm Louisa, am I expecting you?"

"We were told you could clean a picture. I'm just dropping it off. If you could give me a price, I'll let you know if you can have the job."

"I have to see it first, Mrs . . .?" Louisa was not easily roused but recognised bad behaviour when she met it.

"Willoughby, Janine Willoughby. The picture is in my car. I said that. Get your man to fetch it, if you don't mind." That last said with a slight falter.

"No man, I'm afraid. Just me. I restore pictures." Louisa had stood her ground and enjoyed watching the foolish woman, dressed for a ladies' lunch, wrestle the sheeted, heavily framed picture through the door. The relationship did not improve when Louisa declined to make a commitment to do the work until she had had a chance to examine the canvas out of its frame.

Janine Willoughby's mobile phone had rescued both of them when it summoned her away and she abandoned the painting without a backward glance.

Piers Willoughby called next morning to pour courteous oil on troubled waters. Louisa did not bother to imagine what tale his wife had told of their encounter.

He did not flatter her reputation; he complimented work she had done for some of his cousins and friends.

Louisa accepted his implicit apology, amused at the thought of Janine Willoughby's discomfort – it was this gentle malice that made her take the job.

"Damn!" The loft door slammed in a sudden draught; Louisa, startled, knocked over a tiny bottle of water. Before she could mop it up, the clear liquid turned an opaque blue, ran over the edge of the canvas and down the leg of the table. There was barely enough to form a puddle before it ran away down a crack in the bare boards but by the time she had thrown some soft, old sheeting across the sopping surface the damage was done. Or was it?

Lifting the wet cloth Louisa saw what had really been slipping in and out of sight all morning …the face of a wide-eyed girl of perhaps seven or eight, a child anyway. Louisa realised that the artist's original glazing had been overlaid with a water soluble medium of some kind and the adult's dress folds extended to hide the child. A deliberate obfuscation.

A long-haul flight away, Janine Willoughby dozed in the quiet dusk of the spa's treatment room. Her face swathed in moist cloths, she heard only the whirring of the ceiling fan and the occasional click of the irrigation spray on the perfect lawn outside. Afternoons were the best time wherever you were. She had been to every continent since her marriage to Piers and she had to admit life was quite wonderful.

She particularly like the Caribbean; everyone was always eager to please and the climate suited her so well; friends always remarked on how well she looked when she returned to England. God, how awful it would be to live in that cold, damp climate all the time. She so enjoyed seeing the world. Everywhere was so civilised these days one never saw any of the unsightly side of life. Very different from the view she had on the first journeys she took. In those days, a package tour courier, she did the bidding of others. Not anymore.

Mrs Willoughby never ceased to be glad of the day she'd twisted her ankle in Jermyn Street and Piers had stooped into her life. She wondered now how that cleaner was getting on with the wretched painting, she hoped the work would be finished by the time they went home. Miles would be home for the school holidays, she could get on with organizing the decorators: she would choose a colour scheme to complement the painting, show it off: please Piers. It would give her something to do while the boy was around: an excuse to get others to take and fetch him from the summer-school activities. She had urged Piers to enrol his son on the pretext that the boy would meet and make some local friends. The thought of his schoolfellows paying weekend visits, rampaging around the house, made her shudder. She did not feel equipped to deal with a thirteen-year-old stepson and had no intention of doing more than the absolute minimum. She did not think herself unkind. She was not the motherly sort. Anyway, the boy would not take kindly to smothering, much better to keep a distance.

In the meantime, she was getting rather chilly, where was that damn Luella, it was about time she came to finish the facial and repaint nails. She pressed a button to ring a bell …must remind them who's paying their wages.

Louisa had finally got the flesh tone right. It had taken much careful research to establish the pigment needed to blend the child's features into the original. Her friend Ben, who had heard all about Mrs Janine Willoughby, had joked that The Willoughbys would be inviting her to conceal the face once they'd seen it. Louisa thought he was wrong but could not wait to see Janine Willoughby's reaction. She relished the woman's imagined discomfort. On the other hand, Louisa doubted the third son of the old family of merchant traders would turn a hair at the unexpected presence in the family portrait.

Little Uju, as Ben had called her, would be merely another dinner party conversation piece. Perhaps one day the child would be found a branch on the family tree. One never knew with people and their heritage.

Paul Shearer Walmsley

New Year's Eve

Tic-Toc Tic-Toc; the old Grandfather clock in the corner of the room kept up its monotonous beat. It had been doing this for the last three-hundred-sixty-five days without stopping. Old Bill religiously wound it up once a week. It had to be done tonight – and this was coincidence – New Year's Eve.

Bill waited until the first chime of midnight, rose from his chair, and walked over to the clock. Inserting the worn, brass key he started to turn it. All at once, he heard a strange, warbling noise and then the sound of metal grinding against metal.

The clock stopped.

It was one minute past midnight.

New Year's Day and it was Bill's Birthday; he was now 100 years old. Was the clock's stopping a bad omen?

Colin Hall

Murder in the Showers of a Spanish Campsite

If only Fritz had not left his shower gel in the cubicle, he might have got away with it.

The man from the Guardia arrived at the campsite reception at 5am.

He greeted the security man who had telephoned the station earlier, with a nudge in the rib cage to wake him up and said, "Nocho todo." (evenin' all) in an accent reminiscent of a BBC Saturday-night black-and-white television program from the early sixties. The only thing missing was the gas lamp over the doorway behind the copper's helmet (which was also missing but not relevant).

The campsite employee led the Guardia to block number three and they entered together.

The first thing they noticed was the river of congealed blood coming out of stall number four.

They had to use force to open the door and they then stumbled upon the naked, prostrate body of what appeared to be a blonde Scandinavian woman.

She must have been a beauty, before what happened had happened.

Her white, silk knickers and short top were hanging from a rather thrilled looking clothes peg.

Her discarded crocks stood on end against the white tiled wall to save them from being waterlogged from the shower spray. (I mention this because I think it is a useful tip.

There are not many things worse than stepping into wet crocks after you have dried your feet.

Well, apart from being murdered, which is a lot worse and more detrimental to your health.

On the shelf in the small cubicle, stood two shower-gel containers.

The label on one said, 'Dusch Gel'; the other read, 'Dusj Gel'. Our man from the Guardia put his hands behind his back, raised himself up on his toes and said, "Hola, hola, hola. ¿qué tenemos aquí, entonces." Which, roughly translated, means, "Hello, hello, hello, what have we here then?"

The only perceivable difference between this scene and the original, was that this was in colour. The accents were also slightly different of course. Also, back then, people had not heard of shower-gel, no matter what language it was written in. They only had blocks of carbolic soap and rough loofas to scrape the grime off their bodies. These days it was all soft facecloths, but why they were called facecloths when they were used on other, lower, round the back parts of the body, was anybody's guess.

Anyway, back to the plot.

Our hero suggested to the security guard that he might be more useful to the investigation if he went and put the kettle on. So off he scarpered, leaving Sherlock Viviendas alone with his magnifying glass, and the dead bird.

Being a man of habit, and an avid watcher of pólice televisión dramas, and having given up on his pipe, he pulled from his coat pocket, stuck in his mouth, and lit, a cigar.

No lollipops for him.

But hey, *who loves you baby, anyway*, he thought to himself because there was nobody else around who was still alive.

She did not reply.

The next day he had solved this dastardly crime.

The clue was clear for him to see.

Two bottles of shower gel. One from Norway, as in "Dusj Gel" Obviously the one that the Scandinavian bird had taken into the shower. The other, "Dusch Gel", from Germany.

On his walk from reception to the shower block he had noticed the only German registered motorhome on the site.

Our man approached the German's pitch.

He found him looking at a map of Poland and said, "You can't be serious. The last time you went there it started the second world-war." Fritz looked up and saw him holding a bottle with the words 'Dusch Gel' printed on the label and Don Kojak said, "I believe you left this in the shower."

Before he thought about what he was saying, Fritz replied, "Oh thank you for returning my g... ...oh!"

"Golpeo al hico los derechos," nodded the policeman. "Banged to rights, son."

Gail Tucker

Home and Away

The reassuring scent of pine and chlorine lingered with the steamy wash of bleach; Rosa propped the door open with the waste bin while she emptied her bucket onto the steps. Barely pausing to rub her aching back, the woman swabbed the first step with her saturated mop.

Dirty, grey strands swirled into the pooling water caught in a dip on the second step.

Most people skipped the bottom one on their way up so, after twenty years, the middle step was more worn than its connecting fellows.

"Have – you – finished – yet?" The words came separately from an exaggeratedly opening and closing mouth. The agitated woman in bright-orange shorts was waving both purple-nailed hands in an attempt to get Rosa's attention.

"Hola," Rosa hid behind incomprehension and a big smile.

"Can I use it now?" orange shorts advanced.

Rosa moved the yellow and black *wet floor* warning sign just far enough to stop the advance in its tracks. They couldn't wait half an hour, let her careful work dry to a shine before they were in there: polished taps grubby with soap, white porcelain smeared with toothpaste, hairspray sticky on the mirrors – unspeakable filth elsewhere. Some days you could plant potatoes in the shower trays.

Rosa had no illusions about these people who had money enough to holiday all the year round, they were no better than her own family; in some respects, they were much worse. She would have been ashamed to think young Javi would make the campsite shower-block such a mess; she and Javi had taught their children better behaviour. Today she did not allow the topic to trouble her; none of it was her concern, she was just glad of the wage packet.

She refilled her bucket with fresh water from the outside tap near the laundry sinks and flushed away the residual scum on the steps. She turned to put all her cleaning kit back in the cupboard and check the padlock on the boiler room door – it had been found open this morning. There was always something inexplicable happening these days and whatever it was she and Juan invariably carried the can.

"Mind out!" the child on the skateboard skidded behind her and jumped off the clean top step.

The black rubber streak that was left behind only hastened Rosa's own path to clock off.

She nudged the bin aside to release the door, allowing it to swing shut across the almost-dry floor; pocketing the keys she set off up the path to the office.

Tomorrow was another day.

The rat was busy investigating the sandaled foot again. A rainbow of thin straps already lay limp and floppy alongside the arched instep: initial nibbling had tasted of nothing, every colour the same chewy nothing – such a let-down for one of refined taste.

The rat was an optimist to the end of his tail but time and again he had to admit that his mother was right. She had taught him and his brothers to eat what they could when they could; you never knew when it would disappear. He had always been a bit of an artist, tempted by bright colours; his siblings called him 'Rolla, he didn't know why and neither did they.

Great Uncle Dali said it had something to do with their city cousins but that it was so far back he doubted it worth trying to get to Valencia to ask, they'd probably forgotten too. Actually, 'Rolla could have found out much closer to home: his namesake had summered in Xabia, which was quite close to Benidorm, as rat-runs run.

The foot was not twitching so often now, 'Rolla knew he ought to call the family before it stopped completely; nothing pleased his lot so much as a really fresh bit of flesh, blood to the tooth before the flies arrived.

He would be the hero of the week.

They'd not be so quick to mock his future forays around the boiler-room.

After the men came to install blue panels on the roof, the boilers hadn't fired so often and Juan stopped having his break here in the mornings, he went to the bar with everyone else. The pickings became very poor and The Ratuses moved across to Reception where the man was a great devourer of *bocadillos,* lots of lovely crumbs. They slept all day and scavenged all night, 'Rolla's lot were very adaptable and didn't waste energy on lost causes.

There was barely even a shred of tobacco left back here, if 'Rolla hadn't been so keen on the broad, juicy strands he'd have abandoned the place too.

For once his mother had been wrong, "Tobacco will be the death of you, my lad. You'll be found like your father one of these days, dead in the gutter and no girl's going to let you near her with brown teeth like that." On and on she went.

Well, he wasn't bothered about girls.

Waste of time all that preening and whisking when you could get that lovely, warm feeling with a couple of strands of golden delight. He'd been quite blissful with just one strand lately; he knew how to conserve his resources.

The only light came in through the crack in the wall above the door. It travelled slowly and steadily across the floor, a shaft of sunshine, it found the head where it lay beside the fat pipe from the almost redundant boiler.

The right eye tried to blink the bright pain away, the head gave up any attempt to turn. Choking with panic the lungs constricted painfully before giving one frantic gasp to drag in air. The mind slipped in and out of consciousness as it had since its owner was felled with a neck-breaking blow ten and a half hours ago.

Some light, steady footsteps earlier had brought hope of rescue but the sun had not been so advanced then and the flood of light from the fully opened door did not reach to illuminate the area at the back. Metallic clangs and gushing water drowned any unexpected noises.

Unable to do more than whimper, the body stayed undetected; its whole was rapidly losing ability to be the sum of its parts, vital organs continued their fight to survive, identity an irrelevance – for now.

The afternoon wore on. The family from Madrid came back from their day at Aqualandia. Sleepy children, hauled into the harsh sunshine, bounced into life, grabbing scooters and kiddiecars to escape their parents. The fathers sloped off to the bar; the mothers turned on the tellies and set about unpacking wet swimwear, reviewing the outing with each other across the three adjacent pitches where they had made their camp. In the hot, dry afternoon, noise reigned.

A cubicle door banged itself into the semi-consciousness of the dying brain on the other side of the wall. An eye flickered. A knee kicked to jerk a foot away from the pulsing, furry brown, and steadily bloating, cream bellies. The brain had three thoughts in less than a spike, *now ...or ...never.*

Great Uncle Dali whiskered himself to safety before the heel caught the less canny youngsters.

Only he and 'Rolla were untouched by the jet of scalding steam set loose as the foot made contact for a second or so with the tap on the safety valve.

The rolling mass of Family Ratus separated into a squeaking scurry as they abandoned the feast.

Flushing cisterns near-by reduced to a companionable gurgle. Great Uncle Dali nosed himself out from behind the safety of an empty gas canister and looked with considerable interest at the display on the floor.

As he looked, the leg edged toward the open space, it drew wetly through the dark patch left by the steam.

The remains of the foot left the scraps of sandal behind. Dali decided that the bent knee nearest to the steam tap was the point that generated the energy to move the dead leg. As the old rat thought this, 'Rolla scampered up the fat pipe to get a better view. The noise from the head was truly awful now.

Neither rat could believe that the body carried on, it was obvious that each time the bent knee flexed, to move the body another few inches into the light, the effort brought yowling pain.

Humans were indeed weird.

"No damn hot water again! Doesn't matter what time you go these days, it's always the same – useless."

"Expect they've run out of gas."

"Thought it was all solar now, the sun's still shining."

"Well I never! You noticed."

"What does that mean?"

"Nothing. I'm just saying."

"Yes, and I'm just grumpy. Worried actually. Where on earth do you think Jilly is? She can't still be on the beach – since last night."

"She's not a child, Pete, we can't keep her with us all the time. Have to let her go."

No she wasn't. He thought wryly of the little girl they had first brought on holiday to Spain nine years before. Then it had been to encourage Jilly to do well with her Spanish, he could not afford to have a daughter on the list of language referrals, an embarrassment for a modern linguist. "Well this is the last time she's bumming a holiday off me, I'm not paying for her if she's never here. She can go on her own holiday next year – and pay for it, student or no student."

"Why not go and ask about the water, it's really not on – in this heat."

The crowd round the window at Reception was deep and agitated. Pete could only see their backs but he could tell everyone was spitting their sweaty frustration at the unfortunate man behind the glass. A range of languages joined in angry concert.

Pete edged round the back, he would slip into the kiosk and chat to Paco; he was not one for mob rule and over the years had always got on well with the campsite owner.

The shutter dropped with a rattling bang. Silence fell. Before anyone had time to recover, the door opened and Paco's beefy bulk swung through the side door, one hand hoisting his bunch of keys from where it had dangled on the chain at his belt.

"Like a bloody gaoler!" remarked some dry wit, breaking the tension for those who understood English.

Everyone fell in behind Paco now. They were not going to be left out. A kid dragged a scooter to tag along with the crowd. A lad with a skateboard grabbed his arm, "What's going on?"

"I dunno."

Pete tapped at Paco's shoulder, "Can't you fix the water or something? This lot are ready to riot, my friend."

"¿Has visto a Juan? Juan – have you seen Juan?"

"No. Why ask me?"

Paco shrugged. "Su hija."

Pete did not understand, *su hija ...your daughter?*

His daughter and Juan! Just wait till he saw her, the madam. That settled it: this was definitely the last time she was coming away with them.

This was no holiday. He hung on Paco's shoulder unwilling to break connection.

They had reached the bottom of the steps now.

The crowd halted.

They looked up, an audience at an unfolding drama. Observers only, of events they had started with a mundane grumble about cold shower water.

A silence of anticipation held all.

The keys jangled a warning as Paco selected the right one, it scraped in the metal of the keyhole; a flurry of activity stirred the air in the dark beyond.

Jean M. Watson

As Green As Grass

"Effin' Monday again," grumbled Bert, as he slung his lunchbox into his worktable drawer. "She's done flippin' sausage sandwiches for lunch, and I 'ate effin' cold sausages, the car humped and farted all the way to work and wot's more we got an effin' new lad startin' today. I 'ates new boys startin'. Useless the lot of ém.

He glared round at the rest of his gang, daring any one of them to say anything cheerful.

Nobody spoke.

Bert in this mood was unbearable.

He would probably be OK by tea break, but in the meantime each of the four of them got on with getting their section of the paint factory into running order after the weekend close-down.

"What we makin' this week Bert?" asked Pete eventually.

"How should I know?" snapped Bert. Pete did not point out the obvious that Bert was team-leader and was paid a bit more than the rest of them to know.

After a grumpy pause Bert picked up his clipboard of order sheets. "Looks like we're on mint-green and grass-green this week. Be a change from the last three weeks. – 'effin' brown and cream – and that order from the Navy before that. All that grey nearly drove me up the wall. Right, Pete, you get that list of tints we need for grass-green. Fred… Oi, Fred, are you listenin'? You open up vats one and two and we'll make a start. You got that list yet, Pete? Ta. Jim, Roger, you go with Pete to Stores and get what's on this list. Take that big trolley with you, then you can bring it back in one go. Save you skivin' off for half the mornin' and cuttin' short the bonus again this week. My missus, she wants a new carpet, and soon."

Pete, Jim and Roger went off, pushing the trolley in front of them, leaving Fred preparing the vats to take that day's quota of raw materials. Bert glared at the calendar on the wall. She'd got no right lookin' like that on a Monday mornin'. His malevolent glaring at the wall was interrupted by the arrival of Sally Smith from Personnel, trailed by a thin lad who looked scared and extremely pale.

"Hello, Bert," said Sally, not at all worried by Bert's scowl. Just like her Dad, she thought, but had the sense not to say so. Instead she looked flirtatiously through her eyelashes at him. "This is Tommy, your new lad. This is his first-ever day at work, so be kind to him. Tommy, this is Bert. He is in charge in this department so do as he says and you'll soon learn your job. Bye, Tommy. Bye, Bert." Sally went, leaving Bert looking at Tommy, and Tommy looking at Bert. What each thought of the other at that moment was plain on their faces. Neither seemed very impressed with the other.

"Brought your lunch then?" growled Bert.

"No, weren't nuffin' to bring," mumbled Tommy miserably.

"Well, you won't last all day, will ya?" groused Bert, "make sure there's summat tomorrow."

"…'s alright, ain't never 'ad no lunch before," muttered Tommy.

"Well, when you do, put it in that drawer there along with the others."

Pete, Jim and Roger arrived back at that moment with the trolley stacked with cartons of paint powder. Whoever had been in Stores had cheered them up, or perhaps it was just being away from Bert for a few minutes.

"Who's this then?" asked Roger. "You ain't Rhoda Begg's boy, are you?"

"Yea, she's me mam," said Tommy, trying to stand taller, a shade of defiance in his manner.

"Come on, come on," bullied Bert, "you're losin' me my bonus standin' around like this. Let's get going."

"Oh, drat it," said Jim, who was always politer than the others, "we've forgotten the stand. I'll have to go back and get it."

"No, you won't," said Bert, "We'll send Tommy. That's what he's here for. It'll help him learn the job. Now, Tommy listen carefully. Stores is across the yard. Go in and ask for Fred Watkins. He's the foreman. Say the paint mixin' department sent you for a long stand. Got it?"

"Yes Bert," replied Tommy, "…Bert sent me for a long stand."

"Well done," confirmed Bert, "off you go."

Bert and his team at last began the week's work, filling the vats with paint-powder and adding water to mix. The motors hummed and the mixers chortled and thumped. The morning's work was well under way before Tommy returned.

"Hello, lad, where've you been all this time?" asked Bert, laughing as if he had been in stores to see Tommy's long stand.

"Very funny," scowled Tommy. "What d'yer want next? Some elbow grease?"

"Maybe yer not as green as grass, then." Bert looked at Tommy and he very nearly smiled. The team continued mixing paint according to the schedule for the shade known as 'grass green'.

Tommy, not having been given a task to do, watched for a while and then wandered around the shed, exploring. Nobody seemed to remember he was there.

It was nearly lunchtime before the first batch of paint was ready to be tipped from the vats into the channel that led to the canning department.

Bert steered the lip of the vat over the channel and stood ready to guide the paint into the channel.

Jim pulled the lever, which tipped the vat. Slowly the vat started to tip, then, with a sudden rush, the vat slipped sideways out of its holding-bracket.

Paint flooded everywhere, over the machinery, over the floor, over the team standing in front of the machine, but most especially over Bert, who stood gasping for air and stamping with rage.

The only person who was not covered in grass green paint was young Tommy, who sidled out from behind the machine almost choking with laughter.

"Green as grass, am I? Oh, I don't think I'm as green as some people around here."

Colin Hall

Winding Down

Holding hands, they both looked into the fridge.
Most of the shelves were empty.
The freezer compartment contained a half bag of frozen peas, nothing else.
There wasn't much more in the kitchen cupboards.
A jar of home-made jam, that's all.
They were getting used to not eating much.
Not since the visit to the doctor last week.
He said that he was going to be blunt with them.
"I am sorry, but..."
They didn't listen to the rest.
After the tensions and turmoil of the last fifty years together, winding down was so restful.

Avner Kornblum

Midnight Music

Oh! What a night this had turned out to be, Malcolm reflected as he trudged up the hill to his home in the pitch-dark of the unlit street. Fancy beginning the New Year with a blow-out, not an alcoholic orgy as one might expect on Nochevieja but a tyre on his car. He prepared himself for the cascade of laughter tinged with criticism from his wife and family, all of whom had elected to watch the New Year in – or, rather, the fireworks heralding the New Year – from the sun-roof of their villa.

He would be subjected to their cackling derision while his ears were still ringing with the noise of the fire-works explosions in Moraira and it was not even midnight yet.

Well, he would shrug off their comments and join them as they watched the many splendid fireworks from Calpe, Benissa, Benimarco, Moraira, Teulada and even Altea: not to mention the hubbub from the private parties all around them and the blaring nightclubs that would blast out their so-called music, which he would preferably term 'racket', until well after dawn.

Midnight music: How had that unusual expression come into his head just when he was thinking of all the unpleasant noises that humans made to celebrate the passing of a man-made period, completely oblivious of the damage done and anxiety stirred up in their so-called best friends. Of course, it was nearly midnight and, of course, the groups that made this amplified noise were termed 'music groups'. Oh yes, Malcolm was bitter.

Midnight music: As the words emerged from the clatter and clutter in his mind he grew calmer. *"The swishing of the leaves in the coconut trees"* – the gentle melody of that song from his youth was interrupted by a more conscious thought. Were those the words of the song? Wait, didn´t it go *"The whistling of the breeze in the cottonwood trees"*?

Coconut?

Cottonwood?

Oh, what the heck, he couldn't remember another line from the song, anyway. No, not a single line, and he wasn't sure if either of the two now surging through his brain was correct. And what did these have to do with midnight, anyway? The swishing or the whistling could take place at any time of day or night.

Midnight music: "Ha!" he blurted out aloud as he suddenly thought of the grunts and snorts of a loving couple – or a couple making love – giving way to soft words and contented snoring. Now that's more like midnight music.

Ah, yes, the final dance before the band packed up.

A gentle waltz, designed to waft the dancers off the floor and into their beds.

Ah, yes – '*midnight music*' thought Thomas as he sat quietly at his table, fingering his glass, his eyes shifting from the band to the beautiful young woman preparing to leave the hall.

As soon as she was ready he leapt to his feet. "I'm glad we didn't come by car," he said as he passed his arm through hers. "You're not too tired to walk, are you?"

"No, not at all," she replied lightly. "I'm used to it, and anyway, the hotel is close to this building."

They walked along the beach with the waves lapping quietly at their feet, their voices dropping into whispers though no-one was listening.

It seemed they were alone in the world at this time, this midnight hour, apart from the far-off sound of a dog barking.

What was he barking at, they wondered, as they wrapped their arms around each other and gazed into each other's eyes, but feeling rather than seeing each other's presence in the pitch-black darkness.

After a few minutes they disengaged themselves and continued walking along the beach towards her hotel, his arm on her shoulder, hers around his waist.

His mind drifted back to the midnight music of the dance band; it was a waltz, he recalled. Such a pleasant, dreamy way to end the night's entertainment – public entertainment, that is, unlike this…

Then he pulled himself up, this togetherness was private but it wasn't entertainment. Not bidding farewell to someone you have fallen in love with, not releasing her to go back to her husband, not boarding a 'plane in a few hours' time and returning to one's wife and children. Did the band-leader know about their budding but illicit romance, he wondered.

Why else did he choose to sing "Goodnight Irene, goodnight Irene, I'll see you in my dreams"?

Her left hand dropped silently down from his waist and stroked his trousers.

He stiffened – his entire body stiffened.

No, he would not spoil this quiet midnight moment of a real soulmate relationship with anything as grossly demeaning as sex.

He stretched his own hand across his body and grasped hers lovingly but firmly.

This drew them closer together and his right arm slipped off her shoulder and around beneath her right arm.

Gosh, how slim she is, he thought as his fingers rested on her breast, sending him again into a nervous quiver.

She smiled into the night. "You could come up to my hotel room if you're worried about the sand," she whispered. He hastily withdrew both his hands and clasped them behind his back.

"It's not the sand on the beach," he replied. "It's more like the sands of time. Let's rather meet again, sometime, when we've known each other for more than just three hours at the end of the Psychiatrists' Association meeting on *How to Keep Relationships Together*".

At this moment Malcolm reached the gate of his house.

The romance he had invented of Thomas and the beautiful young psychiatrist slipped out of his mind to be forgotten forever.

His wife and three daughters came rushing to the gate.

"Quickly, quickly!" the girls shouted, not even noticing that his car was absent. "You're just in time to swallow the grapes as the church-bells begin to chime."

"What have you been doing?" asked his wife.

"Midnight musing," he shrugged.

Vivien Johnson

The Goatherd

*The Sirocco charges down the valley –
a demented dragon's breath,
dried earth scorched yet again;
goats and sheep munch desiccated rosemary and thyme.*

*Pedro huddles in the cave; battered hat pulled down,
threadbare clothes give little comfort.
He shares his home with geckos and snakes.
His dog will warn him if foxes attack his stock.*

Perhaps Consuelo will come with food?

*The wind scrapes the mountains,
Sahara sand covers glacial rocks –
forked lightning rips the sky
lighting up Sierra needle-crags.*

*The rain comes shyly – apologetic –
disturbing the sun-baked world.
Then torrents lash down – rage –
transparent whips slash from the sky.
Thunder crashes like the sound of battle.*

*Pedro knew the storm would come.
He had felt the changes –
had watched clouds like quilts
rolling over the mountains' lips.*

*Afterwards new shoots force their way to the light;
crystal waters bubble from inhospitable rock.
A mountain pine clings to a soilless ridge –
sheep no longer pant in the midday sun.
Goat's bells jingle-jangle on still air.*

Agnes Hall

Violetta

I think I must have been born with a paint-brush in my hand …not the sort you paint fences with but those that were used to paint pictures. My talent is inherited from my parents, both relatively successful artists.

In our house, you had to make sure that you didn't sit on half-used tubes of paint, the caps carelessly left off and cups had to be carefully examined before use, to check that they had not been used to clean out brushes.

People came and went and I never knew who would be at the table for breakfast, or which rooms not to walk into in the morning in case I disturbed someone who had just 'dropped in' and had forgotten to 'drop out'. Although I was an only child, I never felt the lack of company in our big, rambling house with its purple front door.

I grew up daubing paint on off-cuts of canvas in my parents' studio to the ever-present sound of music, which I could never do without. It was always assumed that I would attend Art College but I loved music so much, as I grew older, that my cello, which I had begun to play at a very young age, became more important to me than my painting.

My father was a big bear of a man with clear, blue eyes and a big, bushy beard.

My mother was the sort that men lost their hearts to. She had long, dark hair and olive skin, was slightly built and very exotic looking. Everyone was 'darling' to her, even if she had just met them and, in return, she was everyone's darling. I took after my father rather than my mother.

My hair was fair, as my father's hair had been before it turned grey and my eyes were blue, like his. I had been born late-on in my parent's marriage and felt treasured, and very lucky to have such interesting, loving parents.

On the day of my sixteenth birthday I woke up in more ways than one. My parents arrived in my bedroom, noisily, as the clock struck midnight, singing 'happy birthday to you'. Nothing was conventional in our house. They had a tray containing 'bucks fizz', smoked salmon sandwiches and a small oblong brown-paper-wrapped package.

My mother passed me a bubbling glass and sat down on the bed. She looked strangely nervous. "Á very happy birthday darling." Glasses were raised and clinked against mine as they drank a toast.

My father eventually picked up the package from the tray and held it out. "The rest of your presents are downstairs. You may want to leave opening them 'til the morning," he said, "but this is something special. We'll leave you to open it on your own." He took my mother's arm and led her out of the room.

They both glanced back at me as they reached the door and smiled.

"See you later, darling." My mother said.

I turned the package over in my hands and examined the label on the front. It was addressed to me and had the name of a firm of solicitors, `Simon Weatherall and Partners` and an address in London, stamped above my name. I tore at the sticky tape and pulled the brown paper apart. Inside was a painted, wooden box. There was a letter taped to the top of the box with the same solicitor's name on it. I read the letter, slowly absorbing what it said, not that there was a great deal to absorb:

'Dear Violetta Mason,

We have been instructed to deliver this package to you on the day of your sixteenth birthday. For further information, please contact me at the above address.

Yours sincerely, Simon Weatherall'

I opened the box and found that it contained a letter written in ink, on now faded paper and also a faded theatre programme for an opera, one that was very familiar to me ...Verdi`s 'La Traviata`. The name of the soprano singing the lead part was Laura Kosminsky.

I began to read:

'Darling girl,

You will no doubt be surprised to receive this letter. You will also, no doubt, be wondering who I am and why I am writing to you. It is a long story and I will start at the beginning but will try to keep it brief.

My name is Laura Kosminsky. I was born in Russia of simple, hard-working parents, long after my parents had given up all hope of ever having children, so I was greatly treasured and they were determined to give me all the opportunities in life, which they had never had themselves.

They discovered that I was gifted, that I could sing, and spent all of their savings on ensuring that my talent was developed. When I secured a place at The National Opera Company of Russia, all their dreams - and mine, came true.

It was a very taxing but exciting life: the applause, the flowers, the admirers and the travel. I saw my parents as often as I could and they always welcomed me with open arms. However, everything faded into insignificance when I met the man who changed my life.'

Violetta paused at this point and wondered what on earth all this had to do with her. She shook her head and continued reading.

'I met him in London, when I was performing my favourite role of Violetta in Verdi's opera, La Traviata. The manager of the theatre threw a party after the performance on the opening night and it was at this party that I met this special man. We were drawn to each other from the first time we met. He asked me out to dinner and that was the beginning of our relationship, a relationship that lasted for many years.

Because of our respective careers, we spent regular periods travelling, apart from each other but, despite this, our relationship grew stronger and stronger. Our meetings had to be discreet because he was an important figure in politics and he was also married with children. He had always said that he loved his wife and would never leave her and I accepted that, because the times we spent together were so precious.

Then I became pregnant! I realised that if our relationship and my pregnancy became public knowledge, his career and his marriage would be over. I could not do that to him so I then had to do one of the hardest things that I have ever had to do. I said goodbye to him. I took time off from performing as soon as I could, feigning illness and hid myself away until after your birth, my darling daughter...'

Violetta paused, her heart racing. What on earth was this...? She began reading again.

'...and then I took another most difficult decision... I said goodbye to you.
It would have been all too easy for whispers to start, connecting me with your father and it would have destroyed him. It broke my heart to leave you but my mother and father, your grandparents, found the people you know as parents, Jonathon and Tilda who were childless and took you into their hearts and home. Over the years they have kept me informed of your progress and regularly sent photographs as you have grown into the lovely girl that you are. They also insisted that you kept the name that I had given you, Violetta, the name of the character I was portraying when I met your father.

I know that this letter will be a shock for you but please do not think too badly of me. I truly loved your father and he loved me and if it had been possible to do things differently, I would have done. If you can bring yourself to contact me, please get in touch with Simon Weatherall, who has been the intermediary between myself and Jonathon and Tilda for all these years. If you have no wish to have further contact, although I hope that will not happen, I will understand.

Happy birthday, my darling daughter,
    Your loving mother,
        Laura.'

Violetta held the letter in her hand, hardly able to believe what she had just read. She was stunned. Jonathon and Tilda not her real mother and father! She realised that she was shaking. She also realised that she was angry. Why had they never told her this?

There was something else in the box besides her mother's theatre programme, which she had not noticed earlier. It was a small object wrapped in tissue paper. She carefully unfolded the paper and saw a gold locket on a chain. When she opened the locket she saw a photograph of a man and a woman... *My mother and father*, she whispered.

There were big decisions ahead of her. What was she going to do?

Gail Tucker

Good Neighbours

The wind-owl was suspended from a branch of the tree that marked the ancient boundary between the properties. It was a beautifully crafted piece of ironwork with two big amber beads set into the head. It had been the thing that stayed with Alice long after she and John had viewed the house.

The woman, of course, was potty but the man was nice; he had a jolly, round face to match his rounded girth – and kind, pleading eyes. He seemed almost always to be asking forgiveness for something; perhaps it was only understanding he wanted, for his wife not for himself. When Alice first met her she was dead-heading the roses and, as a complementary activity, directing where he should fix new tacks to pin the extending trellis higher up the wall.

"Hope you're not going to break the siesta silence like the last people did," it was an abrupt introduction but left no room for doubt. That was when she realised that it was probably best to give-as-good-as-she-got, from the start. Always immaculately articulated, their exchanges never slid below the Plimsoll line. No murky depths with hidden threats. Each recognised in the other a woman of strength and character.

"You must come in and have a drink when you're a bit straighter," one hand clawed to grip faded petals, a glove and secateurs; the other extended across the boundary wall. It was a cool hand, as cool as might be expected, and dry.

Alice took it and smiled, "Thanks, we'd like that."

"I'll ring you. Not changed the number have you? No. Nobody in their right mind 'd do that ...take for ever to get reconnected." The hand was withdrawn and the head gesture dismissed Alice with practised ease.

"Hello."

The figure that had been clinging to the ladder stepped forward to replace his leading lady. Alice put her hand across again and almost made contact before the freckle-backed one was withdrawn. "Oh dear! What a filthy paw I've got, sorry. Good to meet you. We wondered what you'd be like, we saw the van in the lane yesterday."

"Hope it didn't block you in," said Alice lamely, puzzled that she should be apologizing. She wondered what John would make of it.

"Expect you've a lot to be getting on with," even with her back turned, the woman's tone of dismissal was unmistakable. Each, on their own side of the fence, withdrew with a half-wave. That was when Alice first saw the fleeting plea cross the nut-brown eyes.

"Meeting the neighbours?"

"Yes. Next-door, that way. Seem all right. At least they speak properly." Alice said no more. Let him find out for himself.

The phone rang three days later with the invitation for a drink before lunch, "Half-past-one all right? We'll be in the bar, just come in."

By the time their eyes had adjusted to the gloom of the sunless space that would have been called *lower ground floor* by an estate agent in Hampstead, two large drinks stood on the counter. Alice perched on a rickety bamboo stool and John stood to juggle a peanut. Clearly, the bar was not only a relic from life in 1960s England, it was also the anteroom, a place to entertain an unknown quantity, someone who might not be quite the ticket.

The interrogation was by turns direct and oblique.

By the time they had been dismissed again, this time with, "We mustn't keep you," Alice felt she'd undergone an interview to gain admittance to an important club. If there were a next-time, she was keen to see whether they'd get up onto the terrace with the roses.

She knew she'd have to pass the second part first – the return invitation. She also knew that neighbours were not the same as friends but that bad neighbours easily became enemies.

She was willing to play the game Good Neighbours.

It was always like that although over the years the invitations, extended from both sides of the boundary, went beyond tepid – and were infrequent enough to be enjoyable.

"We have very good neighbours," is what each couple might be heard to say to their respective family and friends.

There was little doubt who thought they controlled the situation but after that first sally over the sacrosanct siesta, direct challenges were never again issued.

"If you've no objection, I've got some spare bricks you could use to put up a bit of a wall to hide your vehicle. Rita doesn't like to see it when we come home," the pleading eyes, the half-jolly delivery – head determinedly set to pretend ignorance of the puppeteer on the balcony above.

"Why not just do it?" said Alice to John, later. "Keep the peace."

"That's what he does all the time, why give in so."

"Life's too short…" she remembered a morning she roamed their property prospecting a good site for a washing line; the feeling of being observed that made her look up. It was the wind-owl that moved.

Across the open terrace there he stood quite still, those nut-brown eyes looking down at her, "Nice morning for it!"

"Yes, lovely. I'm wondering where'd be best for the whirligig. Think the sun stays round here most of the year."

"Best not just there," desperate, unbidden advice, "Rita wouldn't like it."

Only later, when she relived the moment, did Alice see how ridiculous it was. By then the laundry was whirling away out of sight, catching on the overhanging fig tree – an intermittent irritation to Alice, the ever-lurking possibility that what she and John did would disturb the status quo next door.

It all came to an end as it had to, of course. The unexpected early morning telephone rang the gasping imperative. John and Alice found her wringing her hands, tossing her head like a fractious thoroughbred. Inside, they found the nut-brown eyes pleading and pleading, in glassy rictus.

Without an ambassador, she shrank into needy-old-lady pose, which worked for a while before everyone tired of it. Having no way back and helplessness not being her true nature, some saw that she had driven herself crazy.

"I'd rather you didn't put laundry out on a Sunday," was her final attempt to keep control. After that, when the cat was found splat in the lane, she howled night and day until her children, unable to deal with the phone calls, took her away.

On the last day, in charge one last time she called Alice, "The people who've bought my house, they are just like us, dear, I know you'll like them."

"How lovely," said Alice as she was expected to.

"I knew you'd be pleased."

The new people brought a camper-van to block the lane and a pair of motorbikes to fill the drive. Soon, the young woman with tattooed shoulders joined the man with the shaved head as he worked to remove the rose trellis from the side wall. Alice looked at the wind-owl and saw in its amber eyes that Rita that had indeed been in control all along.

Vivien Johnson

Pride

It had been months since robins had visited her garden. Silvia loved to see the feisty little birds squabbling over scraps of food. However, now that he had come, all the birds had flown away.

Mr Brown, the new warden, rang her bell and entered her apartment without waiting to be given permission. Sylvia sat on the edge of her chair, straight-backed on the edge of her chair, gripping the arms with whitened knuckles.

"I'm very sorry to disturb you," he said, "but I have to test your alarms."

"Well if you must," she replied. She hadn't liked this man since she had seen him in the corridor, in deep conversation with her arch-enemy Joan Stubbs. Silvia had been furious when she'd bumped into Joan one day at the home and had cut her. How dare that woman move into her sheltered home! Would she never get rid of this snake in the grass?

"Well if you must," she replied. She hadn't liked this man since she had seen him in the corridor, in deep conversation with her arch-enemy Joan Stubbs. Silvia had been furious when she'd bumped into Joan one day at the home and had cut her. How dare that woman move into her sheltered home! Would she never get rid of this snake in the grass?

Joan had been her best friend at school and university until, one vacation, she had inveigled Sylvia's boyfriend away on a trip to London. On their return from what had apparently been a very unsatisfactory outing, Sylvia told him that she wouldn't take back damaged goods and he and Joan were welcome to each other.

"Could you move a little please Sylvia? So that I can reach the bell-pull?" She scowled as he used her Christian name. His overweight arm reached towards the wall exposing a tattoo covering his forearm: two hooded cobras disappearing under his rolled up shirtsleeve. He leaned over her; she screwed up her nose, smelling his sweaty shirt and the peppermint on his breath.

"Would you like a drink Mr Brown? I've got vodka in the cupboard, and no one will know; it won't smell on your breath."

"No thanks Sylvia, no drinking allowed on duty you know."

In spite of her failing sight, he was close enough for her to see the stiff, grey hairs sprouting from his left ear. Then as he leaned closer she noticed the gilt hoop-earring. Couldn't be real gold she thought; he wouldn't be able to afford it on his wages. Her fingers twitched, she had to clasp her hands together to stop herself catching it with her crochet hook. He pressed his meter and the warning rang. He stood up using the back of her chair for support.

"Now Sylvia, can I test your personal alarm? Just slip it off for a moment." He smiled, his face gathered into deep rolls of flesh.

"It's in the bedroom; it makes my neck itch in the heat."

"You are a bad girl then aren't you, what would happen if you had an accident?" He disappeared down the hall. His familiar, patronising tone would go down in her little red book, together with her other grievances. What a pity he hadn't taken the bait about the vodka, then, she really would have reason to complain to the bosses of The Quiet Pastures Home. "That's quite O.K. just the fire alarm now and I'll be out of your hair."

She held her handkerchief to her mouth. The thought of him touching her hair made her gag. The scream of the fire alarm filled her head and she kicked herself for not having turned off her hearing-aid before the test began.

"That's it for now, see you later." The cold draft from the corridor swept around her ankles as he opened her front door.

"Not if I see you first," she said under her breath, pulling a tartan rug around her.

Gail Tucker

Detachment

In about ten minutes, known life would end. This time Tom was ready for it: the final trip in the family car, which had carried them all in their daily round for as long as he could remember.

The battered interior was a swamp of familiar odours. Even now Tom could detect traces of Thomas's long-forsaken cigarette habit, smoke that clung to the coarse fabric of the front seats. A decade or more ago that tang, then fresher, had told him who was in the driving seat when he'd been picked up after college; Tom knew before anyone spoke, sometimes even before he got inside the car. If he were in the right place at the kerbside as the car drew up, he could tell by the slight squeal of the brakes when Thomas had been at the wheel. His father was always in a hurry, Tom instinctively braced himself whenever he sensed the shift into top gear.

Today he had pushed a hand down between the seat cushions and felt for one more time the gritty dust climb beneath his finger nails – a strangely comforting horror. He recalled a time when Dick had grabbed that hand and thrust it into exactly that place where the older boy had held it in a fierce grip. It had often been like that. His brother never attacked him elsewhere. He waited until they were trapped together on the back seat before he took revenge for some notional wrongdoing. Tom understood his own lack of sight was in reality the first and foremost offence. A crime of Nature for which there was no atonement as far as Dick was concerned. He also understood why the older boy chose to launch his assaults here; confined, they were on equal terms, more or less.

Now the old car lurched to a halt and the heel of Tom's hand ground painfully through the grit until the sensitive pads of his middle and index fingers came to rest on cold metal. The car set off apace and the metal slid away, but not before a flash of memory opened a chink in Tom's brain, a kind of internal lightning.

He eased the seatbelt a fraction to shift forward as imperceptibly as possible. He always expected to hear the voice of authority tell him to sit still. Over-protective parental authority, not a malicious attempt to thwart his will – infuriating, nevertheless. Anyone would think he was brain damaged, incapable of assessing risk. There was no utterance from the front seat: Tom moved his hand farther around in the gritty space. He was getting accustomed to it now and rapidly discarded twisted sweet wrappers, a plastic biro top, a rusty hairgrip and a couple of rock-hard, well-textured lumps of bubble gum.

He had almost given up, when he touched the metal again. This time he nursed it into his clutched fingers and made sure that the car was moving smoothly on the straight and flat before he withdrew his hand and slipped the embossed button into his pocket. Something he had not done fifteen years ago when he last had it in his possession.

The woman in the smart, red blazer had got out of the car, slammed the door and walked away without a backward glance. To anyone watching on that autumn morning, there was no sign of the distress she had left behind her. No sound crept from the car. No rocking motion betrayed the anguish of the passengers: the driver slumped over the wheel silently mouthing her name: one figure on the back seat stared dumbly ahead through the windscreen; the other, thrashed about in a futile attempt to free himself from the restraint of the seat belt.

Harriet jumped aboard a passing bus. As she sat down, the woman who had just abandoned her family, noticed that she had lost a button from her jacket. It had been a mistake to reach behind her to stroke the little arm, she remembered the small hand as she twisted out of the front seat.

The bus swerved away from the kerb and a man still making his way along the aisle staggered. *Seat belt* flashed into her mind. She grabbed the metal pole at the end of the seat in front of her, confident that there would always be a hand-hold in her future.

The bus moved more smoothly and she folded back the front of her jacket to check for a spare button. Yes, there it was, safely stitched to the lining. She would have to borrow a needle and thread as soon as she got there. A second thought, more a positive resolve, entered her head. The jacket had a tiny tear where the button had been: she'd not borrow the kit, she'd not repair. Repair was a return, a going back. The future was ahead. She was going forward. She smiled with gritty determination. This was her chance: one shot to be free. The windfall from her mother's lost brother was her ticket to a new life, she could afford to buy a brand new jacket if she wanted. Freedom was hers.

The car driver, left behind, set off with a squeal of brakes followed by the pungent stink of rubber. Little Tom, who had finally managed to unclip the safety belt was thrown across the car, arms flailing as he fought to gain a grip on something, anything. His head thumped the back door post: his world went black.

One more thing altered on that fatal day: Thomas began to use a strange voice whenever he spoke to his younger son. It took Tom years to identify the underlying tone of contrition that infused all their exchanges. No wonder then, that Dick turned resentful. If Tom were his father's favourite, then Tom must pay the price. Dick could not comprehend his father's guilt: he had always been firmly in the jury that condemned their mother, the bolter.

He bolted himself as soon as he could, so he was not around when Thomas finally got rid of the family car. The move was a relief for both Toms. Neither would have to endure the shared journeys again. Public transport would not remind them of *life before.* Neither needed a reminder. Thomas had Tom and now Tom had the button; it would be with him always – carefully passed from pocket to pocket down the years, its tiny clump of red threads hanging from the metal loop.

Vivien Johnson

The Red, White and Blue 2005

A triumph of crowds lining leafy London's Mall.
Five-hundred-thousand British waving to their courageous Queen.
Old men and young, women, children, babes in arms;
Union flags held high above their heads.

Cavalry horses pranced in line, their riders sitting still;
carriages and medals polished, glinting in the summer sun.
Thirty-two degrees, the veterans never faltered –
proudly there – sixty years after they had done brave deeds.
Today their country honoured them, and the now departed.

Spitfire, Hurricane and Lancaster over-flew crowds and palace,
a trail of poppy petals spilled from the bomber's hold –
a peaceful cargo – red snowflakes fluttering to ground;
some gathered up in hats, reborn and given flight.
A commemoration of warriors lost in war, and Britain's victory.

The memory of terrorist bombings on tube and bus
not forgotten – put aside on this special day.
Bands played Land of Hope and Glory;
those who knew the words sang out.
Voices loud – clear – patriotic emotions high.
Old soldiers met wartime friends – wept unashamed.

Her Majesty smiled, waved, picked up a petal from her balcony's edge.
Today Great Britain cocked a snook at terrorists and trouble makers;
showed we still have the grit of former dark days.
Life will continue in our little isle, no matter what.
They will never grind us down.
We shall salute the red, white and blue wherever we may be!

Paul Shearer Walmsley

The Knee Job

John had his operation to exchange the arthritic knee for a new titanium one. "It will take three months for you to fully recover, any problems come back and see me," the consultant told him.

After three months of ice-packs and exercise it was still swollen and red-hot. So off he went back to the consultant. "There's nothing I can do for you here, you will have to go to Valencia, to have a special scan."

On the morning of his x-ray at eight-o-clock, after no food or water, he was given a drink of some horrible tasting liquid, before being taken into a separate room. On the door, as he entered, he noticed the international sign for radiation, the Skull and Crossbones.

Inside, the young radiographer asked him to undress to his underclothes and gave him a hospital gown to wear, the ones that tie at the back and are impossible to fasten, unless your arms are six-feet long. The next thing he knew, he was being tied down on some kind of leather bed where he could not move. *What the hell is going to happen next?* he wondered, as the radiographer vanished into a side room.

On his back, looking up, he saw a camera on a conveyor belt. The belt started to move very slowly over him. George Orwell's '1984' crossed his mind... *Was this some kind of torture chamber?* On the facing wall was a television and as he looked at it, his leg started to appear, built up of horizontal lines; 1984 was suddenly replaced by Doctor Who. This went on for half-an-hour, then stopped at last.

The radiographer reappeared, unfastened him and told him he could get dressed. Now he knew he really must be in a James Bond film because she produced a Geiger-counter and ran it over his entire body. "Just as I thought, you are radioactive, but don't worry it will be out of your body after about four or five hours and will do you no harm. However, you must stay away from children under ten, and pregnant women. Now go and have your breakfast you must be starving."

The hospital cafeteria was almost empty; at least ten tables had no one sitting at them. "You go and sit down, I will get the breakfast," said John's partner, who had accompanied him to the hospital that morning. He sat down at an empty table for six, tucked away in a corner.

He heard someone approach and, thinking it was his partner returning with their breakfast, looked up, to see a very heavily pregnant African lady sitting down at his table and thought, *how on earth am I going to sort this one out?*

Standing up, sighing to himself, John walked away.

She stared after him, but if he told her he was radioactive she would never believe him. He'd bet that, in her mind, he would just be another racist, which, had she known his grandchildren, couldn't be farther from the truth. Never mind you can't win them all.

Gail Tucker

A Son

"Dad, Dad..." the boy's legs carried him across the flagstones to the slowing vehicle. He was bursting with the news, "Our John's dead!"

Frank was never to remember the look on his father's face but he would never forget that the next morning a bald stranger sat at the breakfast table. Oddly familiar eyes held his bewildered gaze and his father's voice had spoken in its characteristic soft even measure. It was only the hairless dome that disconcerted the boy. He was a gawky adolescent, some years later, before he overheard women marvelling at the instant hair loss that had struck a man in shock.

That morning, the morning after his older brother had died on the kitchen table, under the doctor's knife, Frank only knew that he was in the middle of a strange world where his older sister had taken the breakfast porridge out of the range, and a changed man sat where his father should have been. His mother had not come down from the bedroom and it was past the time for school. He and Judith would be late. He wondered if he should venture this but caught Nell's hard stare and decided words from him would not be welcome. He gazed at the brown edged scoop of porridge that sat in his bowl. He smelled the acrid burnt oats, something that usually made him retch: this morning it was a relief, it replaced the horror of the caustic disinfectant that leeched from everything in the house since yesterday. He had dropped to sleep with the evil tang in his nose and woken to it, and John's space in the empty bed along the opposite wall. Other, worse, stenches would stick in his throat in the coming years but that harsh disinfectant was the only one that always made his stomach heave and his heart miss a beat.

His older brother had been his guide and playmate for as long as he could remember. Their scraped knees hung together over the apple tree branch, four feet dangling just out of adult reach. A maddened older sister left to gaze up at escapees from duty was watched with gleeful, mocking gazes. If they were not up the tree, they could be found in forbidden territory beside the canal among the bargees and ragamuffins from King's Row. The irony of the majestic name was, of course, lost on the naturally egalitarian sons of the scrap-metal merchant. They could not know of the danger that lurked in the insanitary conditions survived by their adventurous, forbidden fellows. In any case, what boy would heed womanish warnings of *germs?*

Perhaps if John had lived, his own life would have been different.

Listening to the thrum of the bus wheels and the tuneless whistling of the conductor downstairs, Frank wondered, not for the first time, if that morning had been the moment when guilt cut him from the family circle. He could not know. Sometimes he relived the moment he'd heard his father's car and sped across the yard to be first with the news. Sometimes across a different table, he caught a flash of his father at the breakfast that signalled the shift in all of their lives. Whichever the precise moment, then it was that he became the stranger in the family.

It had seemed that only next day he had been packed off to school.

Adult reason told him that it could not have been so soon, although he had no memory between that breakfast and the day he watched his school trunk loaded onto the guard's van for the first time. The brass-bound, blue leather would make its appearance to signal the beginnings of separations for the next ten years. A separation defined not only by railway miles but by stretches of the sea too.

Frank was not a miserable schoolboy, he enjoyed the company of others and while he was not a great athlete, he was a brave trier, which kept him in the right bunch on cross-country runs. The generous tuck box which he always found at the bottom of the trunk on each return to school had contents carefully arranged to provide variety and comfort across the separating miles. A balsawood box of coconut mushrooms was always there – his mother's calculated way to cherish a child. He had never cared for coconut mushrooms; they were John's absolute favourites.

His parents did not blame him for the loss of their first son but children always see themselves as responsible for disaster, Frank was no exception.

Caught up in school life, he thought little of those at home and rarely glanced at the group photograph on his bedside locker. He wrote the dutiful weekly letter with painful repetitions, *I got good marks for maths prep... Matron says I need a size bigger Sunday shirt and she needs some more name tapes for my House rugger shirt can you put some in my next letter...*

Did his mother ever realise that other, more florid phrases were sometimes – well, – often cribbed? During the holidays, Judith now kept him company. Frank, Judy and John's beloved Major – all three of them took up a kind of unspoken pledge to live life as John might have done if diphtheria had not cut it short. They never went to King's Row. Judy was only a girl but she was game for long hikes. "Buck up, Frank!" she'd say when he flagged on the long haul up Mill Brow. She brewed tea and he scorched his fingers holding bread on spiked twigs in the flames.

Once or twice they stayed out all night up at the top – a single huddle beneath a summer sky, eyes peering at millions of stars. "That one's John," she said suddenly into the silence. "Yes," he said. The dog whimpered in his dog-dream.

The bus ground into a lower gear to negotiate the hill. The relentless whistling was momentarily drowned in a cacophony of metallic crunching as the early morning, almost empty first bus out of the depot made its way through the deserted streets. He thought of the last time he had been on this route, travelling in the opposite direction, clutching the meagre contents of Judy's purse. Well, he'd paid that back years ago – no debts there.

What would the rest of them look like?

He guessed that Nell would still resemble their mother and little Alice might also have her square chin but he could barely recall this late addition to the fold, let alone conjure the mature woman she must have become in the intervening years.

He gazed across the estuary as the mist lifted. It occurred to him that his decision to end his journey this way was a mistake: perverse to have left his car at the hotel. He could even have taken a taxi but last night he felt the strong pull to retrace steps. He had the receptionist check the bus timetable; had asked room service for an early breakfast; and had set his own alarm unnecessarily early – primordial need for discomfort essential to a pilgrimage, for that was how he saw this visit.

Perhaps the whole enterprise was a mistake. He had agreed on impulse to go to the funeral. Judy's phone call had not been to request that he attend, it was more a statement of anticipated fact: he would join them all to spend the night in the family home and the cortège would set out at ten o'clock.

He had not actually agreed to spend the night there – unthinkable. He could stomach this arrival at their breakfast time, it satisfied various aspects of the situation, not the least of which was seeing his loyal sister. It was several years since he had met Judith in Spain, the long arm of coincidence putting them both in an airport baggage hall at the same time. At the end of her holiday he had promised to keep in touch, had given her one of his phone numbers. He almost always returned her call when he finally got news of it. He had called her at Christmas that year they had met in Spain; the next year he was out of everyone's reach and when he did return to England, he did not call her. After that his resolve was lost.

The trace of a frown crossed the face reflected in the window as he thought of bossy Nell when he had not appeared last night. With typical sleight of hand, he had not given any definite undertaking one way or the other but in all honesty he knew that Judy would have believed he'd join them. Now he regretted the hurt he must have caused her as the empty evening had worn on. The worst thing about his habit of disappointing the women in his life was that he knew, as he committed his sins of omission, that they were innocent victims of his emotional cramp. Today he would be in time for the safe formalities. This way there would be little time for inquisition or to stray into dangerous emotional territory. He had at least had that in common with his mother: the facility to close his heart. He saw her now, methodically counting name-taped socks and making a perfunctory wave of farewell each time he went back to school. Today he could do the same for her, name-taped socks being the elaborate gravestone he had already commissioned from the monumental mason. A son's duty fulfilled.

"You couldn't keep away then." The voice landed, sharp between his shoulder blades, and was accompanied by the unmistakable rhythmic tapping of metal on metal. Frank held both his breath and position with practiced ease: the stag who caught the crack of a twig when the unseen stalker moved to get a better aim. Unlike the stag, he had nowhere to flee. His memory spooled through a million possibilities in the space of the next four taps. If he turned to confirm the identity he would see the fifty-pence-piece hesitate for a fraction of a second before the nicotine-stained fingers drove it down onto the shiny metal bar, which topped the back of his seat.

Frank smelled his own fear.

Caught off-guard he cursed himself.

A man used to keeping a safe distance and with the sixth sense essential to any successful undercover agent, Frank Lomax had survived dangers barely dreamed of by imaginative film makers, and in locations so perilous that only a hardened operative was sent to risk their life.

Now here he was, trapped on the upper deck of a local bus, not three miles from where he was born.

For a brief moment he thought he might be able to ignore the ominous presence behind him. He could get up and without a glance aside be down the stairs, step across the platform and onto the verge; disappear before his enemy had time to get out of his seat.

A swift look through the window confirmed that the bus was crossing the open wasteland between the industrial buildings that edged the town and the wooded area that fringed the canal. If he left the bus now, he would have nowhere to hide. Better to stay put. The man they all called Dumbo would not make a move here.

It did not take Frank long to start thinking like the successful survivor he was.

Dumbo must have trailed him here, a careful plan sketched out. Frank wondered what would have happened if he had gone home last night but rapidly buried the time-wasting hypothesis. He took out a packet of cigarettes, his resolve not to smoke on the day of his mother's funeral abandoned like the rest of his pilgrimage. He flicked the wheel of the silver lighter and breathed the sharp smoke into his lungs.

He heard steps on the metal treads of the stairway, the conductor had decided a trip aloft was essential now that he had more than one fare to collect. Frank listened carefully as the ticket machine whirred and money changed hands. He concentrated only on the actions and timings, trying to pick up a rhythm in the conductor's habitual movements – anything to aid the timing of his own escape. He barely noticed that the other passenger named a stop before the one he himself had intended to request, but he did notice the fact and it was stored instantly in his now exceedingly busy brain.

"Top Lock," he said himself, swiftly switching his destination. Throw in the unexpected. Wrong foot the opposition. Make Dumbo wonder. Frank was on home ground here, he had the edge. He rolled the slip of white paper into a tight spool, a fingers and thumb habit.

The conductor moved to a seat at the front of the bus where he could watch the early traffic flow past them into the town. The whistling began again, as did the tapping from behind Frank.

He checked his watch. By his reckoning, he had about eleven minutes to make up his mind. Top Lock was the stop after next. The bus was still moving through open ground. He thought they should have come to the scrapyard by now; he tried to remember what had happened to it. Who had bought it? Perhaps this wasteland was the old site, too contaminated for use. His eyes squinted into the distance for something to help him get his bearings.

Simultaneously, he spotted both the glisten of canal water and the single high-rise. The block of flats alongside the canal, a tall incongruity more ugly than the ill-named King's Row hovels it replaced. He saw the conductor at the front make a salacious gesture-cum-wave to someone on the verge below. The man's head rolled round, apparently following the target of his lust with his eyes. The bus jerked to a halt.

Frank leaped up from his seat and turned. As he passed the bulky figure in the seat behind, he drove the coiled spool of ticket into the man's eye. While the head shied away he stubbed his cigarette into the exposed bit of neck above the coat collar and fled down to the lower deck. The blonde in the leopard skin coat was still crossing her legs and arranging a wicker basket on the bench seat just beside the platform when Frank stepped off the bus and ducked behind it into the roadway. If Dumbo got off he'd probably not look behind but head straight for the flats. With a whiff of blue-black exhaust, the bus drew away. Frank was alone.

It was a short stride along the worn track from the bus stop to the canal path proper. Frank crossed the landscaped patch without a backward glance and swiftly reached the towpath at the point where it went under the disused railway bridge. Inevitable that 1960s planners had failed to consult residents before laying down well-intentioned but poorly aimed footpaths – the one flaw in otherwise well-conceived plans. Now an attractive flagged path curved, ornamental and pointless, away from the bus stop to join the canal bank midway between the bridge and the flats. Nobody would follow its trajectory. Life here was not for idle strolls, King's Row was gone but the people were as narrowly driven to survive as always. They took the direct approach.

Once under the bridge, Frank allowed himself a pause to consult the mobile phone in his pocket. No new messages. Two lads on bicycles were framed in the entrance to the other end of the tunnel and their loud voices reverberated, echoing as they advanced. He stood carefully against the wall, turning aside to appear to light a cigarette as they drew near. Once they had gone, he followed the path through the dripping tunnel and took stock of the situation. It was quite clear that he could not go to the funeral. Apart from his own need to get away there was the safety of his family to think of. Dumbo's words were disturbing, they showed that his enemy had expected him; *couldn't keep away,* indicated that he had known about the funeral. It would not take him long to work out where that was to be held, if he did not know already. This was exactly why Frank had kept his distance from people who mattered to him.

Well that was what he always told himself.

He took a second mobile from his breast pocket; keyed in, '*sorry jude held up, b in touch promise f*', *and* pressed ok. He owed her that.

Vivien Johnson

Europe's Idol

Of course, like most film-goers in Europe, I had admired – no, correction – worshiped him from afar. He had fair hair – charmingly unruly: eyes as blue as the Caribbean and the legs and body of a swimsuit model. It's not appropriate in present company to describe what other endearing features he sported. I must stop this, leave my lustful thoughts and go shopping for potatoes and carrots.

"Tickets please." The foxy man held out his hand. I fumbled in my handbag. "Hurry up, I haven't got all day, I'm tired and I have to complete my shift on the next bus!" He snatched the crumpled paper, which told me where I had to get off, out of my hand. "You passed your stop five minutes ago; you'll have to pay a fine."

"Sorry I wasn't thinking." I handed him a five-pound note which he promptly put in his trouser pocket.

"What about the change?" I enquired.

"What do you think I am a bloody philanthropist?"

I had had enough and reached for the bell pull. The vehicle stopped in a part of town I didn't recognise. Nevertheless, I stepped onto the pavement and decided that I would walk to the shops in future – besides, the walk would do me good.

The wind got up and blew my hat into a square. I ran after it. This definitely was not my day! I hadn't realised that the square was almost as big as a park. In the centre a large bandstand dominated the rolling, grass slopes. A figure huddled in the middle of the platform.

Fearing that he was ill and needed help I wandered over, hand on mobile, ready to summon assistance.

"Are you all right?"

A grunt was followed by deep sobs. I had never seen a man cry before.

"They've thrown me out, the lot of them, taken all my money. I don't have a bean to my name."

"Now, now," I crooned, not wishing to get involved with a

prospective down-and-out. "Things can't be as bad as they seem."

"Worse," he muttered. "I really have no funds and no friends. They have diddled me out of every penny."

At this point I considered phoning the police, or maybe I should phone for an ambulance and a psychiatrist. I really thought he might be deranged.

"I'll call for somebody to help you, perhaps Social Services on the Samaritans?"

He sat bolt upright and pierced me with the most startling blue eyes I had ever seen. This man must be in his sixties I thought: wife walked out with her lover, clearing out their joint bank accounts for good measure …hence his distress.

"You'll get over it in time, I'm sure. Build a new life."

"No I won't. How can I? I've been given the push by everyone. I have tried to keep my appearance, had face lifts and hair implants, which didn't take." He vigorously rubbed his bald pate as if trying to stimulate hair growth.

It was only then that I saw it. He pulled it from inside his jacket and placed the luscious blond wig on his head. I looked more closely at his face, there was a definite sagging under the chin and stretched skin around the eyes and, now that he wasn't choking with sobs, I recognised his voice.

My idol, Europe's idol, had fallen on hard times. His agent and film studio didn't want to know.

Gail Tucker

A Fiction

"When Onistod romped home at a hundred to one, Ted pocketed twenty-five thousand, booked a berth on a cargo boat out of Liverpool and . . ."

All week she'd been wrestling with the plot to carry forward these projected opening lines. She had Ted, who fled reality once too often: the ex-merchant seaman who knew just how to sail away from commitment. There was a scene on a tropical beach where *moonlight was kind to the ugliness of old flesh* beneath which timeless passions surged anew.

The key seemed to lie in *'I wish I knew you before'* – the would-be writer wondered what 'knew' meant here. What if they had known each other before; what if the woman realised all along and thought that Ted did too; what if Ted has no memory except in deep dark moments? He had, after all, spent a lifetime removing himself from responsibility...? *'Chris*t!' *He rolls away and strides into the sea?*

Juxtaposed was the woman, Sally, the girl Ted had met on a train the day he joined his ship in Cardiff. *He had not let her get away before securing a phone number.*

They had enjoyed over a year of pleasure in each other whenever he had home-leave, and they had exchanged increasingly committed letters. Suddenly, after taking her for a weird weekend at his parents' home, he had gone back to sea and she'd ceased to hear from him. The writer thinks her young Sally was rather relieved: she thought his mother very spooky, it might have been the way the woman boiled the milk to make ghastly coffee. The woman had waited until the white mass had bubbled to overtop the rim of an enamel saucepan, snatched the pan from the gas jet and waited for the foam to subside. Twice more, she applied the heat to the pan and repeated the exercise. This was all done with relish: Ted's mother seemed to enjoy the scorching, the changing colour of the milk.

On the other hand, Sally's sense that she had escaped an unknown horror might be due to the strange way Ted looked at her when he dropped her off on the Sunday night – either way, Sally was definitely unnerved.

Forty years later she came face to face with the past.

All of this had churned away for yet another week. The writer juggled with the elements of a tale-worth-telling but remained unable to fix a way in.

'The dark figure on the beach sat up into the moonlight. Sally was chilled to the bone. She peered around, expecting to see his skinny frame amble along the shoreline. There was only the glint of a wave as it rolled to break on the sand.

Where was he? Surely he'd not abandoned her for a second time. They had spent a lifetime apart, this accidental encounter was a rare gift. Sally reached around in the turmoil – aftermath of their coupling amongst the trappings of a day on the beach. She found her flip-flops and slipped them on. Unselfconsciously she scrambled to her feet and looked into the dark. There was no movement to discern. The decision to go to the water's edge was automatic, a reflex action.

At first she thought he was teasing her. His body lay face down, head resting on an arm that kept the face out of the water. Sally kicked water to splash the dry flesh between his shoulder-blades. When he did not move she kicked again. "Come on! I know you're kidding. Don't pretend you're worn out already. Not you, Big Boy."

The only movement was the next wave from the receding tide as it made a little surge up his thighs. Not a twitch moved his body. Alarmed, Sally crouched beside Ted's head and saw that his nose was buried in the wet sand. She grabbed his shoulder to turn him over, to breathe life into this dead thing at her feet.'

Relieved, the writer slid another sheet of paper across the desk towards her and licked the point of her pencil. She always drafted in pencil. Always licked the point. Tasted the metal. Tested her mettle.

'The dinghy bobbed on its tether to ride the swell. Sally knew she was not strong enough to move Ted higher up the beach. The tide was on the turn, by the time she got help, his body might have disappeared, dragged out to sea on the currents of the incoming tide. Their passports and money were up on the sand. The isolated inlet had seemed perfect when they approached it earlier in the day. Now it was a death-trap.'

Sally was still hesitating over her next move when the study window blew open and the draught swept all the writer's papers onto the floor. She looked at the photograph that stood now isolated on the empty, pale-pine surface of the desk. The thin face stared out at her, returning her gaze. It challenged her to continue. "Write the truth," said the sad eyes. "Don't make me fiction. I dare you!"

The writer turned the face flat onto the desk; silence the photograph. She got up and went to the flapping window. Leaning out, she pinned it back to the wall then stayed to gaze down at the beach. The tide was going out. Soon the spot where she had reclaimed her life would be visible. The place where she had fulfilled the dream of her lifetime and buried her past in one gentle push into wet sand would be above water for about ten minutes. The moon's pull controlled the tide as it always would. The writer chose to live in the cottage where she could watch that it did.

Her characters came and went.

The real person stayed, forever dead.

No post mortem could detect such a tender attack.

Colin Hall

The Last Supper

Inspired by Leonardo da Vinci's 'The Last Supper'

Of course, being a woman, I wasn't invited but, since it happened, I have heard accounts of it from all who were there, except from Jesus and Judas. You understand why.

There have been many arguments over the years, why my son asked all his friends round for a meal on that particular night.

Not that it was unusual to have his mates round.

They did it quite often.

Always, whilst eating and drinking, animatedly talking about where they were going off to next and planning on what they would do when they got there.

In the main they were a happy bunch. I won't name individuals but there were one or two who were a bit odd: made me feel uncomfortable; quiet-like and maybe a bit shifty but, in the main, they all got on well together.

They really liked Jesus and he, in turn, liked them a lot. Nobody had any time for girls, but I don't think it was for any wrong reasons. They enjoyed each other's company so much – I think they would have done anything for each other. Well, as it turned out, Jesus did.

He even washed their feet, which seemed a bit odd at the time, but I have since begun to understand why he did it. He didn't always explain things very clearly and I think that is why so many people have put so many varied interpretations on what he said and did.

He knew what he meant, but for some reason left everything a bit blurred; well, to my way of thinking, anyway ...sort of intended everybody to put their own slant on things.

The trouble with this is that there have been so many arguments, even wars, as a result.

Yes, it was a good event. Although there were some sombre moments. It wasn't all laughter. Like when He said He was going away.

They didn't like that. They didn't understand what He was trying to tell them. I have often wondered if that was a fault of His – that is, if he had any faults: not making sure people understood what he was saying. Many an argument followed after he had spoken to people. Some thinking he meant one thing, others that He meant something completely different, but back to the feet washing...

When they told me about that I understood right away. It is not a big deal, just washing someone's feet, but it has a deeper meaning. I try every day to do something for someone other than myself. So, if nothing else, it has made a difference to my life.

I can't remember Jesus ever doing anything just for himself. He was totally unselfish. All right, in the house, He was a bit slow to wash up or tidy His room, but he was only a lad. Then, when he grew up, He was too busy with His mates. I hardly ever saw Him. He was so focused on whatever he intended doing, He didn't have much time for his mother, but that's lads for you.

Yes, the meal went very well. Lots of food and wine, just a bunch of lads having a good time. It was a shame that there was sadness as well. Of course subsequent events have sort of put a bit of a dampener on it all. If He knew what was going to happen, surely He could have stopped it.

Couldn't he?

Vivien Johnson

Christmas

If I'd known that my whole world would be turned upside down, I wouldn't have picked him up.

I had never given a stranger a lift before.

It was a snowy night, a freezing Christmas Eve.

I turned the heater up full.

He was heading for my home town after twenty years' absence.

"It's changed a lot lately," I said. "You won't recognise it. Have you friends there?"

"Well, I had family; I hope they'll still be there.

It's my daughter's twenty-first birthday tomorrow."

I skidded to a halt and stared at him hard.

"Yes," he said, "it is you, Noelle, isn't it? You look just like your mother."

Vivien Johnson

Gone

*Over ditches wide, hedges high,
field tracks – galloping, galloping.
His coat tails muddy and wet,
rain filtered down his breeches;
his leather boots leaked.
Slippery slug reins.
Soil composting in his nostrils.*

*Clouds cleared, the full moon
through winter's branches
cast shadows, shone on iron bolts –
jewels in the rustic door.*

*His mare's lungs heaved; heart pounding,
sought sustenance from drowned grass.*

*Joseph grasped the knocker.
RAT–TAT–TAT
echoed down the passages
to the bowels of the house;
he felt fear, the sound engulfed him.*

*He cried out, 'Hello, hello';
expected a friendly welcome.
The wind moaned around vacant rooms,
through open doorways
and death-watched timbers.*

*He knocked louder – no running footsteps,
no open arms to greet him.
Her father must have taken her.*

He shouted curses of anger and revenge,
but only ghosts heard him.
Joseph's heart, a plant torn from its roots.
He'd kept his pledge to return
and carry away his fair haired bride;
but all he found was emptiness,
bitter–sweet anger assuaged.

Through the clank of steel on steel,
and battles' hardships he'd seen her face,
felt her lips on his;
been united by moon and stars.
Wellington had protected their love;
taken Joseph home a victor.

Avner Kornblum

A Novel Ending

Mortimer had just settled down at his computer to continue with the novel he had started to write ten times before …and, as had happened ten times before, he could not concentrate because of the rowdiness of his next-door neighbours.

There were only two of them but they made more than enough noise through loud-mouthed arguments to ear-splitting love-making – from pans banged into the kitchen sink to nails being hammered into the walls – at ten o´clock at night, what´s more.

However, distracted he was from the passage he was attempting to write, these neighbours did give him a great idea for the ending of his novel.

One of the two villains would perish from a pan of boiling oil being thrown at him, the other would be struck on the head by a hammer.

Even better an ending: the two villains would fall out and kill each other off by those two methods.

That would save tarnishing the cops.

This eleventh time, though, Mortimer could stand it no longer. He got up, wiped his sweaty hands on his shirt, cast a glance through the bedroom door at his happily-snoring wife and marched out of the house.

Joseph and Olga, watching a replay of the day´s motor-racing through bleary eyes, could not hear the doorbell with the TV on full-blast. They were quite surprised when Mortimer rapped on the window pane. Joseph told Olga to hide their joints while he went to the door.

"Hi," said Mortimer diffidently. "I´m sorry to call so late but I´m trying to write and …"

"So what do you want? A pen or paper?" interrupted Joseph. "Olga, fetch this man something to write on, so he can bugger off."

"No need to get nasty," said Mortimer. "All I wanted was …"

"A kick up the bum! That´s what you´ll get!" shouted Joseph.

"Just f... off!"

"Okay, if that's how you want it," said Mortimer, largely to himself as the door was banged shut.

He went home and called Rocky, who was sleeping beside his wife's bed. Rocky stretched his gigantic frame, shook his sleep away and wagged his tail.

"Rocky, I've a job for you. You must frighten the hell out of these nasty folk next door. Come on!"

Placing a strong lead on the Great Dane's collar, Mortimer led him to the neighbours' door and rang the bell – this time more imperiously. The motor-racing having ended, Joseph heard the bell. He flung the door open, furious at this further intrusion.

"What the hell ...my God, it's Charlie! Where did you find him?"

Mortimer was startled by the change in approach.

He was even more startled by the change in Rocky.

That strong tail was wagging; the powerful teeth were bared in what could only be described as a smile.

"Come on in!" cried Joseph. "Olga, come look! Come have a drink with us and tell us how you found Charlie!"

"His name is Rocky. If you hadn't kept yourselves indoors you could have seen this dog almost any day – and I don't want a drink, thank you," replied Mortimer, courteously but coolly. "All I want is peace and quiet while I'm writing."

"Now listen, buster," snarled Joseph, "this here dog is our Charlie ..."

"No, this is Rocky," insisted Mortimer, "and I've had him from the pound for the past two years. It's obvious you didn't care much about your Charlie."

"Not true, fatso," said Olga, who had now joined the group and been practically knocked down by the joyously barking dog. "We had to move, we were loaded up and when we came back for Charlie he'd gone."

"I bet you had to move! Probably a dozen times because of the noise you make and the dope you smoke. Look, what can I do to get some peace and quiet?"

"Just leave Charlie with us and I promise you, no more noise," said Joseph, magnanimously overlooking Mortimer's offensive remarks.

"No way!" snorted Mortimer. "His name's Rocky, he's staying with us, and you can damn well go on making a racket. Come on, Rocky."

But Rocky would not budge, and when a Great Dane won't move few men can make him move. Mortimer was not one of those men.

Rocky stayed and became Charlie again.

Joseph and Olga made a great fuss of him, more noisily than anything they had done before.

Mortimer returned home, wringing his hands in despair.

His wife, awakened by the loud voices and excited barking, demanded, "Where have you been? And where is Rocky?"

Mortimer told her the sad tale of Rocky-cum-Charlie.

His wife said, "That's it! I'm through with you. You just get everything wrong! All for the sake of a lousy novel you'll probably never finish anyway. In the morning, you choose – you go or I go!"

With that, she returned to bed, switched off the light and muttered angrily for an age.

Mortimer left the next day.

Jean M. Watson

Crossing the bar

The mid-afternoon sun shone in a near-cloudless sky. The water in the yacht marina sparkled as it caught the sunlight and cast rainbows across the hulls of the various yachts lying against the jetties. Halliards tinkled against masts in the gentle breeze and somewhere, inboard a yacht, music played softly, emphasising the peace of the afternoon.

Caroline sat in the cockpit of the yacht 'Heavensent', her blonde hair catching the sunlight as she looked, without interest, at a magazine while waiting for Mike, her husband. Mike and Caroline had bought 'Heavensent' some years before. They had found her standing in a boatyard where she had been for a couple of years: varnish peeling, the teak decks grey and dry from lack of oil. Caroline and Mike loved her immediately and gladly paid the bargain-price that she was going for. The owner had died in a car crash and his widow was eager to sell, as she could no longer bear to use the boat on which she and her husband had spent many happy hours. She wished Caroline and Mike good luck and hoped they would have some happy times together on 'Heavensent'.

"How funny," said Mike, "Her ol' man certainly got heaven-sent."

"Oh, Mike, how could you say that?" said Caroline, slightly horrified by Mike's flippancy. "It was all very sad, wasn't it?"

"Yea, it was really, "replied Mike thoughtfully. "It would be awful if anything like that happened to us, wouldn't it? I don't think I could live without you, but in the meantime, get on with rubbing down that rail, woman, or I'll be hell-bent on tanning that cheeky bottom of yours."

"Promises, promises," taunted Caroline, as she picked up the sandpaper to carry on rubbing-down what seemed to be at least a mile of teak rail.

It was now several summers since Mike and Caroline bought 'Heavensent', summers spent in gradual restoration of the boat at weekends and holidays sailing contentedly around the coast. Both Mike and Caroline had grown up around boats and handled 'Heavensent' with ease. Squally weather exhilarated them, although like any good, sensible sailor they preferred fine weather for the comfort and pleasure it provided.

They loved to sail, but their greatest pleasure was sailing together, complementing each other's skills. One sailing without the other was unthinkable. Today, the weather conditions looked ideal for the weekend jaunt to Middlesea Yacht Club that they had planned. There was to be a barbecue and, what Mike called, dancing in a crowd on your own.

Caroline looked at her watch. Mike was late, which was unusual for him, and so were David and Liz who were going with them to Middlesea. "Come on, you lot," sighed Caroline, "We'll be late crossing the bar. The tide will be turning soon and we won't get out." But she spoke only to herself as she looked at her watch again. Twenty-five-past two. Suddenly she saw Mike coming along the jetty. He waved and tried to hurry, but he was holding his head at an angle as if it hurt him.

"Hello, Darling, are you alright?" asked Caroline anxiously. "Where are David and Liz?"

"They'll be along soon. Sorry, I'm late, aren't I?" replied Mike. "I am having a bit of trouble with my neck but it should be OK once we get over the bar. Are you coming with me?"

"Of course," said Caroline, "you know I always go wherever you go. Why should today be different?"

"…'til death?" asked Mike.

"…'til death," replied Caroline in the private ritual they had so often used.

In a flurry of activity, Caroline made the sails ready to hoist and prepared the boat ready for sea. Mike did not help as he usually did and she supposed that his neck was hurting more than he had admitted so she did not complain. With the engine puttering gently, 'Heavensent' left her mooring and passed slowly out towards the harbour entrance. Beyond it, the open sea beckoned, the fresh wind enticing the boat and its occupants away from the safety of the Marina. As the boat crossed the bar, Mike looked at Caroline, his eyes unusually dark, his head still at that strange angle.

"…'til death?" he asked again.

"…'til death." responded Caroline but, somehow, there seemed to be a stronger significance in the words than there had been half-an-hour ago.

Turning the boat head-to-wind, Caroline hoisted the sails and switched off the engine. The wind caught the sails and they flapped furiously until Caroline pulled on the sheets and caught the tiller to turn the boat on-course. "You were late today," she said. "What held you up?"

"Yes," said Mike, "very late. I ran into a problem on the way to the Marina… Still to death?" Suddenly Caroline shuddered.

It was not just that dark clouds had appeared from nowhere and a squall was racing across the sea. Somehow Mike's persistence with the old words of commitment combined with his strange behaviour were making her uneasy. The squall was now very close and Caroline moved to shorten sail but Mike put out a hand to stop her.

"It'll be alright as they are," he said intensely. "You didn't answer my question. Still to death?" Caroline looked at him. She was frightened. Mike, who she had known for so long and always trusted, literally, with her life, was acting very strangely.

His behaviour was so unreal, so distant and his neck still at that odd angle. She knew that to argue with him would be pointless. She must agree with him on everything until they were safely home and she could call for medical help.

"Yes, 'til death," Caroline replied, shivering.

The sky was now black with storm clouds and the sea was a heaving mass of grey waves. 'Heavensent' was rolling uncontrollably under the weight of full sails, then still in sight of the harbour mouth she rolled one final time, throwing Mike and Caroline into the water. Caroline felt the sea pressing her body down and water filling her lungs. Frightened, she knew that she was drowning and that Mike was somehow pulling her soul to him, away from her body, away from the sea that had already claimed it.

Back in the Marina, watchers stood helplessly as 'Heavensent' sank below the waves.

David and Liz had at last arrived at the Marina.

"Oh lord," screamed Liz. "It can't be happening! Caroline! She would never take 'Heavensent' out on her own without Mike. Why, oh why, did she do it? She should have waited until we arrived. Oh, not both of them in one day! Only half-an-hour apart! ...But she couldn't have known about the road accident – Mike being killed on his way here – a broken neck… We were here to break it to her – it happened a little while ago – just before half-past-two, maybe about twenty-five-past."

Avner Kornblum

Flowers in Barcelona

Wearing a suit in Barcelona is not uncommon, just hot. Wearing a hat is both uncommon and hot nowadays. However, suits and hats were not uncommon amongst Barcelona's men-folk sixty years ago. If you were one of those men and were as adroit as you were respectable-looking you could hide a number of purloined articles in your suit pockets and under your hat.

One day in 1955 when Franco's Guardia Civil were not wandering the Rambla caressing their firearms, Juan `Barracuda' Castaño was busy pickpocketing tourists from the more trusting parts of Spain (there were very few tourists from outside Spain at that time). When there were too few curious visitors around – and `Barracuda' was an expert at telling them from the locals – he would lift small items from a tobacconist, a knife from a cutlery store or miniature souvenirs from various stall-holders.

A bench directly opposite the florist's lavish display of blooms afforded him the opportunity to sit down and take off his hat, pretending to be mopping his sweaty brow. The hat held several compartments, large enough to store some of `Barracuda's illicit haul yet small enough not to be obvious as it sat perched upon his head.

Having completed the operation, he placed the hat back on his head, very carefully this time as it secreted sharp nail scissors. Then he sat back with a sigh and looked at the glorious floral display. At first it was a casual glance. Then he looked a second time. Then he peered at it very intently. Then he got up and walked away as quickly as he could without attracting attention.

He was about to turn into one of the narrow streets leading off the Rambla, where a maze of buildings of all shapes and sizes, crammed in against each other, offering wonderful escape routes for pickpockets and robbers, when he felt a gentle hand on his shoulder.

"¿Señor Castaño, no?" purred a male voice. "¿O Barracuda, no es?"

He looked round. Gentle though the touch and the voice were, their owner was a member of the Guardia Civil and he had a large revolver in his hand – pointed directly at Barracuda.

"That's me," answered Juan cheerfully. "Can I help you?"

"Oh yes," answered the guard. "You can come with me to the prison, where you can wait till tomorrow's appearance in the court, where you can explain all the items you are hiding in your hat and, no doubt, filling your pockets."

"Mierda," sighed Juan `Barracuda' Castaño. "It really wasn't fair of you to hide amongst the flowers."

Gail Tucker

Graduation Day

If she stretched out her hand she would touch it. She had no need to. She could feel the texture of the ivory-coloured flank from where she stood. The sensation was so strong that the palms of her hands tingled and her nipples rose against the cotton of her underclothing. The old double-doors had been ajar as always, the automatic closing mechanism as faulty as it had been in her student days when the studio had been her learning ground.

When had the caretaker tired of repairing the old-fashioned mechanism that used to bump part-shut with a characteristic double *whoomp*? It was probably not a caretaker's job any more. They probably had to requisition help from a maintenance department, make out a form in triplicate, get it put on the computer for work to be done on a Thursday; not a Wednesday afternoon; that was bin day, apparently. She heard the ghosts of generations of boisterous young artists as they barged their way through half-closed doors, heads often invisible behind rolls of paper and cardboard, wood and canvases and all the other paraphernalia of their youthful creativity.

Today, this older Lavinia had been on another, altogether different mission and ought not to have been anywhere near the basement. She ought to have stayed upstairs in the long gallery where the current end of year exhibition was set out. Depressed by the sight of so much 'found art', the immaculately dressed figure had meandered away from the assemblages of recycled odds and ends that formed, to its mind, poor approximations of Art.

Lavinia could find little evidence of rigour in a piece entitled, *Wednesday Afternoon,* which carried the 'helpful' descriptor: (Wednesday is the bin collection day. Gary demonstrates here that Art is ever-present if we would only look around us). It was too awful even to raise a smile. She wondered what Gary's portfolio would be like. She looked at the slashed red and black cover lying to one side of *Wednesday Afternoon* and shuddered. She knew that not all student work was so poor and could not understand how one such as Gary had survived the course. In her day, if there had been a Gary, he would not have seen out the first term – perhaps not even the first week. She had thought then, upstairs, of her exacting teachers: men and women who insisted on accurate drawing skills and careful attention to detail in all that their students did. *Wednesday Afternoon* would have been consigned to its own special place one Wednesday afternoon, no question about that.

The Long Gallery opened out into the atrium, the deep buzz of conversion reverberating round its high dome. She wondered how long she ought to stay. She reminded herself that old-fashioned courtesy was not the only reason she was there. Down the years, she had refused several gilt-edged invitations to attend the annual event. This year the simple request from a currently graduating student had been impossible to refuse. The imposing gowned figure of the Dean was making its way relentlessly toward her. Lavinia's heart sank at the thought of making polite small talk: she would be expected to gush. A gap in the throng between her and the statue of Athena opened up; the goddess to the rescue, Lavinia spotted the half-obscured doorway in the wall beyond.

Her willowy form had slipped through the door and down the narrow staircase without a backward glance. The rest had been an automatic transition: like Alice she was in another reality before you could say White Rabbit.

It was a shock to find the piece still here, on the table in the middle of the room. She looked round and saw now that the old studio had been reduced to a store, more like a lumber-room than any formal, organised depository. It smelled of old dust but faint traces of turpentine and size lingered to reassure her that this was the place – if she needed any assurance other than that reclining nude before her.

Noises in the distance, made her step closer, away from the line of sight through the gap in the doors; she felt furtive again. Perhaps it was this room. Yes, after all this time she felt the old guilt, an unfashionable emotion now. An involuntary smile twitched the corner of her mouth, not quite dead yet then. She peered more closely at the figure, it really was that piece, her magnum opus. Looking down at her hands now, she could feel again the encrusted plaster working under her nails, its grit contrasting with the smooth skin of her red-haired model. So much conflict. Yes, no; I will, I can't; I do, I shouldn't.

How young they had been: how naive. He, anxious to encourage his first exceptionally talented student, she, seduced by the excitement of it all – each choked by convention. They both knew that the line was perilously thin, the invisible second between decorum and abandon. For weeks she had drawn and sketched – figures in the park, figures on the dance-floor, figures at work, men in boiler suits, men digging trenches, men on scaffolding. All action caught in the stroke of her pencil.

The light from the windows up at pavement level was momentarily cut off by a passing bus, the traffic noise was another recalled element of student days. Today, the gear-changes masked the foot-fall behind her so that, when light was restored, the new presence was already making its way to the other side of the table. Anyone who observed this neat turn of events, might have thought that she peered into the falling sunlight in an attempt to identify the intruder – they would be wrong.

She had not met him for over forty years but she had kept up with his life through newspaper reports, magazine articles and even *arts programmes* on the BBC. Lavinia had no idea that he had followed her career too, from the moment they had both left the institution.

Each had, in moments of idleness or extreme anxiety, toyed with the idea of this moment; of bumping into the other on the street, on the tube or at an opening in some prestigious gallery. The moment had not come. Until now.

He leaned on his Malacca cane, removed his black fedora, and met her steady gaze. Was it a trick of the sunlight that picked out copper flecks in his snow-white hair? She swallowed. There was time only for the merest tilt of a head as youthful footsteps clattered along the corridor, before the girl with flaming red hair burst through the door.

"Here you are. Honestly!"

"This," said Lavinia unnecessarily, without shifting her gaze, "is the grand-daughter."

"Ah! Yes," he said.

Vivien Johnson

A Walk in the Past

*Gentle folds and rugged crags
where trees cling to escarpments;
and paths of yellow like a child's sandpit
lead to Benidorm to Mediterranean-merge.
One red roof strident in the landscape,
an open wound against the terracotta,
shuttered windows and silent streets.*

*I see El Cid riding tortuous tracks,
his troops Spanish stallions mounted;
armour and weapons creak and clank.
Battle-streets run river-red;
fights' acrid smell on men's
shirts and tattered breeches.
Hunger – unassuaged.*

*Huddled villagers behind closed doors;
children hide in mothers' skirts –
frightened animals.
The soldiers' horses snorting smoke –
the sound of forged iron
clatters on cobbled stones.*

My vision has fled.

*Now, 'Melónes,' a farmer cries;
sells only a few from the back of his van.
It's fiesta, the village sleeps.
Later the people will ogle and exclaim
over fireworks from the square.*

*I scale the mountains to follow El Cid,
my footprints held in silent sand.
A red roof slashes the barren landscape.*

Jean M. Watson

The Ring

I was bored, very bored. I had been asked by Alison, my hostess for the weekend, whether I would like to go with her to an antiques fair. I could have thought of more interesting ways to entertain a guest than this flea-market, held in a vast hall that had once been a corn exchange, but which was now used only for pretentious events such as this so-called antiques fair.

The high-raftered hall was filled with rows of trestle tables covered with grimy tablecloths, old blankets and bedspreads, with displays of articles that I thought should be consigned to the dustbin.

There seemed to be collections of brass ornaments, which would have been more attractive and saleable had someone polished them in the last twenty-years. There were collections of old magazines. Occasionally a set would be complete but, mostly, each set would lack the last two or three issues as if someone had lost interest in that subject, and started the next new and enticing hobby, only to lose interest again before the last few issues. Now here they lay, overpriced and unpurchased.

Bored, bored, bored, I wandered up and down the various aisles, no longer studying the contents of each display. Of what interest to me were rusty collections of tin toys, old clothes, and old tablecloths? The room smelt musty, of unwashed materials, and sometimes of clothes wet from the drizzling rain outside.

Voices bounced and echoed from the bare walls; the slate floor was damp from wet feet. Move too near the main door and the burger van's offering of boiling onions and tomato ketchup distracted everyone from the business of the day.

I had long ago lost sight of Alison, so I continued walking up and down the aisles. She would find me when she was ready to go. A flash of light from a table with a discreet sign reading 'Antique Jewellery' caught my eye and I wandered over to take a closer look. Trays of earrings, brooches, necklaces and bracelets were spread out untidily on the table and, in the centre, a couple of cutlery trays of rings. It must have been something in one of those trays that had caught the light. Most of the other trays were as dull and uncared for as the brass ornaments and collections of magazines on the other tables. My feet were cold and damp, my hands not much warmer, even though I had kept my hands in my pockets all morning. I leaned forward to look more closely at the trays of rings. One ring, an amber oval, set in gold, seemed brighter than any other. My hands came out of my pockets although I had not willed them to do so, and I picked up the ring. It shimmered in the dim light of the hall and I slipped it onto the second finger of my right hand.

The noise around me intensified. Voices shouted fiercely, swords clashed and clanged together, Roman helmets mixed with Barbarian, wild ringlets, and I stood unable to move, my feet covered with mud and slime. I was barefoot, I noted absently, and wearing only a thin shift of beige, coarse material. My ears stung as a horn blared somewhere behind me and all the barbarians turned and fled from the battlefield towards the sound.

Panting and a few curses were the only sounds I could hear, as the Roman soldiers grouped around me. "Where did she come from?" they all seemed to be asking. Although they spoke a rough Latin dialect, I could somehow understand what they said. They all moved a couple of steps closer, like curious cattle. The smell of armour, sweat and blood enveloped me, and I held my breath, feeling very frightened and vulnerable. One of them, obviously the leader, held up his hand and they all retreated slightly. The leader took a step towards me and studied me with dark blue eyes. "You are now my slave," he said, "but first give me that ring. It is too good for a low slave, especially a female." It would be no good arguing with him and there was no escape.

Reluctantly I pulled the ring from my finger. The cold and damp of the corn exchange hit me as I stood there with the ring in my hand. I looked at it disbelievingly. What had just happened had not really happened, had it? Surely not, but it was such a pretty ring and fitted perfectly. Somehow it jumped back on my finger.

At once the air was mild and sunny, just like a spring day. The voices around me were cultured, the air scented with orange pomanders. I looked down at my full skirt, with hooped overskirts decorated with rosebuds. "Oh, there you are, my lady," and there was a gentleman in a brocade cutaway coat and white britches. "I have been searching for you everywhere. I think you may need rescuing from the Countess. She is very angry that you have taken her ring and omitted to pay for it." His dark blue eyes looked down at me. "When we have returned the ring to the Countess and she is no longer angry with you, I will see that you find a suitable position in court, my dear, but I shall, of course, expect repayment of a certain kind. Now take off that ring and we will return it to Her Ladyship." Once more I was trapped by a pair of dark blue eyes. Slowly I pulled the ring from my finger.

The stuffy air of the corn exchange surrounded me once again. It was still damp and malodorous, still noisy. To my surprise nothing had changed. I held the ring in my hand. I had almost lost it twice. This time it was going to stay mine It was a curious thing, but I simply had to have it, whatever the price. "How much?" I asked the stallholder. His dark blue eyes looked into mine.

Avner Kornblum

Mr Grouchy's Holidays

"OK, it's 8.30, let's start now!" Andrew Pilkington called out from somewhere in the middle of the Civic Centre meeting room.

What a cheek! thought Maurice Gresham, Andrew hardly ever comes to our meetings and when he does he slips in quietly, anything from 5 minutes to 15 minutes after we've started. Today he's on time because we're planning a club holiday.

Not for nothing had Maurice's family, friends and acquaintances alike, nicknamed him Mr Grouchy. Even when he had something nice to say it was usually interspersed with negatives. Actually, the name had been coined by Andrew Pilkington, Maurice's most reluctant acquaintance.

Holidays, hah! They're just a pain, reflected Maurice grumpily, like going to Becky's wedding in England. First, that airport delay, 8 hours at Alicante without explanation or apology, then ages at Gatwick just getting through the car-hire formalities. Sure, Becky had a lovely old-time church in an old-time village and a beautiful barn for the reception, but oh, the traffic! It never stopped, not even when we got in at midnight instead of 4pm, nor in the countryside on the weekend, and even worse during the weekdays after that. We needed a fortnight off afterwards to recover. Gary's wedding was another holiday in Surrey. Narrow lane, had to park on a muddy field and, of course, car got stuck in the mud, with me in my wedding gear at that. How embarrassing when Gary's father-in-law arrived just in time to help me push the car out!

Yup, a pain in the butt! Like our trip to Granada. I got a real pain in the butt on that bus – didn't know if it was a converted jeep or an oversized wheelbarrow! The cathedral was so gloomy it was almost scary and what I thought was a *flamenco* concert was a talent contest for tuneless teenagers. Only the Alhambra was worthwhile …made up for all the rest.

It was also a pain in the butt that spoiled our rugby-tour of South

Africa, especially the University of Cape Town crowd. Must have been 40 years ago 'cos I was 19. I'll never forget the party those Ikeys gave us where I met lovely young Monica. I'll never forget her, either. She was so innocent, just turned 17. What a beautiful day the next day was, when we went walking in the countryside and rested under an oak tree. Hah! She would have lost her virginity that day but for a stone she was lying on. Damn stone! Ruined everything just by giving a pain in the butt to *her*.

Ruined! That's the right word. So many holidays were ruined by some lousy little event. Like those filthy campsites in the Camargue and their disgusting toilets! We were in such a small tent that when Vera needed a doctor, he had to lie alongside her. Anyway, I'll never forget my first trip to France …first time I'd ever seen a woman topless in public! Of course, it wouldn't be some beautiful babe, oh, no, a blessed fat 80-year-old woman knitting on a beach in Normandy and having to swing her arms past her enormous breasts at the end of each row. Now I think about it, I did have some fun. We went to…

"What's that you said, Mr President?" said Maurice Gresham, out loud. "The details for our group holiday in Cordoba? I – I – I didn't realise you wanted me to speak about them today. They're in my house. Yes, of course I can fetch them. I'll be back in 15 minutes!"

"Ah, well," sighed Andrew Pilkington in a stage whisper designed to reach Maurice's ears. "It's only a couple of minutes past eight-thirty, so it won't be too late."

"Come on, Andrew," said Judith from the chair alongside. "Let's all go into the lounge and have a drink while we wait for Maurice."

Vivien Johnson

Faded Pictures

She knew it would be the last time they would be together.

Holding hands, Emma and Nick wandered up the field, kissing and laughing in the moonlight. The sweet smell of the dewy grass and scent of honeysuckle in the hedgerows, seemed to bind their love.

Emma shuddered as they entered the forest where the moon's rays cast eerie shadows on the ground. The dead twigs and last autumn's fallen leaves crackled under their feet. Was it a touch of guilt that made her clutch Nick's hand so tightly? He put his arm around her waist to comfort and reassure her.

When they reached the clearing, Emma forgot her fears; she instinctively knew it was right to spend the night with Nick. It would be the last time they would see each other. He had told her months before that he and his parents were moving to South Africa. The intervening time had flown by all too quickly, and now they were spending their last hours together.

"You see Emma, I promised you I could find this place at night." She touched his mouth with her fingertips; he held them for a moment between his lips. "I do love you so much." he said.

"I love you too." she replied.

"Just a minute," Nick reached up into a tree and pulled down the tartan rug he had put there during the day. He laid it in a mossy dell. "We can sit on this; I would hate you to get chilled."

"You are wonderful Nick; you have thought of everything."

They sat in silence for a while looking up at the stars.

"I want you to have this locket, so you will never forget our love. Our pictures are inside." He fastened the chain around her neck.

"Oh, thank you Nick. I promise I could never forget you." She felt an inner glow, and snuggled closer to him.

When he spoke again his voice had changed. "It's so awful; I can't bear the thought of never seeing you again. Mum and I are sailing early in the morning. I can't think why Dad has bought a farm out there, when he already has this one." Clinging together, their tears mingling, they tried to think of a plan to keep them there forever.

At dawn they heard Nick's parents calling him, and then Nick's father appeared.

"What do you think you are doing?" he ranted. "Your mother and I have been worried sick. Come home immediately! As for you, young lady, I shall see your father about this. Now, get off my land at once." He took Nick by the collar and dragged him out of sight.

She pressed the locket to her throat, as floods of tears poured down her face, soaking the front of her dress. She made her way home, alone. Hardly daring to turn the key in the lock, she quietly let herself into her family's cottage.

At breakfast time smothering copious yawns, she forced herself to smile the usual greetings at her parents, hoping they had no idea of the last night's escapade. For weeks afterwards she shook every time the telephone rang; she lived in dread of Nick's father telling her mum and dad. Months later, Emma discovered that Nick's dad had let the farm, and departed for Africa as soon as the deal was settled. Shortly afterwards Emma and her family moved up north.

At first the couple wrote to each other every day but, as time passed, the number of letters dwindled to once a week, then once a month, then every six months and after that, just Christmas cards. As they both matured and made new friends, they lost touch until, eventually, that whole chapter in Emma's life faded into the past. Then she met her husband John.

Now, thirty-five years later, their two boys had left home.

John had been a kind and generous man. They had been very happy together. After John's sudden death from a heart attack, Emma decided to sort out her things and start a new life. She smiled when she came across the locket tucked at the back of her dressing-table drawer, still wrapped in a silk handkerchief. The pictures had faded, but the fond memories of her first love came flooding back. She knew she would have to take the locket and return to the special place, where she and Nick had innocently spent the night together. She made plans to move south.

She should not have trespassed the previous day, then she wouldn't have lost the locket. She shouldn't have given in to the temptation to ride her horse, Fred, up the side of the field. Now she had to do the same thing again today. She hoped she would get there early enough to find her treasure before someone else got there. It was only a cheap trinket, but it meant such a lot to her. She let herself through the gate and, once inside the field, she let Fred have his head. He felt the soft turf under his feet, took hold of the bit and galloped up the hill, into the wood. She knew she could find again, today, the clearing where she and Nick had spent the night under the stars, professing undying love.

Nick's caring ways were what she remembered most about him, even after all these years. It all came flooding back to her now. Yesterday, she had found the place. She had sat there just the way they had that night and she had placed the locket around her neck, just as he had done. The trinket had only come from Woolworth's, but it was the only thing Nick had ever given her. It was silly to get so sentimental over such a worthless object but it was the picture of him she treasured so much.

Fred pulled up as they reached the glade. Across the early morning air, plumes of hot breath snorted from his nostrils. Emma dismounted as she had done the previous day and let Fred graze. Once more she felt the thrill of her first love.

"I know I had it yesterday," she said to herself. "I put it round my neck, I sat here." Fred continued to graze. "It must be here somewhere." She ran her fingers around the mossy depression.

"Have you lost something?" The male voice made her jump.

From her kneeling position Emma saw the muzzle of a double-barrelled shotgun pointing at the ground. Shaking uncontrollably, she couldn't take her eyes off the gun.

"I watched you sitting here yesterday, I didn't like to interrupt. You seemed to be deep in thought." Emma had heard that voice before. Her mind flashed straight back to that fateful night. It was Nick's father's voice!

"Sorry... I'll go, sorry ...I haven't done any damage; I only rode around the headland, I didn't ride the plough. It was nostalgia, you see, it got the better of me." Emma felt embarrassed; he must have heard her talking to herself. She made herself look up, as the man stepped out into the glade. He caught her horse and handed her the reins. She looked straight into his eyes and there was no mistaking those kind eyes. It was her love of thirty-five years ago! Her memory stripped the years away, bringing back vivid thoughts of their last night together. The old feelings came racing back, all the love and the tenderness. To her surprise, she found that her love for him was stronger now, than it had ever been.

"I think you were looking for this, weren't you?" Her locket shone in the sunlight on the end of its chain, as it dangled from his hand. "May I put it around your neck?"

"Oh, yes please Nick." Tears of joy flowed down her cheeks. Choked with emotion she whispered, "Ever since I found it hidden away in my drawer, I had a feeling that you would come back some day."

He fastened the chain around her neck as he had done years before. It felt as if they had never been parted. Her eyes hadn't left his face then, without being aware of it, their arms were around each other: kissing on the lips as though they had never been apart.

"I will never leave you again, I promise." he said.

"And I promise, I won't let you." Emma replied.

Colin Hall

My Gloves

When I was little, like very tiny, the gloves I wore were connected together by a piece of string. This string ran all the way up inside my left sleeve, round the back of my neck, inside my collar and then down the inside of my right sleeve. Nobody, apart from myself and my mother, knew there was a string, as it was concealed from public view throughout its entire length.

My grandparents and aunties and uncles would peer into my pram and say things like, "Oh look at him. Isn't he cute?" and, "Does he know anything yet?" Well, I remember thinking to myself, *I know something you don't,* and hoping that my mum wouldn't spill the beans about the string. Thinking back, the string served a security purpose, ensuring that if I lost one glove, I would also lose the other. Something I got quite good at. Of course, as the years went by and my body grew, the string would get lengthened by my mum. Eventually, when I got married, my wife took over from my mother and assumed responsibility for the string but, by then, my arms had stopped growing so it only required minimal maintenance.

I remember one particular winter when the snow was many feet deep.

Well, it seemed to me at the time that that was the case.

It may have been that, as I was not very tall myself, it only appeared very deep.

Taller friends of mine didn't think it that deep at all.

Whilst perfecting the art of snowball manufacturing and chucking, my gloves became very wet and soggy and cold. Every so often I would go into the house, remove my gloves and hang them over the metal fireguard, which surrounded the roaring fire.

There they would steam away until they were dry, by which time I had thawed out sufficiently enough to want to go back outside into the freezing cold.

Throughout most of my sporting life I wore two pairs of gloves. A thin pair, made from fine, white cotton, and known as 'inners'. Over these I wore a heavily padded, thick leather-covered pair. These were robust enough to absorb the thudding impact of the hard cricket ball.

Now approaching my 70th year (from which direction, I hear you ask), I am into my fourth pair of gloves. They are black, padded and covered in a thick material to give warmth and safety. I wear them when I am riding my moto on the way to the Writers Group meetings. Unlike all my previous pairs, I have to remove these to do what I have decided to do. You see, I can't write whilst wearing gloves.

Vivien Johnson

Inquisition

"Isn't it a terrible day?" The young woman said, as she sat down beside me. She ordered a black coffee. "Been shopping?" she asked.

"Yes, I've been shopping for my daughter; she's getting married next week." I was thrilled that at last Sheryl and Gordon were getting hitched. They'd been living together in my spare room for the last six-months, and I couldn't wait to get them into their own flat. I'd paid the deposit as a wedding present.

"A wedding, how exciting. Have they known each other long?" The young woman, Karen, crooked her little finger and sipped her drink delicately.

"Just over six months," I replied. I didn't see what business it was of a complete stranger, but I supposed she was only being friendly.

"Did they meet locally?"

"Oh no, they met at a fishing competition. Sheryl went along with her dad and met Gordon there; it was love at first sight," I replied. I hated fishing. I thought it was pure Nazi-style torture of defenceless creatures.

"Fishing? An unusual hobby for a girl," Karen said, pulling a face.

"Yes well, I suppose you might say that Sheryl is an unorthodox girl." Why had I told her that?

"Church wedding is it, with all the trimmings?" she asked.

"Oh, good heavens no, nothing like that, they are going to the registry office, on Tuesday, here in Hibble. A quick *'I do'*, exchange of rings, and it's all over."

"I must go now it's stopped raining, nice to have met you." The young woman got up and, once outside, merged into the crowds.

Gordon's future mother-in-law had been surprisingly open about Gordon's relationship with her daughter. Karen's pushy nature had always worked; interrogation seemed to be in her blood. As child, she'd hunted all over the house for her Christmas and birthday presents, her mother could never keep their whereabouts secret for long. She'd been a difficult child, played truant from school, shoplifted and had stolen cars. Now as an adult and with her marriage, in a kibbutz two-years before, she'd steadied down.

She had followed the woman into the café. When the waitress brought her black coffee, she'd stuck out her little finger in what she thought was a sophisticated manner. She'd turned her lip up at the coffee, she would much rather have had tea, but coffee was another of her pseudo-sophisticated ideas. This is going to be easy she thought. She had to have her fears justified, and they were. Now she knew what she had to do. She'd wrapped her coat around her and hurried from the table.

On Tuesday morning she put on a new pair of tight jeans, a short, red t-shirt, which exposed her navel stud, let her long, straight hair flow around her shoulders and tottered down the High Street on her four-inch heels. She was early and sat at the back of the room, waiting. Soon, people started to arrive and sit down. Then the registrar greeted a couple and the ceremony began.

"Does anyone know of any reason why these two people should not be married?"

Karen's big moment had arrived at last. She jumped to her feet.

"Yes I do," she screeched, "Gordon is my husband!"

Jean M. Watson

Driving Home at Night

I had stayed too long at the party and was anxious to get home. My mother would be waiting for me. In spite of my twenty-six years and a responsible job, leading a team of six historical researchers, my mother insisted on staying up to lock the door behind me. What a good job she had not accompanied me to university. She would have had to sit up for many a late night or early morning in those days.

Tonight, however, I would be home by one-o'clock probably, and the lecture would hopefully be short. Even so, I pressed the accelerator a little harder and flicked the lights onto main beam as I drove along the dark road leading to our village. The road curved up and to the left, an old barn hiding the next stretch from view.

BANG! My car stopped suddenly and I hit my head on the steering wheel. For some moments I stayed with my head down, dazed and shaky. I raised my head slowly and looked at my hands. I was gripping the wooden bar that ran across the front of my coach. I looked through the narrow window and saw Henderson, the coachman, lying over the side of his seat, his head hanging very close to the big front wheel, the big iron band smeared with blood. More blood dripped to the ground from Henderson's head.

"Oh, my goodness," I breathed and, gathering the skirts of my ball gown into a bundle, I opened the carriage door. Just in time I remembered to drop the steps to the ground, which Henderson would normally have done for me, before stumbling out of the carriage. The carriage lanterns flickered in the light breeze, but I was able to see enough to ascertain that our horses appeared to have run into a small hay-cart collapsed in the road, its wheel leaning against the axle. The horses were tossing their heads in fright, although they did not appear to have been badly hurt, the hay-cart having plenty of its load hanging down the back.

"Oh, my goodness," I said again, "whatever will Mama and Papa say about this? And what should I do now? Henderson! Wake up,

Henderson. The horses, Henderson."

Henderson did not stir, and I looked around for assistance.

Where were the watchmen when you needed them? I looked once again at the barn, and was relieved to discover that I had indeed been mistaken in thinking it to be so. The door opened, revealing, by lantern light, the tables and chairs of an hostelry.

"What be 'appening 'ere, then?" came a loud voice. "Oh, Miss 'Amilton. It be you. An' that 'Enderson. 'E do look badly. Come on, you 'orses. Shh now, shh." The stocky innkeeper, minus his apron because it was late and the inn closed, soothed the horses until they stood steadily, although still snorting and moving their heads up and down at intervals.

More lights appeared quickly in the downstairs rooms of the hostelry as someone with a commanding voice took charge. "Come along now, young lady. You had better come inside. That is a nasty bump on your head. Hey! You! See to the coachman. Take him round to the stable and have Bessie Wilson look at his head. Looks like a very nasty cut. Oh, and get Sam to see to the horses. And get that damn cart moved. It should never have been left there. Whoever left it is going to lose their position as soon as I find out who it was. Come along, Ma'am."

I stumbled towards the inn door, the gentleman's arm beneath my elbow, and in spite of my sore head, regretting the mud ruining my ball slippers.

"Come along, Ma'am." A new female voice urged me into the main room of the hostelry.

A stout woman with a white mob-cap over ginger curls helped me onto a settle where I leaned back with some relief. I did indeed feel quite dizzy.

The stout woman brought the lantern close to my face to peer at my forehead and I tried to push it away, impatient with the bright light so close to my eyes.

"It's OK, it's OK, can you open your eyes?"

"Of course I can," I thought impatiently. Slowly I raised my eyelids. The woman's ginger curls framed her round face. She held a bright torch.

"Where am I? This isn't the inn."

"What inn is that?" asked the woman. "You have been in a car accident. Do you remember it? You ran into the back of a car parked without lights. It had broken down and the driver had gone off to find help. You are in hospital now. You're going to be fine. You were lucky you were found as soon as you were, so late at night on that road. But your mother 'phoned the police when you did not turn up and there was quite a to-do to find you, hidden in that old barn. However did you get in there?"

"What barn? It happened outside an inn." I said. "The people there helped me. They were so kind.

"Well, dear, I'm sure I don't know what you are talking about. There hasn't been an inn there for nearly two hundred years …just that old ruin of a barn."

Vivien Johnson

An Encounter

He passed my car in the traffic: an azure Lycra streak, head down over the handlebars: leg muscles pumping, tight buttocks.

Lusting, I followed him into the mountains.

He stopped at the spring, removed his crash hat and drank.

He was a she!

Crest-fallen I drove past.

Vivien Johnson

The Woman

*The first time I saw her
our trolleys collided – we didn't speak.
I noticed all her brightly coloured comestibles –
packets of chips and fish fingers,
red peppers and corn on the cob.*

*The second time I saw her
she was wheeling an empty baby buggy
outside the school gates;
a small girl ran into her arms.
We smiled, didn't pass the time of day.*

*The third time I saw her
we were at the hairdresser's
heads down over basins,
junior assistants working fingers into our scalps;
we grimaced as we came up for air.*

*The fourth time I saw her
was in the estate agent's office;
she sat behind a desk
covered in papers and five phones –
she was speaking into one and waved at me.*

*The fifth time I saw her
was at a charity reception.
She was talking to my husband –
he looked embarrassed, and she turned away
before we could speak.*

Colin Hall

Boulevard Montmartre

Inspired by 'Boulevard Montmartre' by Camille Pissarro

The year is 1897.
"It's no good. All this rain is making my colours run," mumbled the artist.
"Be that as it may, my dear Camille, you have captured the sounds and atmosphere of the boulevard very well. I can almost hear the horses' clip-clopping along and the shouts of the newspaper vendors. Listen to them."
"Read all about it!
"Batley beat St. Helens in first Rugby League Challenge Cup Final!
"Oscar Wilde released from prison!
"Enid Blyton born!
"The Gold Rush starts today!
"All the half-time scores!
"Read all about it!"

..."By the way, Mr Pissarro, if I may be allowed one small criticism?"
"Why, of course, Mr Cezanne."
"You have missed off the McDonalds on the corner!"

Colin Hall

Married Bliss

Jim was sprawled on the settee in the lounge watching his favourite programme, 'Match of the Day'. This was his down-time.

The previous night he had been in his local.

The eight pints with his mates had tired him out.

Today, Sunday, he needed a rest before Monday morning's trip to sign on.

The wife was in the kitchen. He heard her ask, "What would you like for dinner my love? Chicken, beef or lamb?"

He shouted, "I'll have the chicken please."

She replied, "You're having soup, you fat bastard. I was talking to the cat!"

Vivien Johnson

The Cooper's Art

When Mr. Jenkins told her what was in the barrel, Jan was dumfounded.

The old, oak barrel had stood in the corner of the basement for as long as Jan could remember. Behind it the red-brick arch stood like the menacing halo of a wicked guardian angel. She could never work out whether it was the damp in the walls, or the smell of rotting wood that gave the area that acrid smell. When she was a young girl she had asked her mother what the barrel was doing there but her mother had never given her a satisfactory answer. Perhaps she couldn't, maybe she'd inherited it from the former owners of the house. Jan's father had been a merchant-navy captain and had drowned in a terrible accident before she was born. His ship, carrying a cargo of dynamite, had exploded. There were no survivors.

The barrel had become part of her young life, she'd tried to remove the bung and look inside but it was stuck fast. She'd hit it with the poker from the sitting room, trying to work out if it was empty.

She had no idea what an empty vessel should sound like but imagined it would be like the bass drum that drum-horses carried.

Now, thirty-years later, she thought the barrel must be rotten. Surely the woodworm had had a good feast, just like they had everywhere else in the house. For all she knew the woodworm had spread from that sinister object.

Upstairs in the kitchen, Jan made herself a cup of tea and carried it into the hall. She sat on the bottom step, leaning against the newel post of the flight leading up to the first floor. As a child it had been her favourite place. The front door was straight ahead; the light through its stained glass made colourful patterns on the beige wallpaper. How could her mother have lived with that dull stuff for all those years?

Then there was that awful hallstand dominating the passage. She remembered it covered with raincoats, like a vulture with wings outstretched ready to scoop her up. An old umbrella was still propped on one side. She opened it. A cloud of dust flew out and, as she tautened the fading cotton cover it, split into holes and the fabric dropped away, exposing the spokes. The silvering on the hallstand mirror had almost completely disappeared. She remembered her mother preening herself in front of it, patting her immaculately coiffured hair, saying, *'Father promised we shall be rich one day'*. Now, green mould could be seen through the glass.

She took her mother's address book from the telephone shelf and thumbed idly through the musty yellowed pages. Names of people from Jan's past jumped out at her. Auntie Gladys Porter, their next door neighbour. She wasn't an auntie really, just a local busy-body, whose husband ran the paper-shop on the corner of the street. Mr. Siddington the butcher: on Saturday mornings his boy used to deliver the meat by bicycle – white paper bundles, wedged like baby rabbits in their nest, in the wicker basket over his front wheel. She flicked the pages back to the beginning and one page glided gently to the floor; she followed it with her eyes and felt for it under the hallstand. It was the page headed 'C'… Cooper, barrel-maker. What on earth did her mother want with a cooper? Did he make the barrel down in the basement? Jan read on: 79, Brewery Street, Longton. Brewery Street wasn't there anymore; blocks of high-rises had been built on the site years ago.

She wanted to sell the house, but who would want to buy it with a barrel in the basement?

The estate agent she had shown round was very disparaging about the upper floors and when he saw the basement, well …words had failed him.

"What's in it Mrs Black?" he had asked.

"I don't know," she'd mumbled. He had given her a very old fashioned look.

"Then have it taken away," he'd replied.

After he had gone she returned to the basement with the kitchen step stool. Once again she tried to look inside the barrel and shone the torch over the end. She couldn't quite read the foreign words burnt into it. Well the only thing to do was to go to the pub and ask the landlord if he would tap the barrel for her.

Mr. Jenkins, the landlord of the Crown and Anchor, looked mildly surprised at the request but got his equipment together in a bucket and followed her down the street.

"Well bless my soul," he declared when he saw her problem. "What a whopper!" He carefully placed the bucket under the bunghole and inserted the metal tap, giving it a series of sharp blows with his wooden mallet; a little strong-smelling, golden, liquid seeped out before the tap was fully secured. Mr. Jenkins wiped a drop up with his fingers and held it under his nose, licked his fingers and grinned.

"That is incredible. I don't believe it! Smells and tastes like the real stuff to me."

"What stuff Mr. Jenkins?"

"Well, matured French Cognac of course," he replied.

The barrel had to be lifted out of the basement by crane, breaking the paving, the house wall and the brick wall to the street. Jan had always wondered how the barrel got into the basement; it was far too large to get through any of the existing doorways.

Now, a pile of red dust and rubble lay in the yard outside. The drayman had handed Jan a stained, smelly envelope that he'd found stuck to the bottom of the barrel.

It was addressed to her father.

She read the sheet of paper inside:

To Captain James,

One hogshead best French Cognac, in payment of a debt.

Signed,

John Smith (Merchant).

"Bottled up this will make you a rich woman," the man said, as he turned on his ignition and drove away.

Vivien Johnson

Autumn Tandem Ride

"Mavis wake up, it's Tuesday!" Eric whispered softly to the sleeping figure beside him.

"It's too early, go back to sleep," she grumbled, "last night's party exhausted me."

"Yes I know Dear, but Andy is coming for me at ten!" He walked to the window, opened it wide and filled his lungs with cold, sea air. "I'll make you a nice cup of tea, then you'll feel better. I'll start the porridge too." Mavis sank down under the covers.

Andy peddled up at exactly ten o'clock and, as Eric opened the front door of his bungalow, the acrid smell of the extinguished bonfire filled his nostrils. Last night there'd been the ritual firing of the rotten, dismantled garage. Next week it would be replaced by a smart concrete one. The burning had been a good excuse to have his three daughters, their husbands and seven grandchildren round. He loved to hear the children's whoops and 'aaahs' as the fireworks exploded into myriads of patterns and colours. Now, standing in the doorway, he could still taste the charcoaly-flavour of the sausages and baked potatoes his wife had cooked in the glowing embers.

"Hop on Eric, we'll get going straight away. Got your picnic? I know a beautiful spot where we can make ourselves comfortable in the dead bracken."

"Bye Dear," Eric turned and waved to Mavis as the two men cycled off up the hill and away from the coast.

On reaching the wood they dismounted. They pushed the tandem through the deep leaf-litter, puffing at every stride, and couldn't help breathing in the earthy, pungent smells of the disturbed, rotting vegetation. "Any Fly Agaric toadstools around here?" Eric asked. "When I was a child I used to think they were fairies' houses, where these magical beings would sit cross-legged on their bright, red roofs warming their wings in the sunshine."

"There are some on the other side of the wood," Andy replied. "There's a hedge there too, where gossamer cobwebs are often covered in dew. That really is fairyland."

After lunch of hot soup, pork pies and tomatoes the two men lay back on the dry bracken and dozed, listening to the trickle of a nearby stream. A robin serenaded them from a nearby gorse bush.

"We'll go back via the church," Andy suggested.

"Fine with me," Eric nodded his agreement. "Where you go, I go. The swallows' nests under the eaves 'll be empty now, but it's good to know they'll be back next year, with their constant whooping and twittering."

As the two friends dropped down into the town and stopped outside Eric's house, beams of yellow light shone through tightly-fastened windows; picking up the russet colours in his garden's trees and bushes.

"You'll stay for supper won't you Andy? Mavis said she'd cook roast pork and fruit crumble, as a thank you for getting me out from under her feet."

"Wonderful. My favourite!" Andy smiled in anticipation.

"Oh good! You know, I really enjoy our outings. Not only for the exercise, but you describe everything so beautifully. I'm one of the lucky ones; I can picture everything around me. It's a sad fact that so many of my friends in the Blind Association have never been able to see those things for themselves!"

Jean M. Watson

Obsessions

The sofa was plumpscious, folding itself around them. Mary and Joe sat side by side, their feet on the coffee table, a packet of crisps between them, and their hands dipping alternately into the bag and taking crisps to their mouths, while watching a murder-mystery on television.

"That's the one that did it," said Mary, pointing to a dark-haired woman in a cream suit.

"No," said Joe, "it wasn't her, it was that fellow with the scar on his face. He wanted the old man out of the way so he could have Cream-Suit for himself. Hey, you've just eaten the last crisp!"

"Have I?" said Mary in surprise. "That packet didn't last long. Hang on until the end of this. Whoever is wrong will have to get the coffee and there's those chocolate and orange biscuits in the cupboard."

The programme continued its devious way. Neither Joe nor Mary spoke again before the end of the programme, although occasionally a hand would stray towards the crisp packet as if forgetting it was empty.

"There see, I told you it was him," triumphed Joe.

"Yes, okay," grumbled Mary, "but he didn't get Cream-Suit, did he? Turned out she really, really loved the old man after all. Ah well, I guess I'll have to make the coffee. Give us a shove off this couch, will you? It is so deep and comfortable."

"Yea, once you get your behind on it, it is sheer weight that keeps you down," grinned Joe, supporting Mary's ample hips as she struggled to her feet.

"It's alright for you, you're such a skinnymalinck," she puffed as she went towards the kitchen to make the coffee and open the new packet of biscuits. "There's karaoke at the pub on Saturday. Shall we go?" She called through to Joe. There was no reply. "What's the matter? You gone deaf or something?" She asked sarcastically as she took the tray of coffee and biscuits through to the living-room.

"Just look at her." Joe's voice was reverent as he gazed at the television screen. "Isn't she gorgeous?" 'Gorgeous' was wearing a white shirt tied just below the bulging, tanned bust, with designer-tousled hair. Gorgeous, with a waistline that dissolved into not-really-there hips.

Just gorgeous. Joe was smitten. Each evening he would turn on the television for his nightly ogling at the blonde vision. When she appeared on the screen, he became deaf and blind to anything else. Once or twice Mary tried shouting *'Fire'* and banging on a saucepan with a wooden spoon. Only Mary heard it.

Then, suddenly, enough was enough. "I will fight fire with fire", thought Mary. Two days later the campaign began. Biscuits and crisps were strictly for Joe. He did not notice that Mary would eat an apple while watching television, and that he was eating a whole packet of crisps instead of half the packet that he had previously shared with Mary. Sometimes he noticed that she was not sitting beside him on the sofa. He was vaguely aware of grunts and puffing from behind the sofa, but Gorgeous would claim his attention again and he neither saw nor heard anything else for the duration of her stay on the screen.

The one thing Joe did notice, however, was that three or four times a week his dinner was not ready at the normal time and that would make him late sitting down in front of the television, but it was never so late that he missed watching Gorgeous. Had he thought to ask, Mary would have told him why his dinner was late, but he did not ask and Mary did not say.

"Mary," Joe wriggled about on the sofa, trying to get more comfortable, "Mary, my trousers have shrunk. Have you washed them all wrong?"

"No, of course not," replied Mary, settling down beside Joe. "You must be putting on weight. Look at all those crisps and biscuits you keep eating."

"No more than usual," protested Joe. "Anyway, you eat as many as I do."

"No, Joe, not any more. I used to, but I gave them up and now I eat fruit instead," answered Mary, mockingly waving an apple in front of Joe.

"Hey, that's not fair, making me eat all those crisps by myself." Joe looked at Mary reproachfully. Then he looked again. This time he really saw Mary for the first time for several weeks. He saw a slim woman in a close-fitting red dress with loose blonde hair to her shoulders, and bare, brown legs in strappy sandals.

"Well, just look at you," breathed Joe, "how did you change so much without me seeing? Was it magic?"

"No, of course not! While you were so taken up with Gorgeous on the television, I have been dieting and doing exercises at home. And I go to the gym down the road four times a week. Oh, Joe, my trainer is wonderful. He is all muscles and so fit I dream about him all the time."

Joe looked at Mary. Reaching for the remote, he turned off the television. "I don't need to watch that any more," he said, "I have my own beauty at home." Watching Mary serve his dinner he frowned. "Hey, who is this trainer-fellow you're on about? Just remember you're married to me".

"Oh, I do, I do," said Mary, "but, as I said, he is superb."

"Hmm, I see." Joe looked thoughtful for a moment. "Well, as he has done such a fabulous job on you, perhaps we had better see what he could do for me. When do we start at the gym? I am not in too bad a shape, so it won't take too long."

Joe did not see Mary's dismayed look at the idea of Joe sharing her dream sessions at the gym, but she answered gaily, "Tomorrow evening at five o'clock, so don't be late."

The following evening Joe and Mary arrived at the gym. To his amazement, Joe was weighed, his chest and waist measured and a programme, designed especially for him, was drawn up. A seemingly impossible level of training was suggested. Looking around for Mary to tell her how ridiculous it all was, Joe was amazed to see her on the running machine, apparently moving with ease, and laughing at something the young man standing beside her in a shining white vest had just said.

That was the moment Joe snapped. He had only just discovered that he had a beautiful wife – and that it was possible that he might lose her to a set of over-grown muscles in an over-white vest.

"Come on then, let's get going," he growled at his own allocated trainer. From that moment Joe was dedicated to improving his chest and abdomen, not to mention his legs. There was no question now of packets of crisps in front of the television because Joe was never in front of the television. Instead he spent his evenings at the gym, pounding and stretching, running and sweating until he was as fit and toned as Mary's wonderful trainer.

Feeling pleased with his new body and level of fitness, Joe went home for his dinner. The house was incredibly quiet and there was not the usual smell of cooking coming from the kitchen. The dining table was set, but only for one. On the empty plate in Joe's place was a note. Wondering where Mary was, Joe picked the note up and read it.

'Dear Joe,

I am leaving you for my trainer. I do not suppose you will miss me, as you have been so obsessed with your own training and personal image, that you have not known whether I have been at home or not.

How I have missed those evenings on the sofa, sharing a packet of crisps. Goodbye Joe.

Mary'.

Mary took a deep breath and, before she could change her mind, she pressed *'Send'*. It was done, sent, she was committed now. Committed to what, Mary wondered. After she had left Joe for Paul, her fitness instructor in the white, shining vest, life for a time had been exciting. She had been admired for her slim body and her shining blonde hair.

How different it had been from her life with Joe, the evenings on the sofa sharing crisps and chocolate in front of the television. That is, until Joe had fallen for Gorgeous, and she had retaliated by losing weight and going to the gym and in her turn fallen for Paul.

At first it had been fun with Paul. She had felt glamorous and it had been fun being known as Paul's girlfriend but soon she realised that Paul was obsessed with his image and, to Paul, time way from the gym was time wasted. One evening, Mary finished her routine on the exercise bike, then rested for a few moments. She looked around for Paul. He was at the weight-lifting machine. Mary walked over to him. "I'm going now. Are you coming home soon?"

"Shan't …be …long." Paul's voice was strained as he lowered the bar slowly. "I just need to do one more routine, then I'll be home."

"Okay," said Mary, "supper will be on the table."

Supper was on the table – long before Paul came home. Mary wanted to be angry, but was afraid of driving Paul away; their relationship was still so new. Then the same scenario was repeated over and over again. Paul was obsessed with his own personal image, and had no time for a life outside the gym, or for Mary, except as a reflection of his own beauty, a symbol of his success.

Mary had had enough of men and fitness. First Joe had become obsessed with getting fit after Mary had left him behind in the fitness stakes, and next Paul had shown himself to be even more fanatical. Passing the paper-shop on the way home one evening, Mary went in and defiantly bought a bar of chocolate. Tearing off the paper wrapping, she bit the bar savagely. Never had chocolate tasted so good. Never had she felt so free and in charge of her own life. Bother Joe, and bother Paul …but what to do next, she wondered? She did not want to go back to Joe; she did not want to stay with Paul. Mary walked back towards the newsagent and searched the noticeboard for a flat to rent or share.

A month later Mary moved into a small bed-sit, which she had made as comfortable as possible. She did not intend to stay there long, but for now it was her home, and only hers, until she decided what she was going to do next with her life. It was, however, quite lonely in the bed-sit, and she decided that some company would be nice. For the time being television and chocolate were her companions, the gym no longer the place where she spent her leisure-time. Programme followed programme, requiring no intellectual response from the viewer. The commercial breaks provided momentary shocks, simply by the suddenness of their appearance but even they failed to distract after a time. Opening a packet of crisps one evening, slouched on the sofa, Mary wondered whether or not the last commercial break was more or less interesting than the sit-com she was watching for at least the fourth time. Suddenly she sat up, the packet of crisps fell onto the floor.

An advert for computer dating! For Mary? Why not? It might even turn up something (or someone). Mary grabbed the evening paper, the only kind of paper to hand, and a pen. It was another half-an-hour before the ad appeared again Mary wrote the website address in the margin of the paper and turned off the television. Tearing the address from the margin of the paper, she switched on her computer. In the corner of the room the screen flashed into life and Mary opened the Internet connection. From the scrap of newspaper, she copied the address and was rewarded with a brightly-coloured page of successful dating results. This looks promising, Mary thought, and scrolled through the whole website. It invited her to enrol and to send a description of herself and of the kind of man she would like to meet.

"Well, I am blonde – with a little help," she murmured and wrote 'blonde' in the box. "Eyes?" Running to the mirror she decided they were green, and wrote that in the correct box. *Describe yourself: thin, slim, plump, fat, slightly obese, obese.* Slim, of course. No, perhaps not nowadays. Too much chocolate and no gym… *Plump.*"

"What sort of date do I want? Not slim, not in the least sporty, sense of humour etc., etc." The questionnaire completed, Mary pressed *'Send'*. There, it was done.

A few anxious days later Mary received an e-mail from the dating agency.

Should she open it?

Should she delete it?

Of course she opened it.

There was a potential date for her.

Who could it be? Would she go? Of course she would go. That was the whole point of joining the dating agency, was it not? Mary e-mailed the dating agency, asking to be put in touch with her 'match'. Tall, dark, with a sense of humour was his description. That will suit me very well, thought Mary… Hmm, he can't really be called Maximus. That's a disguise. I know, I will call myself Claudia. Here we go… She typed in Maximus' e-mail address into the computer and wrote:

Dear Maximus,

Hello, I am Claudia and the dating agency seems to think we would be a good match. Do you like watching murder mysteries on TV? Or are you very fit and take a lot of exercise?

Best wishes,

Claudia.

Five minutes later Mary got a reply.

Lummy, he is keen!

What does he say?

Dear Claudia,

Thank you for getting in touch. You sound just my kind of girl. Although I am fairly fit I do not work out any more. I had a bad experience at the gym once. Now I prefer watching murder mysteries on TV.
How would you like to meet for a drink? The Red Lion in Mafeking Street suit you?
Regards,
  Maximus

Bit of a fast worker, thought Mary, but I'll go anyway. How will I know him? I know, I'll tell him to wear a blue shirt and carry a copy of the local paper – less obvious than the Times.

I will wear a green dress and carry a large, white handbag. Friday evening would suit me.

Maximus agreed by e-mail that Friday evening would be best and thus it was arranged.

On Friday evening Mary walked into the Red Lion. She was wearing the green dress, her blonde hair loose on her shoulders. She felt that she was looking her best, which helped her to feel less nervous. The room was crowded with groups: some having a drink after work, some drinking before a meal. There were not many people on their own. A girl in a pink dress, another in red, a chap in a grey shirt, and just one in a blue shirt, holding a newspaper in his left hand as obviously as he could. That must be Maximus, thought Mary, and moved to stand in front of him. Maximus looked up.

"Mary?" he gasped.

"Joe?" asked Mary, "why are you here? You can't be…?"

"Yes, I am Maximus. So you must be Claudia."

Suddenly it was all very funny, and Joe and Mary laughed and laughed, then talked and talked as they had not for many years.

The sofa was plumpscious, folding itself around them. Mary and Joe sat side by side, their feet on the coffee table, a packet of crisps between them, their hands dipping alternately into the bag and taking crisps to their mouths, while watching a murder-mystery on television.

Vivien Johnson

Hamburg Christmas

It was minus 15° C in Hamburg; flurries of snow covered the streets in a white blanket.

My English cousin wanted to show off her new German husband. He took us sightseeing, recklessly driving through red lights. Six people squashed into a five-seater Mercedes. In the port, I stood in my nylon stockings and court shoes, gazing at the inky water: ankles blue from the icy, Siberian wind.

On Christmas Eve we celebrated with traditionally cooked carp. The fish is boiled until the flesh turns to grey jelly. The head and brains are said to be a great delicacy. Encouraged by Siegma's mother, the rest of the family watched while I nauseously refused a second helping.

Teeth chattering in the freezing house, my elderly aunt and uncle, being used to central heating set at 25°C at home in England, tried to look cheerful.

Christmas Day came, more snow had fallen in the night. It seemed to be colder than ever. My cousin's mother, my other aunt, suffered a detached retina and was carted off to hospital. Vandals broke into the car in the hospital car-park.

Christmas was different that year!

Colin Hall

The Hot Dog Stand

Inspired by the painting 'Hot Dog Stand' by Lisa Gade

Having experienced a very slow morning, in terms of hotdogs sold, the owner of the business took himself off to the Palm Readers studio, just to see if things were going to improve in the afternoon. Quite frankly, he thought, he might as well call it a day and go home if things remained the same for the rest of the day. It had been a quiet week all through. People weren't spending the same as they used to. What with the global economic downturn and a plague of obesity, nobody wanted hotdogs anymore.

The government was to blame for it all. No wonder core businesses like hotdog stands were failing. Government ministers were not showing any sign of supporting the small business in the street. No cabinet minister had bought a hotdog from him all month. At least Margaret Thatcher would eat one in the morning, on her way from number ten to the Houses of Parliament.

"A hotdog with onions and ketchup, please, my good man," she would shout from her limousine.

"Right you are, ma'am, coming up. Send your driver over for it in a minute," he would shout back.

Those were the good old days. She might have brought the mines to a halt, but she supported the small entrepreneur, and defeated the Argies.

The palm reader told him that she couldn't see much hope for the future of hotdog businesses in this area. Not until after the election and the Tories got back in. She did say, however, that he was going on a long journey. That gave him hope and an idea. He sold his stand and went on a cruise around the world which left him feeling a lot better.

Colin Hall

Snoring

You have my wife to thank for my contribution to this short story collection. Had she not developed her knack of snoring loudly, I would have still been asleep. However, always looking for ways to inspire me, she has persuaded me to leap out of bed at 3.49 a.m. and turn on my computer.

I count myself more fortunate than a lot of fellow sufferers in that I have been endowed with the ability to write. By that I mean, if I'd had the gift of a modern day Premier League soccer player, I could not start kicking a ball against the wardrobe door at this unearthly hour. So in spite of his trappings of flash cars and huge mansions, I am better off than he is.

Had I been blessed with the ability to play music, I would not be plugging my twelve-stringed strato-something or other into my mega-amp and strumming and plucking some amazingly riff in the dead of night. Despite his following of screaming teeny boppers in short skirts and bobby socks, I count myself better off than he is.

To possess the gift of being able to write short stories such as this, is a far more valuable thing to have than the gift of being a brain surgeon: regardless of his being surrounded by pretty nurses and driving his Porsche Turbo Bimbo-Pulling-machine out of the hospital car park. Where would he find a brain to dissect at this time of the morning? I consider myself better off than he is too.

So, poised as I am, with my fingers hovering over the keyboard, wondering what to write about, I open a web-browser and start searching for some inspiration.

Shall I write about my early life? Here is a picture of me at primary school in the fifties. Shall I recount my experiences of being a milk-monitor and having to chip the ice off the tops of the third-of-a-pint bottles?

I could come up with a tale of Manchester in the sixties, where I started work. Let's look at some images of the old streets around

Piccadilly and Ancoats. Oh look, I remember that building and those old, red, trolley buses.

What about something about football? Manchester City's website is full of facts and figures. In 1961, Denis Law scored six goals in a cup-tie against Luton Town. Unfortunately, the game was abandoned because of the weather and Luton won the replay. Later he went to play in Italy and on his return to the UK played for United. I knew all that of course, but it is still good to read about it.

This is fascinating stuff.

A voice from the dark bedroom, "Hello Colin, what time is it?"

Glancing down to the bottom right hand corner of my screen, "Err, eight-o'clock, darling."

"All right, I'm getting up."

Yes, to be gifted with the ability to write short stories must be a source of envy to a lot of people, especially those whose wife snores.

Vivien Johnson

A Surprise Trip

From my seat the Pullman, as the train pulled out of Victoria station, I watched an empty cigarette packet blow along the platform.

Neil sat opposite me with that silly grin he had, the one I had put up with for all those years. Now, the pretty, shaded, table light between us showed up his double-chins. If only he'd stayed an Adonis would I still love him? Perhaps not with the original passion but with a gentler love. I suppose I did still love him, in my way; after all, we'd been married for forty-years. This anniversary trip had been a complete surprise. I thought we were going to one of those boring, shareholders' meetings in town. Neil usually spent most of his mornings on our computer studying the stock market.

We decided to go by train, it was easier. "Parking has become so difficult," he'd said.

"We'd probably have to leave the car miles away from our destination."

Now, I heard the 1930's engine puffing away, as the carriage rocked into a gentle rhythm. We passed through suburbs of Victorian terraces and, after Purley, we chugged into the Surrey countryside. Occasionally we stopped to let a fast diesel train rattle past. The whistle blew and we were off again. I could see billows of acrid smoke floating past the carriage window, reminding me of childhood journeys, when my mother had said, *'Always sit with your back to the engine Alison, then you won't get smuts in your eyes'.* Of course I never took any notice; I always wanted to see where I was going.

"You enjoying yourself?" Neil asked. He didn't hear my answer, as the waiter came to take our order for lunch. "No soup, thank you," Neil looked up at the man, pencil poised over his order book. "Just the main course please, poached salmon, peas and boiled potatoes for two, thank you." Neil turned to me, "That all right for you dear? Oh yes and a half bottle of champagne."

"I would really have liked the curry," I'd said. However, as usual,

Neil ordered for both of us; he thought that spicy food was bad for the digestion and to drink more than one glass of alcohol, or to get a little tipsy, was a sin. I bet he orders prunes and custard for the sweet course, I thought. I shivered and snuggled deeper into my coat.

I sat back in my seat and gazed out of the window at the passing green fields. My mind wandered. A pity Brighton has a shingle beach... Fancy Neil arranging this anniversary surprise, he usually forgot important dates. I wondered what life would have been like if I had married Joe.

I'd met Joe in the foyer of the Regent Street Poly all those years ago. My collection of photographs had fallen out of their folder and had skidded like ice-skaters over the polished marble floor. I was squatting down to retrieve them when Joe's face appeared in front of mine. "Can I help?" he asked, a wicked twinkle in his deep blue eyes.

"Oh thanks," I replied. "I can manage." He took no notice and gathered my pictures together, took the folder from my hand and popped the pictures into it. "You can probably guess which course I'm on," I blurted out. I couldn't help myself giving a cheeky grin.

"What a coincidence! I'm on the I.B.P. photographic theory course, I failed it last year but I passed the practical, so here I am having another go... Fancy a coffee?"

We climbed the stairs to the canteen, sat at a plastic-covered table and chatted. We had both come to London to train. The difference was that I was living comfortably with my aunt Bess in Barnet and commuted on the Northern Line every day, while Joe was living in a Y.M.C.A. hostel in Walthamstow, until he could find a cheap room somewhere.

Over the weeks we fell deeply in love. One day he asked me out for a meal. Of course I accepted but wondered how he'd managed to raise enough money to pay for it.

We met after class; he held my hand as we ran down the road to the Oxford Circus tube station. He bought the tickets, so I had no idea where we were going, except that we boarded a south-bound train. We changed trains at Charing cross and alighted at Clapham Common and kissed and kissed as we walked towards the trees and grass.

"This is home," he said proudly, stopping at an ancient, parked, Ford Popular. He opened the back door and got out a cardboard box, which he set up-side-down on the grass. Then he unhitched the two front seats from their mountings and put them on opposite sides of the box. Next, he spread a paper table cloth over the box and laid two places. "Just a minute," he said, "sit down and make yourself comfortable, I'll be back in a jiff."

He retraced our steps, running towards the station. A few minutes later he hurried back with two newspaper parcels. "I'm afraid I could only afford hake," he said, as he unwrapped the fish and chips and placed an opened parcel in front of me. Before he sat down he put a fish-paste jar filled with daises in the centre of the makeshift table. The sun glowed orange and pink clouds scudded across the sky. As dusk came on, Joe lit a nightlight. "I always have these," he said as he took my hand, suddenly serious. "I love you so much. When we qualify will you marry me?" He separated my fingers and placed a twisted grass ring on the third finger of my left hand.

"Of course I will," I replied. "I love you too."

We kissed and climbed into the back of the car...

In the middle of the night, three months later, while Joe was asleep, a heavy truck crashed into the old Ford, and he was killed.

I cried for weeks. I was so lonely.

So, when Neil came along he helped to take my mind off Joe. A little while later when he asked me to marry him, saying that he had a good job, a house and an E-Type Jag, I said yes ...on the rebound I suppose.

I still have that grass ring and always wear it in a silver locket. It's my secret, I have never told Neil about Joe, the boy I still love.

Jean M. Watson

The Photograph

Ellen, totally unaware of the market-day bustle around her, gazed into the window of the junk shop. Dusty sofas and scratched tables, mock Japanese vases and strings of amber beads had been thrown together as they arrived in the shop. No longer wanted in someone's home, it seemed as if they could never be wanted again anywhere.

"Just like me," thought Ellen, pushing her hands deeper into jacket pockets and hunching her shoulders defensively. "I was beautiful once and loved so much – for that one summer."

For a while she gazed unseeingly into the window. Before her, ash trees swayed in the breeze as she ran laughing towards the photographer. He pressed the shutter repeatedly, securing the image of her long hair flying in the breeze, her skirts clinging to her thighs and flaring out behind her. As she ran closer, the pictures blurred and he stopped his work, or his 'great opus' as he later called it. Still moving joyously, Ellen ran into his arms. The impact of her body knocked him backwards, and they staggered some paces together, then fell to the grass.

"Hey, mind the camera," the photographer complained, pushing it carefully to one side.

"Oh, Anton," said Ellen, "it'll be alright."

"I am sure I have the perfect picture among that lot. Pictures of you cannot fail to be anything but magnificent. You are so beautiful." He stroked her suntanned arm as she turned to lean back into his chest. She felt secure there in the meadow with Anton.

The photographs Anton took that afternoon yielded a picture of such youth and innocence that it became a symbol of that summer, the last before the world was plunged into terror and destruction for six long years. The picture was reproduced in newspapers and magazines, and framed prints hung in many a drawing room. Sadly, Anton did not make the fortune from it he thought he deserved, although any photograph by Anton in later years was heralded and feted by critics everywhere.

Now Anton was dead, but Ellen had never forgotten him, even though he had forgotten her. Slowly, she came back to the present and the meadow disappeared behind the glass window of the junk shop. Ellen blinked and refocused her eyes. There, amidst the grime of the junk shop, propped against a dirty jug, was her picture, the frame grubby and dull, but the joy of the day shone through the smeared glass. "Yes, I was loved once," she said aloud, "One summer".

Vivien Johnson

Comfort

We lay on the bed. I caressed his bristly chin and looked into his brown eyes.

"I love you," I said.

He closed his eyes and slept; my arms around him.

At seven the alarm rang.

He woke and pulled away from my embrace, ran to the door and barked.

Colin Hall

Something Uninteresting

I saw something completely uninteresting yesterday. It was so uninteresting that I thought I should write about it. Have you noticed how writers write about interesting things? Rather, what they find interesting or what they think those who read their stuff might find interesting.

Well I thought that if I wrote about something that I didn't think was interesting and I didn't think that anybody else would find it of any interest, it would be a breakthrough in modern literature: something completely different from the ordinary run of the mill, interesting garbage, which is flooding the market.

I know that people are different from one another and each finds something different to interest them. However, there are some things around that are of no interest to anybody. I think I have discovered something that no-one on this earth would find the slightest bit interesting. I also think that if I wrote about it, not one person would think it of interest to them.

My question is this …should I write about it?

Vivien Johnson

My Friend

At nine years old we climbed the pine tree and stared into the turret room, sneaked apples and soft fruit from under the gardener's nose, played tennis badly – hitting balls over the fence and smoked Woodbines in the garage loft.

At nineteen we met again.

He called at my house; embarrassed strangers in an adult world.

Vivien Johnson

Opera and the Secret Service

It was a Monday morning; dad had been home for the weekend.

He had to return to London where he had a room.

He said his work was of National Importance. I thought he was a spy because he never talked about it.

At four a.m. I saw him onto his train, then realised he had forgotten his breakfast sandwiches.

Later a policeman knocked on the door. He said that Dad had had an accident at work.

Had he been shot?

No, he'd been portering in Covent Garden and a fork-lift truck had run over him.

Gail Tucker

Knowing

A fearful known, unknown birth.
An unknown known, fearful death.
Falling in love, a willing leap into the unknown.
Filing for divorce a plunge to regain a better known.
Spring is harbinger of summer, each well known,
a temporary state.

Vivien Johnson

The Fall

Because of the fall, two years ago, my legs are now partially paralysed and I can no longer show-jump.

The day had arrived at last and the lorry loaded for the long journey from Yorkshire to Hickstead. Solo Tiger and I had trained all year for the qualifier, which would get us to The Horse of the Year Show. Of course I had been to the H.O.Y.S. but years before, in a pony-club display and also on the team in the mounted games.

Today was different; we would be competing against senior, international riders in the main ring.

Daniel my groom came with us in the lorry; it was O.K. though, there were two bunks. We took Domino, my childhood pony, now aged thirty-two, for company for Solo Tiger, who was always happier travelling with a friend.

The Hickstead atmosphere was fantastic: as I walked the course the crowd buzzed with anticipation. I knew that the ring was larger than any I had jumped in before but this was huge and the fences enormous. I knew they would be, of course, but the bright paint made them look bigger than they actually were.

Anyway, we started our round. Number one was a stone wall with a rustic pole over, number two, a blue and white parallel bar and three, an upright of red and white planks. Well, everyone knows what that ring looks like, so I won't bore you with the others. Solo was jumping out of his skin until we came to the double of water ditches. He backed off a bit as he saw a reflection in the first ditch. I spurred him on and he stood off a little too early, lost impulsion, landed short between the fences and slid into the second ditch: catapulting me over his head and through the rails.

I landed heavily on my back.

I remember the faces of the crowd rushing past and a sort of moaning noise that must have been me!

Then everything went black.

However, I haven't given up with the horses.

I'm teaching able-bodied students to jump and Daniel helps; he moves the stands, poles and fillers…

Oh didn't I say? He's been wonderful, such a help with everything. We are now living together and hope to get married in the spring. That's by-the-by.

I've bought an experienced dressage-horse who is teaching me.

We train hard, five days a week.

On Saturdays Daniel takes him for a long hack over the moors. On Sundays he is turned-out. We have been lucky enough to be short-listed for the next Para Olympics dressage team.

So watch this space!

Colin Hall

Water Lilies

Inspired by the painting 'Water lilies' by Monet

"Isn´t it about time you cleared that pond out? Those water lilies are starving the fish of any daylight!" bellowed Mrs Monet: not so much a question as an order.

Claude heard it more like, "You will clear that pond out!"

Since he had taken up his new hobby of splashing paint on canvas, his previous pastime of keeping the garden up to scratch had gone by the board. He needed to find things to do outside the house, well out of sight from his wife. She was always looking for jobs to keep him busy and it wasn´t in his nature to do as he was told.

Not that he was any different from any other man, but our Claude thought he had hit on a good idea. Something he was good at and which brought him friends from all over France, namely, 'Impressionism'.

So he got an idea. Instead of clearing out the lilies, why not paint them? He had recently given in to his wife´s constant nagging about not taking her anywhere. So he took her to Venice and London and Paris, only to leave her in a cafe and go and sit with his easel and brushes and paint the local scenes. She was quite happy sitting there doing her tapestries.

The pond never did get cleared out and old man Monet continued to paint the water lilies well into his eighties.

Colin Hall

The Zip

The awning zip unzipped with that zipping sound so familiar on the campsite.

She stood, provocatively holding her wine glass in her raised right hand.

From somewhere behind her there shone a light.

Whatever it was she was wearing wasn't very thick.

The pessimist in him saw that her wine glass was half-empty.

The optimist saw that her nightdress was half-full.

He zipped the zip closed with that identical zipping sound, trapping those familiar guilt-feelings outside.

He thought smugly to himself, "These zips are guaranteed for ten years. I should be all right."

Vivien Johnson

An Act of Kindness

Robert entered the smoke-filled bar. He'd been wandering around the village weekly-market, inspecting the bright array of Mediterranean fruit and vegetables, thinking how his wife, Mildred, had she lived, would have loved to cook them. As it was, an unfortunate road crash in England had taken her and he'd come to Spain to try to make a new beginning. He shook himself, enough of these melancholy thoughts. He was now in great need of a coffee before his walk home through the campo.

He entered the only bar in his village and was immediately convulsed with a bout of coughing. He could hardly see across the room through the thick, smoky fumes of cigarettes and cigars favoured by locals. He wondered how working men, retired to the hostelry for breakfast and brandy or two, could tolerate such an atmosphere at ten-o'clock in the morning.

His thoughts were interrupted by a strong blast of air blowing across his face; his coughing stopped almost immediately. A fellow sufferer had switched on the fan! As the smoke cleared he could see more of his surroundings …plain Formica-topped tables and stick-backed chairs. Posters advertising bullfights past and future plastered the walls; not at home with this different culture, he shuddered. He wanted to leave but where else could he find a drink? Another thing struck him, the babble of voices he'd heard from the street, had ceased; now there wasn't a sound. He studied the silent men around him, no longer swigging brandy and tucking into half-eaten bocadillos. One further fact occurred to him about this place, there were no women present. He felt uncomfortable, as a dozen pairs of eyes followed him to the bar. He decided not to buy a coffee but instead, as he had no Spanish, he pointed to order a bottle of water. He'd only been in Spain a couple of months, the language was still an anathema to him. The barman frowned, grabbed Robert's euro and threw it into the open till. Clutching his water, Robert strode out into the sunny market square.

The loud clatter of the stallholders made him feel better; the combined smells of ripe fruit and vegetables laid out in the warm, summer air were a tonic to his senses. He bought locally-grown tomatoes, lettuce and oranges for his lunch and looked about him. A little disorientated, he couldn't remember which street the pharmacy was in, even though the village had only eight streets. He took the prescription out of his pocket and stared at it. A feeling of hopelessness engulfed him. He was an Englishman in Spain, only able to say *por favor* and *gracias*. He wasn't sure that he was going to stay in this gobble-de-gook country, where the language seemed to be incomprehensible and the habits very foreign. He thought perhaps it was a mistake moving to an isolated village. He probably should have gone to the coast, where more people spoke English.

He felt a tug at his sleeve, he couldn't see anyone. He ran his fingers over his trouser pocket, fearing that he was being pick-pocketed but his wallet was still there. Then, looking down, he saw an elderly lady beside him, dressed in black from head to foot and carrying a sleeping, tan puppy under one arm.

¿Señor, farmacia? Smiling, she took him by the arm and led him up the street, her stick tap-tapping on the cobbles. She jerked his sleeve outside the shop, smiled, waved, turned and retraced her faltering steps back to the square.

He knew now, that there were kind, welcoming, people around and perhaps he would like living here after all. He decided to book up for some Spanish lessons when he got home.

Vivien Johnson

Valentine's Day

It had been six years since she first sat on this bench in Weston Park with Alex, when they had promised to love each other for ever.

At sixteen their emotions had been so strong that they couldn't ignore them. Arms around each other, they kissed. Not the sort of kisses that either of them had experienced before, but the sort of kisses Sharon had only heard about... Tongues!

To her surprise it was so natural.

Alex had got out his penknife and started to carve a heart on the back rail of the bench.

"No Alex, you mustn't, you'll get into trouble."

"I don't care, it'll be worth it," Alex replied.

Soon a slender arrow thrust through the heart, with their initials underneath.

This was to be their special place.

"I've got something terrible to tell you," Alex said one day, choking on his words. "My dad's got promotion, to manage a branch of the Insurance Company in Sydney. We're leaving for Australia next month!"

Sharon clung to him. "You can't go," she wailed. "What am I going to do without you?"

"I shall always love you Sharon, remember that. We'll send e-mails every day!"

The month rushed past. Sharon's mum and dad noticed that she was moody: not eating, and slamming doors. "What's the matter Love?" Mum had asked several times.

"Don't worry Mum she's only got growing pains, that's all, I expect." However, her dad was worried.

The wrought-iron park gates had had an air of foreboding on that last day.

"Let's walk around the pond," Alex said, "and then go to our seat."

Everything was a blur through Sharon's waterfall of tears. Sitting on the bench together she soaked the front of his shirt. He sobbed silently into her hair.

"I've made something for you," he said, gently wiping her eyes with the ball of his thumb. "Give me your hand." He slipped a carved ring on the third finger of her right hand. "We shall never forget each other, shall we?"

"It's beautiful, thank you, I'll wear it for ever." Sharon burst into tears again. "I haven't anything for you Alex but I'll come here every year on the fourteenth of February." She took his right hand and stroked the carved heart with his fingertips.

Over the years, the correspondence had dwindled to Christmas and birthday cards. Sharon put the ring away in her drawer, wrapped in red silk, only wearing it on her annual pilgrimage to the park.

She was moving to another town so this was the last time. She kissed the tips of her fingers, ran them over the heart and down the arrow on the bench back.

"Goodbye my darling. I will never forget you," she said out loud.

"I'll make sure of that." A voice boomed out from beside her; she hadn't noticed the approaching figure.

He had changed but there was no doubt who it was.

He held her hands and removed the wooden ring from her right hand, gently replacing it on the third finger of her left.

"Will you marry me?" he asked.

Gail Tucker

Impatience

The clock ticks, the brain itches,
papers flick, heads bend.
My heart beats.
Be still my beating heart,
a friend.

Each in his world seeks resolution,
a friend.

Beyond the bars distraction beckons;
a sniff, a sigh, easy digression.
My heart beats,
my eyes flick,
reality bends, the brain itches,
the clock ticks.

Vivien Johnson

Old Faithfuls

They were comfortable you see. I know I'd had them for a very long time but was that any excuse to chuck them into the basura without even asking? I was fond of the old-fashioned beige-plaid fabric although, admittedly, the red stripe had faded and the linings had become a little lumpy. My feet were used to them; my corns had burrowed their way into the material's worn recesses. My left big-toe nail, upturned, had drilled an adequate niche through the front. Of course the left back was broken down, but who cared? I didn't.

"You'll break your neck in those old things one day." Prue, the wife, often said.

"No, I won't," I always replied. "There's still some wear left in them."

"It isn't as though you couldn't afford a new pair," she retorted. "I give up...!"

After every such conversation she left the room slamming the door behind her.

Settled back in my armchair earlier, legs resting on the coffee table, I'd been watching TV. The advertisements came on, so I turned off the sound and contemplated my snug feet.

The right slipper looked comparatively unworn compared with the left one. I had the habit of rubbing my itchy left foot on my right leg; it happened when the heating came on. Only the previous night we had rowed about it again.

She often sneaked the radiators on when I wasn't concentrating but I knew... my foot told me everything. She said she did it because she was cold.

"You can't deny it. Turn them off and wear more sweaters."

"I thought you wanted me to look nice." Her face puckered as if about to cry.

I pretended to be immersed in my newspaper.

She handed me my coffee and a biscuit.

I couldn't let it go at that. A cup of coffee and chocky bics didn't get round me.

"Do you pay the oil bills? No, I do!" I continued.

"We've got plenty of money in the bank, so surely our comfort is important?" Her lips quivered.

"That money is staying there for a rainy day. Conversation over." I'd said.

I had thought that was the end of the matter; I was mistaken. Today, when I came in from the garden, I discovered that she had walked down to the bins with my slippers and a brand new pair resided where my old ones had been.

"Where are my b....... slippers?" I yelled. "I want my old ones, not these characterless things!"

In truth, I thought they looked rather smart but I wasn't going to admit it.

They were comfortable too.

I won't bore you with the details but I didn't speak to her for a week.

Imagine my surprise when we went to the supermarket ten days later and sitting there, outside, was my right-slipper on the foot of a one-legged beggar.

I wanted to ask for it back but the other one was nowhere to be seen. So I pretended not to notice.

Deborah Grant

Not Fade Away

It is November 2008 and I'm stuck here with nothing better to do than read The Daily Mail. I should not have been too surprised to see another article reporting on the death of a famous, sixties rock-star who reportedly drowned while under the influence of drink and drugs. The star's death was originally ruled 'misadventure' but, given the way he lived his life at the time, it could have been an accident, suicide or even murder. His fame and the circumstances surrounding his death have always fascinated speculators and there have been plenty of salacious stories over the years.

Now I read that a new witness has decided the time is right to disclose that it was she who actually found the star dead at the bottom of his swimming pool after a squabble with a builder. The article says that gaps in the Police account and their lack of persistence in pursuing several witnesses has made this new version of events plausible. The nurse putting forward the new account was the girlfriend of the band's tour manager, so I'll admit she does have some credibility.

A brief laugh at the audacity of her claim didn't stop the churning in my stomach and the shortening of my breath. No amount of time stops those malign thoughts and visions from going round and round in my head. Nothing is worse than losing your own child and nothing fades the memory of seeing my promising son going downhill.

When I first tried to stop him ruining his life, I came across plenty of debauched people preying on naïve souls, too young to know where their habit was leading. No amount of encouragement could lift him out of the most pitiful of situations, although he did give us a couple of brittle shards of hope when he attempted cold turkey and rehab. I can't describe the progressively worse desolation that followed each failed attempt to bring him back.

Later, less than six months after I found out that he was dealing hard drugs, he suffered a turbulent death and my life was effectively over.

This tragedy was in violent contrast to the earlier, golden times experienced by the two handsome boys from the Cotswolds. The middle-class prep-school boy latched onto the working-class 'street cred' of the charismatic scholarship boy. Later on, the days of one riding on the other's coat tails were reversed dramatically when one became a member of one the most famous rock bands of all time and the other became his drug dealer. But before that, our proud family were full of hope for my special boy's future.

What I haven't said is that I didn't feel entirely blameless – although I was a drinker myself, I fatally didn't recognise the early signs of addiction in my son's case – but there is someone else I blamed more.

So as I sit here in a stinking nursing home as an increasingly debilitated wheelchair prisoner, a complete non-person, I'm going to set the record straight and tell you what really happened.

A few months after my son died, out of pity, the rock star gave me a job cleaning at his mansion in Sussex, where I was one of an army of people keeping his increasingly erratic show on the road. I could see that the recreational drugs had deteriorated into something more sordid since he had been thrown out of the band. The wild parties continued but the hangers-on became less famous and the girls were hookers and not the beautiful starlets or Playboy Bunnies of better times. The whole atmosphere was one of desperation and dependency, rather than unfettered hedonism.

By the time my son was found dead, I should have had plenty of time to get used to the idea that he had been at risk, but no mother wants to believe the worst of their child. I've never said anything before because I didn't want to be considered bitter or unhinged, but I held that fading rock star completely responsible for my son's death.

So it actually happened that, one breezy summer's day, when the formerly beautiful star was looking pallid, edgy and wobbly on his feet – high as a kite as usual – I heard him arguing with the builder, who appeared to be just as stoned. Then, in an incredible moment of clarity, I saw an opportunity. It was easy for me; I was totally invisible as usual. So while he was briefly alone at the poolside, I tipped some soapy water around the edge nearest him. No-one saw me with my mop and bucket and after a few of the longest seconds of my life, he slipped and fell into the pool. I didn't hang around to see whether he got out again, I disappeared as inconspicuously as I had arrived.

I know that nowadays the Police are more methodical and have lots of technology, but in 1969 they couldn't have been more inept. Despite the high profile nature of the tragedy, they didn't even interview all the likely witnesses at the mansion on that day.

The question is, will they find me now that it really doesn't matter? Could jail possibly be any worse than this?

Colin Hall

That Day Long Ago

Inspired by the painting 'Bellagio Promenade' by Howard Behrens

We met here.

It was just after the last war. Everything was getting back to normal after the upheavals of the last few years.

Winston was our hero, but we had all lost someone we knew.

It was a time of victory and yet not many of us rejoiced. There was too much sadness.

On the Sunday morning, I came out of the 'bed-and-breakfast' and strolled along the front.

It was a warm, sunny day and the seagulls were making the most of it: soaring and diving, bothering the holiday makers, frightening the little children and messing the benches and promenade.

I strode out, getting some fresh sea air into my lungs, expelling the smoke from my customary post-breakfast cigarette. My eyes were focused on the far end of the promenade, with its tea-rooms and the promise of company – someone to share my experiences with: possibly start a friendship that would last.

I was slightly excited by the prospect of meeting somebody, perhaps a celebrity, a big name or even a nobody who might have an interesting story to tell.

I had not noticed the female form heading towards me. Not until we almost bumped into each other.

We were mutually embarrased by the unexpectedness of our near collision.

We offered apologies to each other. After the exchange of pardons we were soon sipping tea and eating cake together.

After our marriage the following year, we lived and loved in a riverside cottage. I still hold, in my memory, that day we met, sixty-years ago. I thought about it the other day as she was laid to rest.

Vivien Johnson

The Birthday Tea

"How about asking Edwin and Amanda over for a birthday tea tomorrow?" I asked, as John finished his lunch.

"Good idea! I'll go outside and do a bit of tidying up before the frost comes down. Edwin's garden always looks so immaculate, no matter what time of year it is."

"I'll make a Victoria sandwich with a chocolate filling. That's Edwin's favourite isn't it?" I said, pushing open the kitchen door.

I knew the recipe by heart. Two eggs, their weight in butter, sugar and flour and a little warm water. Freshly labelled ingredients shone out at me; everything easily to hand. In a couple of minutes the mixture was ready. I scooped it into tins and feeling rather pleased with myself I popped them into the oven. I could hear John raking leaves and knew that I'd have at least half-an-hour to put my feet up while the cakes cooked. He always got tetchy if he found me resting during the day. Since his retirement from the bank, his favourite saying was something about the devil and idle hands... Anyway, I never paid much attention except that I liked him to feel that I was busy, even when he wasn't looking.

At the tea party we scoffed our way through cucumber sandwiches and scones; Edwin managed to get strawberry jam and cream all over his fingers and face, and everyone laughed. Having hidden the cake in the kitchen I made the GRAND ENTRANCE, candles blazing over the chocolate icing. Edwin ceremoniously cut it, while John and I sang the birthday song. Amanda hid her face behind her napkin.

"I know you like chocolate," I said. I couldn't help noticing the embarrassed look he gave his wife. As he mouthed,

"How can I tell her that my birthday is not till next month?"

I pretended not to notice. John was bumbling on about polishing the car, or some such equally boring subject. Men do have the strangest idea of what makes interesting conversation, don't they?

"Well Edwin, you must be the first to taste it," I continued, and ignoring everyone else put an over-sized slice on his plate. I had to admit I was feeling hurt that there had been no oohs and aahs from the birthday boy. I'd made a real effort with the cake decoration. Garlands of cream, coloured flowers intertwined around the six, blue candles, one for every ten-years of Edwin's life. "Is it all right?" All eyes expectantly fixed on Edwin's face, he took a huge bite and after a moments chewing, grimaced, spluttered and rushed to the bathroom; closely followed by his worried looking wife. I couldn't stop laughing. John looked at me with a puzzled expression.

"Shouldn't we go and help?" He asked. "Call the ambulance or something?"

"No, it serves him right! I purposely used salt instead of sugar. I've been waiting a long time, to pay him back for propositioning me at last year's Christmas party."

Gail Tucker

Parched Cures

From an apothecary chest
I can offer balm –
Sweet almond oil,
Unguents,
Emollients,
A calamine lotion
but no rain to bathe the cracked earth.

Avner Kornblum

When Budapest Became Istanbul

One January, Vera and Maurice Gresham, known to their family, friends and acquaintances as Verra Grouchy and Maur Grouchy, decided to take a week's break in Budapest. Vera spent some two hours on the Internet looking at places to visit, suitable hotels and other items of interest.

"It is an extraordinary city," she told Maurice, "and well worth a visit."

Then Maurice took her place at the computer to organise flights. It was so easy. He looked up 'Cheap Flights' and there they were, a whole list of options. He carefully chose the dates, filled out the several panels of required information, added his credit card details and awaited the result.

"We are sorry," appeared on the computer, "but we only accept American credit cards. Please insert your American card details."

"To hell with you!" snarled Maur Grouchy, "and to hell with Budapest!"

A brief discussion with Vera and a much longer session at the Internet decided them on Istanbul instead. It was a very good decision.

Their flight was uneventful and dull, mainly spending six hours in the gigantic, uninspiring airport at Rome being bored out of their wits and shifting from one hard seat to another, interrupted by going for walks along never-ending corridors in order to get their bums back into shape.

From Rome to Istanbul they flew in an old, smaller, tatty plane, much more comfortable in spite of the creaking cardboard sound of the backrests. Arriving at Ataturk Airport at 01.20 they had to buy Turkish visas before the passport officials would let them through… "Bye-bye thirty Euros," growled Maur.

They finally emerged out of airportlandia and got a whiff of fresh, icy-cold air and lots of snow after nearly fourteen hours. "The Internet told us it would be cold but didn't tell us there would be snow!" muttered Maur. The taxi-driver had to wait for another passenger from France, then the trip to the hotel was interrupted by several stops to clear ice off the windscreen. They eventually got there at 3.00am.

A pleasant man at Reception hurried through the formalities then a pleasant young man escorted them to a warm, pleasant suite. At last the Grouchy's washed away what remained of their tired grumpiness in gratifyingly hot baths. The cheerful mood was spoilt a little when they looked out, expecting to see a city of turrets and domes. Instead, the windows opened onto an ugly building site. Nevertheless, they pampered themselves with chicken sandwiches and wine, which Vera had smuggled in, in her suitcase, and they finally got to bed close to 6am.

They woke at 10.30, the exact minute when the breakfast area closed, but the charm of their reception had not yet worn off, so Maurice and Vera dressed and went down to Reception. There, a friendly young woman had no difficulty placing them in a magnificent suite with its own lounge.

"But," growled Mr Grouchy, "it has only a shower."

"Indeed," snapped Vera, "And it also has a balcony."

On the balcony a plant-pot full of flowers attracted a family of russet-coloured doves, enchanting Vera and Maurice.

From this vantage-point they enjoyed a spectacular view of a section of the city. Going out for lunch, they virtually skated down the street on snow turned to ice. Having expected cold but not snow, Vera's smart boots were warm – but soon also very wet so her feet grew cold and she decided to line them with plastic bags. Thus armed (or footed) they visited the Galata Bridge to view the masses of wonderful ferries and boats, and enjoyed an excellent meal there for two, for five Euros.

Interestingly, the city had wrought such magic upon them in the few hours they had been there that, despite the discomfort the plastic bags held for Vera, they took the whole inconvenience in good spirit. They agreed that when they encountered a shoe-store she would buy water-proof boots with the money they had saved by not being able to do many of the things they would have done had they not been snow-and-ice-bound.

Vera e-mailed her daughter.

*"Having changed to a much, much nicer room, the snow on the balcony above our room melted, and water dripped in **through the central chandelier**. Oh my goodness, how your father went on, at the Reception Desk! It poured in to such an extent that we had to put the waste-bin below to catch the water. We were asked to move to another room because of the danger of the water dripping onto the electric wires. This time they gave us – guess what – the best room in the hotel – the Honeymoon Suite! By the way, the Honeymoon Suite is called 'Topkapi Palace' because it is a miniature of the Sultan's suite up the road – everything in red plush velvet, golden sequin curtains, crystal chandelier drops, etc – Oh, and a **huge** bed."*

Vera still preferred the rained-out room, which was decorated in black and silver, and had a separate lounge where Maurice could grumble into the computer while she slept. Honeymoon couple indeed.

Later that night even Maur Grouchy was smiling. "We've just had a superb dinner in the hotel restaurant on the sixth floor with windows covering about a 300-degree view of Istanbul, European and Asian," wrote his wife.

Maurice and Vera had walked to Topkapi Palace earlier, so they recognised the room. Afterwards, they walked to the Spice Market. It was very close to their hotel and full of an amazing variety of things quite apart from the many stalls featuring huge piles of spices. They even discovered a speciality called 'Viagra -5 Turkish Delights' in the crowded *souk*.

Their final day in Istanbul was their best in every way. It started with the sun shining and the temperature being acceptably warm – very different from the previous days.

After another excellent breakfast they walked several miles to visit the other – still European – side of the Bosphorus. This time they crossed the Galata Bridge, missing out the delightful restaurants on the lower level. Reluctantly, they climbed the many, many stairs that nobody had told them about, to reach the Galata Tower. From the top of the Tower one can see the whole of Istanbul, but Maurice and Vera decided to take the scriptwriter's word for it.

The best activities of the day, and perhaps of their whole stay, came in the next couple of hours. From the Tower they walked to the famous and recently bombed Neve Shalom Synagogue, then travelled by Metro (the equivalent of London's Tube but clean), then by bus (wonderful views of the places they hadn't time to visit) and then by Tramvay to the Blue Mosque. *("Note: it's Tramvay, NOT Tramway,"* wrote Vera in her next e-mail.) This was near their hotel, so they could walk the final stage of their tour. In the midst of their peering from left to right so as to see as much as possible of this wonderful ancient city, they had time to observe that the trams in Istanbul are like two-carriage to four-carriage Tube trains.

Vera particularly wanted to go into the Blue Mosque, the exterior of which they had visited the previous day. However, she was distracted by a fashion shop and some sights to photograph, so they arrived at the mosque as the janitors shut the doors in their faces.

Remarkably, Maurice remained angelic and gave no hint of the Mr Grouchy lurking within.

Throughout their stay Vera was captivated by the diminutive shoe-shine man near the hotel.

Each day she had her shoes shined there, mainly to have an excuse for giving him money. He in turn had no objection to polishing her shoes three times, but he certainly recoiled from having his photograph taken.

The Greshams also managed a cruise on the Bosphorus around Istanbul. They were too cold to take the six-hour return trip all the way to the Black Sea and the Russian border.

They were amazed at the variety and vast numbers of birds, the many cats, all well-behaved, even in close proximity to birds, and the scarcity of dogs. Above all, though, wherever they went they were overwhelmed by the lovely warm, friendly Turkish people including all the staff at the hotel and the shops they visited.

Although they didn't see the Istanbul of touristic fame, they saw enough to convince them to return there in the spring or summer. Maurice, however, retained his Maur Grouchy title by grumbling that a summer trip would be much more expensive.

Gail Tucker

A Fib

'You set my heart aflutter,' a young man used to say,
while gazing at his lady love agoing on her way.
But that was many years ago when poems talked of bliss
and long before the critics panned a rhyming scheme like this.

Good boys might tell a little fib while a bad lad told a lie
language learnt through nursery rhymes – a young man now would die!
These days the only hearts that fib are those that suffer flutter
that medication keeps in check when sinus rhythms stutter.

(Dedicated to my husband's cardiologist.)

Vivien Johnson

A Painful Thumb

Jimmy liked his garden, not his friend's next door. His tree house was a place of refuge from his kid sister, Alison; his own private place. Indoors he had to share his bedroom with Alison. She cried at night and wet the bed. He wished his mum would buy the night training-pants they advertised on T.V.

"I can't afford them now your dad has left," she'd say, and quickly change the subject.

He reckoned Alison would always be a pain, girls were soppy anyway.

Granddad had taken over Jimmy's bedroom since Grandma died. At first it was fun having the old man living with them; he came a year ago. They used to play together but not now. Since Granddad broke his hip the accident had made him miserable; he was always going on about dying.

Today Jimmy was alone in his tree house, rubbing two sticks together. He'd heard about making fire that way and wanted to see if he could do it, on this cold January day. His friend Pete called from over the hedge.

"Jim come and see the goldfish."

"Okay." He struggled through the laurel bushes.

"What's up Pete?"

"Look Jim, they're frozen in the ice, we've got to rescue them!"

"How do we do that?" Jimmy didn't wait for an answer. "I s'pose we'll need a bucket."

"Right, you get the bucket and I'll get a hammer so we can break the ice. It took some time but eventually large pieces of ice floated into the bucket.

"I'll use my fingers to get the fish out." Pete said.

"Me too," Jimmy replied. Ow! I've got a splinter in my thumb." He grimaced and struggled back through the hedge.

"Mum, Mum!" He burst into the kitchen, where Maureen was

slicing carrots for lunch. I've got a splinter in my thumb!"

"Go to the bathroom dear and get the tweezers. Don't go in if Granddad is in there, you know what he's like."

He returned to the kitchen clutching the tweezers but, for some reason Jimmy couldn't work out, the little swelling and the pain had disappeared.

His Mum smiled wryly, knowing that it must have been a splinter of ice. She also knew full well that the shock of the hammering had probably killed the fish! Boys thought they knew everything... Jimmy was such a little tyke.

Gail Tucker

A Puzzle

Tiny worrier, you wait in the dark –
sharp, alert, inert.
Plucked into the light, you rescue
the torn, the broken, the chewed.

Vivien Johnson

Grand Exit

Tammy had moved to Spain not knowing anything about the country where shooters fired at any wild thing that moved.

She'd just wanted to go, wanted have an adventure.

Now, she missed the birdsong, the sweet smell of wild flowers and mown grass back in Britain.

She remembered the rolling Surrey heath-land and pine forests, where she had ridden her trusted horse, Darcy.

Today she sat in the boiling sun with no respite from the heat, even in the shade.

She hated it, all of it.

She swam in the pool, the water temperature thirty degrees Centigrade and planned her return to constant rain and people speaking her own language.

Gail Tucker

Setting Out

On journeys by foot, head or heart,
lucky the traveller with companion in step;
fortunate, one to journey with like mind;
rare, the pair stepping out in tune.
Keep company you can – that will not hold you back.

Vivien Johnson

Darkroom Senses

Marion pushed the prickly, wool curtain aside and let it fall back behind her, sandwiching her between it and the door. Her hand knew instinctively how to find the round wooden handle; the door's smoothed, wooden path showed her the way. She slipped inside the room, into the blackness.

She knew where everything was, years of working there had trained her mind, two steps to the lead-lined sink, six sure steps to the enlarger. Now she ran her hand around the smooth, Formica table, for the box of exposed colour negatives. She discovered the lid of the cardboard box and levered it open. The acrid smell of the chemicals made her sneeze, she fumbled in her white overall pocket for a handkerchief and blew her nose. She knew the subjects of the photographs and was excited at the thought of printing them later.

They'd travelled from Africa in her suitcase, at the end of Mr Smythe's contract in the Northern Rhodesian copper mines, where she'd been his assistant. Marion was glad to be back in U.K. and be with her husband for their first wedding anniversary. Careful not to cut herself on the tinfoil lined packet, she extricated each sheet of film, its nicked right-hand corner came easily to hand in the dark; she clipped each sheet neatly into a developing frame.

One stride to the wet bench, her right hip brushing its edge, she traced the bench with her right hand for the two steps to the developing tank, she'd already pushed her sleeves up to her elbows, and donned her rubber gloves. Before loading the films she'd removed the tank's plastic outer lid.

Now she lifted the air excluder.

It rocked on the solution like the boat on the lake that she and Dave had hired at the weekend.

With her left hand she inserted the films and *shuckled* them in the warm developing liquid.

Funny word that onomatopoeic, *shuckle*, her Prussian boss often used it. Mustn't forget to press the timer, she thought. Leaning forward, arm outstretched, a splinter from the rough wooden shelf pierced her gloved thumb. Toxic chemicals prevented her from sucking it out. Had she been nearer to the wash-bath she would have held it under the water she could hear hissing – the tap must need a new washer.

She fumbled along the shelf, curling her fingers away from the roughness.

The clock was there, she knew it was, two seconds and her hand touched its metal base. Running her hand up its shiny face, Marion's fingertips found the lever; she heard the familiar crunching sound as she pressed the metal down.

Then the ticking began. Fifteen minutes – tick, tick, tick. How many ticks in fifteen minutes she wondered? One day she would count them. Now she was deafened by her heightened imagination, making the ticks seem louder and louder; until they became something unworldly.

Pring!

She knew it was going to happen, but it still made her jump every time the bell went. Momentarily forgetting her terrifying worries, her next move ran through her mind.

Feel for the stop bath; hold the developed films like a bunch of dog daises, heads down.

Drop them into the next tank and agitate them as before, then into the bleach-fix; vibrate again for ten minutes.

She rubbed her eyes with the backs of her gloves. Even after all these years the pungent chemical smell of fixer made her eyes smart.

Next, the wash-tank.

With one hand tracing the snaking path of the water pipe to the condensation covered tap, she heard the 'snake' hissing as the water surged out.

Marion put her hand into the tank to make sure, felt the power of water from the hose end and immediately relaxed, she realised that her brain had been working over-time; she'd been watching too many horror films!

The fix-bath being so close, her hand went immediately to it, no need to feel around; she gathered up the frames and dropped them into the cold water.

Icy droplets sprayed onto her bare arms.

The contrast of comforting warmth of the night-storage heater reminded her that it was still early in the morning.

She raised her hand, pulled at the light switch and instantly saw something else that had travelled from Africa in the negative box ....a baby cobra coiling around the table leg.

Deborah Grant

Purple Haze

I forced down the strangest cocktail I've ever tasted.

I'd never done this before, so maybe it would help.

He made me put on something embarrassingly scanty and lie down. I obeyed.

His words were reassuring, his voice a seductive foreign lilt.

The heat flashed through my mouth, my stomach and loins were on fire. I imagined my body glowing purple, like a science fiction creature. It wasn't exactly pain, but it was deeply disturbing.

Suddenly it stopped – was that it? I opened the package he gave me.

Relief flooded through me. The CAT scan was clear.

Gail Tucker

Spanish Spring Haiku

One

Sturdy trunk holds hard
to fluttery pink of frail
almond blossom flower.

Two

Coarse bark offers pink
delicacy, cruel wind
tears petals away.

Three

Candyfloss billows
fill a springtime valley now,
rock mountain looms.

Four

Siskin's flash here, brings
a gold spring from Africa
to bounce my clothes-line

Vivien Johnson

The First Day

It was April 10th, 1956 when Angela stepped through the back door of the Bond Street commercial photographers building. Her dad had left her at the corner of the street. She was on her own in an adult world for the first time in her life. She'd got her first job and now there was no one to chivvy her along and metaphorically hold her hand. She waited by the desk until a stout man in his fifties, wearing a tweed suit, turned and smiled. "Hello Angela, thank you for coming."

"Good morning Mr. Robinson." He was the man who had interviewed her. His smile reassured her.

"Just take the lift to the second floor; you'll be met there."

She pulled the lift gates across, then listened and watched as the service-lift rose slowly past the first floor, clanked its way up its shaft and came to a shuddering halt at the allotted level. Once more she heaved at the heavy concertina gates. Taking a deep breath, she stepped out uncertainly. She was greeted by a tall, thin woman with a foreign accent.

"What's your name dear?"

Angela was so tight with fear in this new situation, if it hadn't been for her long skirt, the woman would have been able to see her knees knocking. "Angela, Miss."

The girl didn't quite know how to address this imposing-looking woman and thought that to address her as if she were a teacher she would be on safe ground.

"Now Angela dear, there is no need for formality here, my name is Margo and I'm in charge of printing, retouching and mounting. I'll introduce you to your colleagues and they'll show you round.

A few moments later Angela's coat hung on a hook in the cupboard and her new, pink, nylon blouse and grey, pleated skirt were covered with a green, cotton overall. Looking in the speckled mirror, she patted her short-cropped, dark hair into place. Judy, a girl about her own age, seventeen, pulled wet, photographic prints from a tank of cold water and fed them onto a heated, revolving drying-drum. "Just be careful to put them the right way up and don't crease them," she said, "okay?"

Once Angela got into the swing of the job she began to relax and enjoy herself. She kept reminding herself that at the end of the week, she would have three pounds ten shillings in her pay packet, less Tax, and National Insurance. Even after paying her train fare and giving her mother ten shillings for her keep, she would have money left over!

At coffee time the photographers came up from the first-floor studio. At the same time, blinking in the bright light, the printers emerged from their nearby darkroom Angela felt overwhelmed and a little frightened by all these men; she had been convent educated and men were an anathema to her. As an only child she'd missed the rough and tumble of brothers and sisters; she didn't know how to deal with the present situation but they seemed to be friendly enough.

They all smiled at her and asked her questions about where she lived and where she went to school. It was different with her father's friends, they were older and she knew how to be polite, which with them, was all that was required of her. Now, choking back tears of embarrassment she hurried to the lavatory, to give herself a talking-to and compose herself.

She applied a fresh layer of face powder from the compact her parents had given her at Christmas and returned to her work, hoping no one would notice her swollen eyelids.

At lunchtime she felt much more self-confident, she hadn't creased any prints. In Joe Lyons café she ordered beans on toast and reflected on the morning. The other girls had told her not to be frightened of Margaret, they also confided that they had all found the men a bit daunting on their first day. Beside Judy, two other girls, Susan and Jane, worked in the darkroom. Angela began to like the girls a lot.

At teatime, when the young men came up from the first floor, she felt more comfortable until she noticed Rodney staring at her hands. She promptly hid them under the table. "Angela you have lovely slim hands," he said. "I would like to use them on some shots I'm doing this afternoon. Would you mind?" She felt herself flush to a deep crimson. "Please say yes, the professional model has let me down. It won't take long." Angela looked at Margaret for permission, and reassurance.

"You go. Judy can manage to dry the prints." Then she added, "You'll enjoy it."

It was quieter in the studio. Richard placed a large jewel in the palm of her hand, positioned the lights and took two shots. Next, she had to hold the diamond up to the light with her fingers tips. It sparkled in the brightness; spectral colours shot across the studio. A couple more pictures and the session was over.

Angela returned to the second floor, her head held high. Now, she would have something exciting to tell her mum when she got home.

Agnes Hall

A Table for Two

The whole journey, starting in Calais and driving down through France in the yellow Citroen, had been carefully planned. They stopped at different places each day, to experience culinary excellence. The climax of their holiday was to be in a small village near Toulouse, where they had heard about a particular restaurant renowned for its special fare and where, as in so many famous restaurants the proprietor would not divulge the secrets of the wonderful dishes that he created.

Hilary was a chef, as was her new husband Gregory, and this was their honeymoon. Their interest in food was demonstrated by the circumference their waists and, indeed, it was their mutual interest in food that had drawn them together in the aftermath of their disastrous marriages. The honeymoon was part holiday and part work, the idea being to research as many restaurants as possible in the four weeks available to them. Their aim was to attempt to discover new recipes that they might themselves be able to use in their own restaurant, which was due to open a few weeks after their return.

"This must be it." Hilary said as they approached a large sign at the side of the road. The sign, displayed a steaming bowl of food and the words 'Le Bon Chasseur'. An arrow below the sign directed them down a narrow gravel track to a double storey building, where red and white roses competed with each other in their efforts to cover the warm, red brickwork at the front of the house. As the car drew to a halt at the main entrance, a large, smiling man with a long, white apron appeared in the doorway.

Hilary and Gregory introduced themselves to the smiling man and they in return were welcomed. "I am Jacques Thierry, the proprietor of 'Le Bon Chasseur'." He gestured to the man who had appeared in the doorway and was making his way towards them. "And this is my good friend and helper, Henri. If you would like to show Henri the bags you would like taking to your room, and give him your keys, he will park your car for you. I have taken the liberty of putting you in the honeymoon suite and have another little surprise for you when you come down to eat later."

"You have a delightful place here, Monsieur Thierry." Hilary said, as she glanced around, and her praise flowed even more as she saw the room where they were going to spend the night. "It's absolutely perfect, Monsieur. If your food lives up to its reputation, I am sure that we will have found an absolute gem."

"Believe me madam, you won't be disappointed. All my recipes have been handed down to me by my father and they are very special. Please when you have refreshed yourselves and before you dine, I would like to offer you a celebratory drink on the terrace." Jacques inclined his head and left the room.

A few moments later, a knock on the door heralded Henri with the luggage.

"Is there anything more that you require from the car, monsieur, before I put it away?"

"I think that we have everything that we need for the night, haven't we darling?" Hilary nodded her head whilst Gregory felt in his pocket for a tip.

"Thank you monsieur," Henri said staring boldly at Hilary as he left the room.

"I don't like him." Hilary said, pulling a face and shuddering. "Looking us up and down, examining us. Maybe we're not the sort of people who normally stay here."

"Maybe he fancied you." Gregory responded, laughing.

"Yuk!!! Anyway, I'm not going to let that slimy toad affect my enjoyment of this lovely place. I feel all hot and sticky, darling, so I am going straight into the shower." Hilary undressed and went into the bathroom. When Gregory eventually took her place in the shower, Hilary dressed and began to put on her make up. As she sat in front of the mirror she noticed the reflection of a yellow Citroen, in the distance, driving down the gravel track, away from the hotel. She shook her head. There must be more than one Citroen in the area, the same colour as theirs.

When they made their way downstairs, Jacques awaited them on the terrace with a rather plump, jovial woman who he introduced as his wife, Cecilia. "We have a large party occupying the main dining-room this evening, but we have a separate dining annex, which I think would give you more privacy and less noise. A special surprise for the honeymoon couple. You will have it all to yourselves." Jacques poured champagne into two glasses. "With our compliments! Please sit and enjoy your drinks. I will bring you the menu unless you would like to take a stroll in the garden first."

"I think that we might be more in need of a stroll after our meal than before it, if what we have heard about your wonderful food is true." Gregory said.

"We are very proud of our food and we serve only the freshest produce available."

Hilary and Gregory sat in the early evening sunshine enjoying their drinks until Jacques called them to their table in the little annex room. "How absolutely delightful," Hilary said, as they were escorted to their table. "Thank you so much for the wonderful care you are taking of us."

"It is my pleasure." Jacques said. "Our guests are very important to us."

Excellent course followed excellent course and despite cajoling by Hilary, Jacques would not give away any of his culinary secrets. The evening passed delightfully with Hilary and Gregory trying to outdo each other trying to determine the ingredients making up the exquisite flavours that they were sampling. Finally, satiated, they both sat back.

"What a wonderful meal," Hilary said, slurring her words and giggling. "I'm a little tipsy."

"Me too," said Gregory. "In fact I feel a little strange. Quite light-headed in fact. I didn't think that we had that much to drink."

"The food was superb. What flavours!"

Gregory closed his eyes, his face ashen.

"Are you okay?" Hilary asked anxiously, knocking her chair over in her haste to get to his side.

Jacques appeared in the doorway. "Is everything alright?" He asked. "I heard a loud bang."

"I don't think my husband is very well. I'm afraid that I knocked the chair over as I went to help him," Hilary replied. Jacques went to the door and called for Henri, who appeared almost immediately.

"Don't worry madam, we will look after him." Jacques said, as they led Gregory from the room. Hilary struggled to follow them, stumbling down a narrow flight of stairs until they arrived at what appeared to be a refrigeration unit, where a large stainless steel table occupied the centre of the room. Madame Thierry stood alongside the table, a gleaming set of butchers' knives in front of her.

"What's happening?" Hilary struggled to keep her eyes open as Jacques pushed her into a chair. She heard him say, as she slipped out of consciousness. "Sit down and relax, madam. We will take care of you both. You're in good hands."

He turned to Madame Thierry and they smiled at each other.

"Another job well done, my dear," she said.

Gail Tucker

Nets

A solitary palm rises above an ocean of nets,
chestnut waves of fresh cording swirl and stretch
in quiet afternoon sun.
Garlanded by big bright beads, swathes of dense brown
float dry in optimism of their first catch.

Islands of spent fishnet break this harbourscape,
careful mounds – careworn skeins
could tell those flashy newcomers of all
in deep dark beyond the breakwater,
too limp and frayed these nets dully silent.

From empty sky no shadow is cast,
no bird circles to land, no cat stalks.
Dredge shovels shed iron;
a spray of dull rust betrays
harsh reality that will strip away
gloss of bright newness in a single trawl.

Just ropes and entanglements.

Vivien Johnson

A Short Break

I was thrilled when Jake invited me for a weekend in London. He had phoned to say I could stay with him and if I'd get a cheap flight from Alicante to Gatwick, he'd meet me at the airport. So the trip wouldn't cost too much.

We had originally met on Spain's famous Denia beach. He was on his summer holiday. To say we met isn't quite true. I was taking a breather from a very busy day waitressing in the Bar Juan.

So there I was wondering along gazing out over an azure sea, watching the yachts tacking in a warm breeze, trying to work out how I could pay next month's rent ...when wham! I fell over this sexy pair of masculine legs stretched out in the sunshine. I found myself face down on the hot, Mediterranean sand, spitting out grains of silica.

Jake, the owner of the legs, was very nice about it. He took my hands, helped me up and gently dusted me down. "Fancy a coffee?" he asked, grinning broadly; I could see he fancied me. "There's a free table at the bar, over there, under the palm trees." Well, I couldn't refuse this Adonis, could I? It all started from there.

I chucked the holiday job. Daddy would pay the rent if I spun him a good story. Jake and I spent the next two sex filled weeks together. He left his hostel on the other side of town and stayed with me in my apartment. He paid for our meals, nothing fancy, mostly burgers and pizzas and I showed him the local sites. Like me he was an impecunious student. He was reading humanities at London University and I was studying Spanish literature at Alicante. Although both my parents are English ex-pats, from Carlisle, I had never been to London and relished the opportunity to visit the capital, with someone who knew their way around.

The flight had been delayed five hours, so it landed in the middle of the night. Jake looked different from the way I'd remembered him. Three months earlier his muscular body rippled under a golden tan, his long dark hair tied back in a ponytail. I could read his thoughts in his laughing, blue eyes and sensitive mouth.

Then of course he only wore shorts. Now, in November, filthy jeans hid those gorgeously strong limbs, his loose hair straggled from under the hood of a torn parka.

"Come on," he said, kissing me on the lips and sticking a beery tongue down my gullet. I felt sick. "The Rolls is outside," he continued, as he strode off to the car park, leaving me to carry my grip. "Well what do you think? I rescued her from a scrap yard." I didn't know what to say. Even in Spain a rusty heap like that wouldn't be on the road. "Throw your bag in the back and jump in."

I clambered inside the cab and sat on a spring poking through the seat. "Ow!" One of the springs had sunk into my behind.

"Sorry, I should have warned you about that," he laughed. That's the end of my sex life I thought. Jake started the pickup and we roared off into the darkness.

"How long will it take to get to London?"

"Oh, didn't I tell you? We're not going to London. My aunt's place is in a village about an hour away."

"But you said a few days in London!"

"Well yes, perhaps I did, but Gatwick's a London airport. We'll have to stop for a minute, it's started to rain. I have to start the windscreen wipers manually."

"This way," Jake said, pushing open a five bar gate. He was carrying my bag this time. A porch light beckoned to us through the rain. I looked forward to the warmth of the farm kitchen and a bed with dry sheets. Jake fished in his pocket and produced a glimmering torch. We walked across a concrete yard and turned between two corrugated iron barns, away from the light. "Here we are, home sweet home." He kicked at a stone and reached down for the caravan key.

Well, caravans can be very cosy, but this one wasn't. He lit a gas mantle; I could see a bucket in the middle of the floor and immediately identified the dripping noise. "The bog's round the back, be careful, it's a bit muddy where the cows walk. The bunk's comfortable though, so we can cuddle up for warmth," he said, giving me a smirky sort of smile.

I was too tired to argue and fell asleep fully clothed on top of the blankets.

Things weren't any better in the morning. I had to push through the smelly milkers on my way to the outside cloakroom for an ice-cold wash. After breakfast of cornflakes, bread and marmalade, no butter, Jake said he had planned an outing to Brighton.

It was raining harder than the night before and a gale force wind whipped up the sea until it broke over the pier and promenade. All the amusements were closed. We returned to the caravan wetter than ever.

"Never mind," Jake said, "we can go to bed for the rest of the day. If the weather's bad tomorrow, we'll spend the day there too!"

"No Jake, I want you to take me to the airport," I said, tears welling up ready to overflow at any moment.

I have to admit that I'd been a bit naive about this trip.

I had really fancied him a few months before.

Maybe it'd been the attention and relaxed atmosphere, coupled with the hot Spanish sun that made me blind to Joe's many by faults.

Now I didn't fancy him at all, in fact I found him quite repulsive and couldn't wait to get away.

Gail Tucker

Missing

(For widowed friends)

They sit, these women, amid the detritus of their lives
picking over the objects of a past
that yesterday was present.
Their wandering hands strangely disconnected from their brains:
movement no longer a synchronicity
of impulsion and desire.
Competent women suddenly bereft.
Their eyes flicked out of focus in that eyeblink heartstop moment:
he is he is not.
What does it do to them, where
have they gone?

Vivien Johnson

Train to Work

It is seven-thirty a.m.
 We wait, freezing, on the crowded platform.
 One stop from the terminus, the carriages are cold. We huddle inside, teeth chattering.
 We speed through the tunnel, the lights go out.
 In daylight again, we approach the next station; more people pile in, treading on toes and jostling newspapers.
 Conversation dwindles as the train rushes on.
 The rhythmic drumming of the wheels on frozen tracks sends the readers to sleep.
 We stop many times, the temperature rises as more bodies squash together in overcrowded compartments and corridor.
 Warmed, we alight at Victoria Station.

Gail Tucker

Sedge

Sedge, hear it
saturate
steel blade slides
betwixt fine grit
sharp edge glitter
barely touches
invisible particles
revolve
as blade slices
below
root thatch
down
to final
thump
sump
whump!
Guillotine Revolution

Avner Kornblum

Pitchblack and the Giants of Dedlysinz

King Totiltrooth and his beautiful wife Luvenlite were honest and generous rulers, and all their subjects led happy, harmonious lives. One day, a charming outsider named Iggo arrived at the court. She was as attractive as Luvenlite yet completely different in appearance. Whereas Luvenlite was tall and well-built with large, brown eyes and blonde hair, Iggo was petite with flashing, green eyes and glossy black hair. Her speech was silvery and flattering whereas the queen spoke clearly and directly.

    King Totiltrooth was instantly so enraptured with Iggo he did not notice when the slimy, slimy newcomer dropped a poisoned pill into Luvenlite's cup of nectar. Luvenlite's passing was mourned by all the court and countrymen, and nobody suspected the delightful Iggo ...nobody except the royal couple's young son.

    Prince Pitchblack knew she was the murderous culprit for he had seen her drop the pill into the cup but Totiltrooth was so captivated by Iggo that it was clear to Pitchblack, he could not tell his father. He decided to look for a poisonous mushroom he had heard about, with which he could avenge his mother's death. Early next morning he left the palace and made his way into the nearby forest, which his parents had previously told him not to enter.

    Some decades earlier Dedly, an ugly brutish giant, met an equally ugly yet very magical giantess named Sinz. They had been instantly aroused and decided to live together. They chose an almost impenetrable forest as their home and named the forest Dedlysinz after themselves. A year later Sinz gave birth to a daughter and they named her Iggo. She had her mother's gift of magic and could transform her physical body into whatever form or shape she wished in order to obtain whatever was her objective.

After Iggo, they parented seven more one-eyed monsters. Their brood grew up and dwelt in the forest of Dedlysinz, sometimes venturing out to collect food and benefits for themselves and to do what mischief they could whilst they were about it. Iggo instructed them in the use of a special magic called Deception, enabling the young monsters to use a wide variety of shapes and appearances to achieve or acquire anything they wanted. Unfortunately, Pitchblack did not know that.

Picking his way through thick vines and searching for the mushroom, he was deep into the forest when he stumbled across a narrow path. He was about to walk along it when he heard the giants' roars of laughter and bellowing voices, so he stepped back and concealed himself behind a tree.

Five male monsters moved in file along the path, the oldest leading the way, while two fat females, obviously twins, changed places with each other and with their brothers from time to time.

Pitchblack listened intently to their speech but he could not understand their language. In his mind he named them, according to their appearance and attitudes, Pride, Envy, Gluttony – oops, her twin sister, Greed, ambled off behind two males who he'd called Lust and Anger and there, well behind the others, was a painfully slow monster whom Pitchblack named Sloth.

As the procession passed him by, Pitchblack reflected that he had better find the poisonous mushroom and scoot off quickly and take care to warn everyone at the palace about them. However, Greed, moving back and forth in ungainly fashion, focused her eye on some twitching vines and said to herself, "There's something there that might be edible. I'm going to get it for myself and not tell the others." With that, she rumbled towards those vines and Pitchblack did well to climb a tree hastily to avoid her penetrating gaze.

Sloth, being far behind the troop, saw Greed's action and followed her, but lay down in the grass along the verge of the path and fell fast asleep. It was Gluttony, waddling behind Lust, who noticed that her sister was missing and sounded the alarm. The four giants ahead of her turned round and at a word from Pride they spread out into both sides of the forest along the path, searching for Greed and Sloth.

By this time Pitchblack, terrified – almost petrified – decided to get out of the forest as quickly as he could, mushroom or no mushroom. However, Lust saw him and, seeing such a handsome young lad, was overcome with desire. It took him two leaps to catch up with Pitchblack and enfold him in a tight and pleasurable embrace. Pride came along and beamed at the sight. He said something incomprehensible as he touched the young prince with his wand. The effect was immediate. From that moment on, Pitchblack would never tell anyone of his degradation by Lust.

Envy emerged from the vines and trees and immediately wanted to emulate Lust, but Anger arrived and stopped him, shouting at his elder brother. Only timely intervention by Pride stopped Anger from punching Envy.

Meanwhile, Gluttony had found Greed and the sisters gorged themselves on berries while their brothers argued. When they had eaten their fill they made their way back to the path and stumbled over Sloth. Awakened, he accompanied them and they soon found their way to where their brothers were arguing or gloating while Pitchblack sat on the ground, sobbing.

Once the seven Dedleysinz family were together each of them touched Pitchblack with their wands and spoke sounds he did not understand.

Then they appointed Anger to return him to the palace. There Iggo had stroked Totaltrooth with her wand and the bemused king had appointed her Supreme Ruler, allowing himself to become a powerless figurehead.

The humiliated Prince Pitchblack was brought before Iggo, trembling and fearful of what she might do to him, but Iggo greeted him with a warm and pleasant smile. "It was brave of you to enter the forest of Dedlysinz and to befriend its occupants. You may think that Lust was the only one to embrace you, but believe me, all their wands are as powerful as his, and your genes have been impregnated by them forever."

That is why, as long as there are humans on this planet, while many will attempt to embody total truth and love and light, for many others their actions will be pitch black forever.

Avner Kornblum

Lost Sons

I envy men who have lost their sons
through fighting wars or through disease.
I've lost my son for no better cause
than that he simply disagrees.

Vivien Johnson

The Scoop

"Pay up you shit, or I'll get you!" The hoodie shouted, as he and another young man struggled in the poorly lit, narrow alleyway. Fists flaying, they fought like stallions over a mare in season; rearing up at each other, kicks and punches raining and connecting. Suddenly, Fiona saw the flash of a blade. The hoodie slashed repeatedly at the other's face."Gi'me the dosh," he panted.

"Ain't got none," the other rasped back, blood pouring from his cheek.

Photographing violence was part of Fiona's job but she had to stop this before they killed each other. She stepped out of the shadows, still clicking her hidden shutter. "Stop this at once," she yelled, staring straight at the knife carrier and pointing her index finger in his face.

"You slag," he shouted back, grabbing her by the throat and holding the knife against her larynx. She struggled and kneed him in the groin. Yelling in agony he let go and crumpled onto the damp cobbles clutching himself. The other young man fled.

Pausing long enough to get a shot of the moaning heap on the ground, Fiona ran down the alley. Careless of taking risks by walking alone in the inner city, she had taken some of her best shots there, with her hidden camera. Her editor had often said, "For God's sake be careful!" However, he wanted stunning stories and Fiona thrived on scoops; the adrenaline rush had always driven her on.

With the film camera still focussed on her, the director shouted, "Cut."

Avner Kornblum

Alcalali, 1990

Narrow streets we see, bedecked with flags:
It's fiesta time, the poster brags.
Yet the town lies silent in the noonday sun
and of human beings there are almost none.

Here and there a woman goes to shop
or perhaps to chat
Now and then a bird will chirp, or hop
past a blinking cat.

Scruffy dog lies stretched out in the street
listless, panting, full of fleas and heat.
Indoors, a puppy yaps and plays
undaunted by the humid haze.

He takes his chair outside his door,
the old man who can work no more,
and plants himself there with back to wall
where he can see and be seen by all.

In the Jalon valley nothing's changed
for a hundred years or more, it seems;
save for cars and foreigners (deranged)
who intrude into siesta dreams...

As did the German woman, sculptress friend
of Canadian Joe
Restoring work for her will never end –
everything goes slow.

While her builder's working at Alcoy
from her plumber there will be no joy . . .
Soon the Northern stress will pass:
urgency will seem a farce.

The English, sipping their cups of tea,
are so 'at home' in Alcalali
yet the town lies silent in the noonday sun
for here, midnight sees the start of fun.

Gail Tucker

Holiday Snapshot

The overnight parking area for motor-caravans was almost full that hot, Spanish summer evening. The late arrival drew to a halt. It was a well-used four berth affair, designed for an average family. Three children tumbled out first with the pet labrador, all laughing to be free. An older girl handed a toddler onto the grass and joined the rest. A final child appeared with a cat in its arms. The woman stepped down just before the pregnant goat jumped out and began to crop the adjacent grass. It was the driver who climbed out with the parrot cage.

Avner Kornblum

Do Fish Have Feelings?

*Female fish don't fuck
or fuck about, stroking the scales,
feeling the fins or teasing the tails
of shoals of piscine males,
nor merge themselves in a mad embrace
with so-called sole-mates, nor do they extend
romantic lures ("Come up to my plaice")
then their fishy honour fight to defend.*

*Manly fish don't screw
or screw around, or float and strut
or tie themselves into an ungainly knot
with even the sexiest little halibut
nor whistle, call or wink with watery eyes
at swirling eels or girlie rays,
nor drink themselves silly or pretend to be wise,
nor form special clubs for aquatic gays.*

*Perhaps fish don't pray
to some distant Cod in deepest deep
nor flail their frilly fins and weep
if they're jilted for some scaly creep,
nor make waves of protest when rejected,
nor write wishy-washy wads of verse
nor hang their heads and feel dejected
and complain each day of feeling worse.*

But surely fish have feelings –

*Males must feel thrills as they gyrate
around their loved ones, and vibrate
until, impassioned, they create
in females highly orgasmic surges
through which they discharge all their roe.
Do virile fish have some mighty urges
of which we humans cannot know?*

Sheila Skinner

What Will The Neighbours Think?

Through the open window I watched him. There he was, him, at his age, in the full heat of day, dragging huge planks of wood and lengths of thick rope down to the bottom of our small-holding.

The boys had come home from the far pasture. As hot and tired as their own work had made them, they felt obliged to help him. Watching with me though, they agreed, this was some kind of madness that had possessed him.

"I'm his wife but still he won't listen to me," I said, "perhaps we should all try to reason with him. He can't go on like this, the whole village is turning against us."

Our three sons stood, sad and troubled, nodding in agreement. They were already embarrassed by the protests over the animals he had insisted they collect together.

The smell of them from the fields was bad enough, now this. They knew what the people were saying – that the sun had gone to their father's head and he was suffering delusions.

Now we watched horrified as clouds of noxious smoke belched from the cauldrons of pitch he was boiling up.

"What is that devil's brew," I cried, "the stink of it must have reached the village by now. They'll think us in league with Satan himself."

"Father said it was for caulking the planks," my eldest replied. He wouldn't look directly at me, none of them would.

We all feared the same …that the head of our family was under the influence of some evil force.

"Oh the shame of it," I sobbed. I sank to my knees in prayer. After a few moments my sons raised me to my feet. Knowing that we had only our own strength and Faith to help us now, we had to speak to him. Pulling cloths across our faces to protect us from the acrid fumes, we walked together across the fields towards him. My eldest took my arm.

Occupied, carefully stirring the bubbling pitch, first in one cauldron, then the others, he didn't hear them approach.

Turning, he was surprised to see his wife with their three sons, standing just feet away. He knew her to be the good woman and dutiful wife she was, he was even more surprised when she, not their eldest, raised her voice to him.

Her arms spread wide with palms open, her eyes beseeched him …but it was in desperation, not anger, that she addressed him. "Noah, gentle husband of mine, good father to our three sons, we beg you …stop this madness".

Gail Tucker

Summer Storm

The air is heat-heavy.
Silver undersides of leaves are
wind-whipped into view as we
close the windows against the greening
light of a gathering storm.
The dog flattens its ears,
winds into its basket.
Senses stand on end, alert with static;
we beg for thunder clap and sky crack –
for relief of rain.

Vivien Johnson

Big Mistake

I was walking down King Street one afternoon when I came across a young boy.

"Hello," I said, "what's your name?" I paused, not expecting an immediate answer. "What are you doing here?"

"Nuffink," he replied, wiping his nose on his sleeve.

"Come on now, you're too small to be out on a busy street on your own."

"No I'm not! I'm five today, it's my birfday."

"My word, you *are* grown up. Have you started school?" No reply... "Where is your mummy?"

"Gone wiv Uncle Dec."

"Where have they gone?"

"Dunno."

"Well you'd better come with me and we'll try to find them." I took him by the hand and felt how cold it was.

For years I had worked in a children's home as an assistant, and prided myself on being able to recognise a hungry, unhappy child. Letting go of his hand for a couple of moments, I rummaged in the bottom of my handbag.

"Would you like a Mars bar? Here you are." I didn't expect any thanks and didn't get any.

He snatched it, tore off the paper, and wedged the end into his small mouth. Chocolate oozed out of the corners and ran down his chin like tram lines; eventually dripping onto his rather worn, over-large school blazer.

"That's a smart blazer you're wearing." He nodded and continued to munch.

When he'd finished I said, "Come on, we'll have to try and find your mummy."

"Don't want to," he spluttered.

"Why not?"

He didn't answer.

When I took his hand again, a dishevelled female figure suddenly appeared from behind a wall.

She was followed by a tall young man.

The boy threw his sweet paper over the wall.

"Joe, what are you doing? I've told you never to take sweets from strangers!"

She glowered at me and dragged the boy away.

Gail Tucker

Transhumance

(villanelle)

The campo[2] seems to move again today
Last week the trees were still and green.
Last month in England they were making hay,

In Spain the goats moved on their way –
Twice a year they pass – almost unseen.
The campo seems to move again today,

Not goats nor sheep now make the branches sway
But men who reach for fruit amongst the green.
Last month in England they were making hay.

Across the world to divers gods men pray,
For hungry pickers there is little left to glean,
The campo seems to move again today.

Earth's bounty picked and thrown away
Rich houses sit apart – aloof, serene.
Last month in England they were making hay.

In Spain, the sun shines – come what may
Whilst city folk can only march and scream;
The campo seems to move again today
Last month in England they were making hay.

---

[2] **campo** - in Spain, unfenced land used for agricultural purposes

Meet the Authors

All in the Mix

Sheila Skinner

Sheila Skinner was born and raised in Paddington. Convent Grammar School educated, she left after GCE's, with English a favourite subject. Despite the school curriculum of set books, Sheila developed and retains a love of reading.

Only much later in life, with more leisure time, did she discover the addiction of writing. "I Enjoy setting down the short stories that burst out of me, but find the discipline required for the longer haul very tough. The ongoing support of the Jalon Valley Writers Group, through my membership of the U3A, has been as valuable as it has been enjoyable over these past few years."

Avner Kornblum

Avner was born in South Africa and graduated from the University of Cape Town where he majored in Law and English Literature while serving as a sub-editor on the Cape Times, a major South African daily. He spent 18 years as an advertising copywriter (gaining two international awards) and public relations journalist. During this time he studied metaphysics and edited a variety of publications from philosophical to technological. In 1980 he was appointed Spiritual Leader of South Africa's foremost metaphysical organisation.

His wide range of interests are reflected in his writings – from motivation manuals and philosophical essays to political satire, from metaphysical adventure novels to humorous, romantic and children's poems.

In 1991, after five years in England, he moved to Spain.

Gail Tucker

Gail has been an English teacher, shopkeeper, sometime cook and a guide at Roman ruins. She has lived in and explored Spain for over ten years with her husband and his camper van. Most recent published prose appeared in Picked and Mixed, Short Stories, a U P Publication 2012.

    A life-long scribbler, Gail is never far away from a pencil; when at home in Orba, she shares her fondness for prose with the Jalon Valley Writers. Stanza Alicant is where she shares her love of poetry. If pushed, she will admit to having a couple of incomplete novels on her desk and is almost ready to set everything else aside to finish at least one of them this year.

    A life-long observer of others, it is always the people who fascinate wherever they are; so it is the characters she creates that provide the pulse for her short stories. She invites the reader to explore beyond the narrative to find more than might at first appear. Life is rarely what it seems.

Vivien Johnson

Vivien has lived in the mountains of the Spanish Costa Blanca for fourteen years. She has had poetry and prose published in Spain and in the U.K. and has been runner up in both genres. She has also broadcast poems and short stories on two radio stations in England. In 2013 she won the Segora International poetry competition.

With thanks to the following Publishers for their consent to include Vivien's poems in this book: McFarlands Publishing; Through the Mill; www.poetryproseandplay.co.uk; The Salopian Poetry Society; Writers' Forum; Select Publisher Services Ltd and Costa Blanca News.

Acknowledgements: One of Vivien's poems was broadcast by Bradford Community Radio and 3 stories were published by My costa Blanca Info and and were also broadcasted by Bradford Community Broadcasting. Several stories and poems were read/ performed on Basingstoke Hospital Radio

Paul Shearer Walmsley

Paul came to live in Spain in 1988 living first in Benidorm and then in Alfaz Del Pi, at first he worked in a British bar for 2 years then in his own bar for a few years.

In the early 90s he met his future partner who fancied owning and running a Casa Rural. So the next six months were spent looking and visiting villages in the mountains for ideal properties. At last they came across a ruin in a village by the name of Beniaya which was perfect so after 18 months and untold thousands of pounds the ruin was converted into a six-bedroom bed and breakfast Casa Rural.

At this time Paul did a lot of walking and joined a painting group. In 2006, he joined the Jalon Valley writing group, retiring in the same year. When his partner died, over four years ago, he decided to carry on living in the same property and still lives quietly there now.

Jean M Watson

Like most people, Jean spent many years earning the crust, and sometimes the butter too.

Then, when she and her husband, Gordon, were offered early retirement at almost the same time they decided to sell up and buy a boat and roam around the Mediterranean for a while.

Their wanderings brought them to Calpe where they made many friends and decided to settle there, where they were very happy.

After a number of years, they moved to the Jalon valley, where Jean still lives.

Agnes Hall

Agnes Hall was born in Liverpool and after a Grammar School education, pursued a course in Design at Liverpool College of Art, Nottingham Polytechnic and Leeds Polytechnic. This culminated with a B.A. Honours degree in Three Dimensional Design.

After a short period working freelance in Advertising, Toy Design and eventually Set Design (for the BBC and Yorkshire Television), she was employed as a member of staff by Yorkshire Television where she worked for 20 years before retiring to Spain in 2000 with her husband and 2 dogs.

Retiring brought with it an opportunity to write and she has had one novel published 'The Canvas Bag'. With two others in the pipeline, her work is not progressing as quickly as she would like but as a member of The Jalon Valley Writing Group (a U3A Creative Writing Group), she remains part of the creative writing scene and still pursues her love of design, drawing and painting

Colin Hall

Author and publisher, Colin Hall came from Oldham in the north of England where he was born in 1945. He attended various schools where he played a lot of football and cricket which left very little time for anything else. Achieving an "O-Level" pass in Engineering Drawing, he wisely took his teacher's advice and left school to join the family shop fitting business. For some years in the sixties and seventies he was responsible for the design of many shop-fronts and restaurant interiors in Lancashire. Most of his working life was spent in the building trade, writing specifications for building projects. Colin retired in 2000 and, together with his wife Merril, set off from the UK in a campervan. They settled on the Costa Blanca where Colin started to write of their travel experiences. These articles were serialised in a local magazine under the pen-name "Colincampsite". Encouraged by those around him, he started writing short stories of a humorous nature and at one stage had a fleeting ambition to write a serious novel. The feeling passed.

Most of his time is spent producing books for children. He quickly discovered his niche in "Personalised Children's Books" and has a portfolio of stories written about football, visits to the zoo and many more adventures that he personalises to order.

What is more pleasing than to give little ones a personalised gift and to see the pleasure on their faces 'scoring the winning goal' for their favourite team. Colin plans to expand the list of titles in his children's books and then maybe write some more serious stuff.

Deborah Grant

Deborah's only early writing experience was producing marketing copy as part of a career spent launching naughty but nice food and drink products on to an innocent but receptive public. Latterly she used her big company expertise to help small businesses, culminating in the start up of her brother's brewery in Sussex. After moving to Spain with her husband in 2006, she was persuaded to try creative writing and found that having been a voracious reader of fiction, she loved creating stories herself. The Grants spend half their time in Spain and half travelling, often to Australia.

All in the Mix

Author Index

Agnes Hall

17, 41, 68, 98, 105, 115, 153, 282, 317

Avner Kornblum

15, 23, 36, 55, 81, 90, 101, 111, 123, 149, 187, 194, 203, 264, 293, 296, 298, 301, 312

Colin Hall

57, 80, 122, 136, 148, 182, 209, 218, 219, 233, 234, 242, 248, 249, 260, 318

Deborah Grant

257, 277, 319

Jean M. Watson

26, 66, 145, 190, 200, 213, 225, 239, 316

Gail Tucker

16, 21, 32, 40, 52, 73, 84, 113, 117, 131, 139, 158, 164, 170, 179, 196, 245, 254, 263, 268, 271, 273, 278, 286, 290, 292, 300, 305, 308, 313

Paul Shearer Walmsley

114, 135, 168, 315

Sheila Skinner

13, 33, 45, 60, 74, 99, 303, 311

Vivien Johnson

14, 22, 25, 29, 35, 39, 51, 59, 65, 71, 83, 87, 100, 108, 125, 152, 162, 167, 177, 184, 185, 199, 205, 211, 216, 217, 220, 223, 232, 236, 241, 243, 244, 246, 250, 252, 255, 261, 269, 272, 274, 279, 287, 291, 297, 306, 314

All in the Mix

www.AllintheMix.info

Lightning Source UK Ltd.
Milton Keynes UK
UKOW06f0356100516

273911UK00002B/99/P